The Summer Boy

A novel of Texas

D1016207

Rhamey, Ray.
The summer boy : a
novel of Texas /
©2011.
33305238956324
ca 08/18/17

The Summer Boy

A novel of Texas

Ray Rhamey

Unbeaten paths to worthy reads.
Pullman, WA FtQPress.com

The platypus breaks all the rules—it's the only mammal that lays eggs, is venomous, has a duck bill, a beaver tail, and otter feet—and it does just fine, thank you very much.

It can be the same for novels that don't slip tidily into genre pigeonholes. Platypus authors take readers on unique paths to entertainment, truth, and enjoyable reads.

This book is a work of fiction. All characters, organizations, and locales, and all incidents and dialogue, are drawn from the author's imagination and not to be construed as real.

The Summer Boy Copyright © Ray Rhamey 2011. Manufactured in the United States of America. All rights reserved. No part of this book may be reproduced in any form or by any electronic or mechanical means including information storage and retrieval systems without permission in writing from the publisher, except by a reviewer, who may quote brief passages in a review. Published by Platypus, an imprint of Flogging the Quill LLC, 845 SE Spring Street, Pullman, WA 99163. First Edition.

ISBN 978-0-615-49906-2
Library of Congress Control Number: 2011934872

Book design by Ray Rhamey

Dedication

In memory of my best friend, Cy Lloyd, my partner in many adventures, including the dream of a ranch of our own.

For my son Dan, who was sixteen when I wrote this story. This is the world as it was when your pappy was that age.

And to Loretta McGuire, wherever you are.

June, 1958

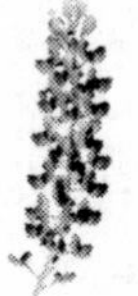

A time of innocence.

1

The air was as still as it was hot—only the whir of a grasshopper's flight troubled the quiet. Jesse felt like an overcooked chicken, his meat darn near ready to fall off his bones. Mouth so dry he didn't have enough spit left to swallow, Jesse croaked, "That guy tryin' to kill us?"

Dudley's answer took a while coming. From where he slumped against the other side of the tree trunk, he said, "I'm beginning to wonder."

The live oak's skimpy shade was as good as it got there in the south yearling pasture—wherever the hell that was on the Box 8's ten thousand acres of ranchland. A half-dozen red-brown Herefords, a broad white blaze down the center of their empty faces, grazed on parched yellow grass. Jesse had tried a friendly moo, but they paid him no mind.

Jesse said, "Doesn't seem like a foreman should be leavin' people stuck out here with no water."

"Maybe Buddy ol' buddy doesn't know what he's doing. He's not much older than us."

"Oh, he knows. You hear him laugh when he drove away?"

Dudley chuckled. "You mean right after he said, 'You ain't bothered by snakes, are you?'"

"Yep." Jesse tossed a stone at a prickly pear cactus the size of a laundry basket. A dry rustle started up, whispered through the air, and then faded away. It didn't sound like any kind of bug Jesse knew about. "You hear that?"

"Yeah."

"Rattler?"

"Sure sounds like it."

Jesse thought about taking a look, but his legs were like empty sacks. It had been a good three hours since Buddy dropped them off to dig a hole for a watering trough, and it had taken two of those hours to hack one into the rocky ground with shovels, leaving their hands blistered and their arms and faces cooked medium-rare by the sun.

They'd sung "summertime summertime sum sum summertime" along with the Jamies on the car radio all the way from Dallas, but now he was thinking they had a little more summer than they'd expected.

After they had dragged the galvanized steel watering trough—four feet tall, three wide and five long—into the hole, they had stomped around under the live oak to scare away snakes and then collapsed against the trunk.

What if they really were dumped out here? It was at least a mile to the ranch house down dirt roads with no signs and Jesse didn't know if he could find his way back. His imagination fired up thoughts of rattlesnakes seeking the warmth of his body when night came.

He scanned the landscape in hopes of a dust plume signaling Buddy's return in the Jeep. He saw no sign of rescue, but did find reason to smile—the hill country west of Kerrville was so blessedly different from home in flat, suburban Dallas. Under a white-hot afternoon sun in a never-ending blue sky, the green of live oak and cedar trees bordered yellow-gold meadows. Sprawling patches of bluebonnets prettied up hillsides here and there.

Jesse inspected his hands; his blisters were definitely prize winners. Digging holes was not his idea of cowboy work, and it sure wasn't what he'd imagined when Dudley's mother found them a summer job on the Box 8 Ranch. With their dream of becoming ranchers one day, they'd thought an invite to work on a real ranch as junior ranch hands was like a pass through the Pearly Gates. It hadn't mattered that they only got paid room and board.

That was then. He said, "Some fun so far."

Dudley stayed quiet for a spell. Then he said, "That Lola's something."

So Dudley had been thinking about Lola Braun, too. Jesse had figured the rancher's daughter to be about sixteen, same as him, when they met at the ranch house that morning. And she was already the kind of girl a boy undressed with his eyes.

It wasn't her body that had started his mental peep show, although she was fun to look at. Lola was little, five feet tip to toe, if that. His gaze had roamed happily down and back up slender, tanned legs exposed by short shorts, but on top she was no Playmate of the Month.

It was a boldness in her green eyes that promised the stuff of daydreams. And then, when they shook hands, her fingertips had trailed across his palm as if she didn't want to let go.

Who was he kidding? Dudley would be the one she'd go for—he'd been on lots of dates and had a Cadillac. Jesse had never been on a date and had no car. He glanced at Dudley. "You think you'll ask her out?"

The corner of his eye caught a shrug. Dudley said, "She was looking at you."

Jesse could think of only one word for what she had seen—medium. Medium tall, medium brown hair, medium brown eyes, medium looks, medium build (if he could shed a couple pounds). Medium nobody. He said, "Probably wondering how anybody could possibly be that dull."

Dudley laughed. "Yeah, that would explain her giving you the twice-over with those big ol' eyes."

"The what?"

Dudley hitched around and gave Jesse a look. "You don't know, do you?"

"Don't know what?"

"What girls say about you."

Jesse couldn't imagine any girl saying anything about him. Why would they? And say what?

The whine of the Jeep's engine butted in before Jesse could ask. That dust plume he'd hoped for was here. Axel Braun, the owner, rounded the hill and pulled up beside the trough. Dust drifted over them. Jesse had to steady himself with a hand on the tree trunk when he struggled to his feet.

Dudley moved in even slower motion. Big and powerful at six feet and on the fat side, every year the Wildcat football coach came after Dudley for the offensive line, and every year Dudley was too lazy for all that exercise. But his strength hadn't seemed to help today.

Mister Braun got out and inspected their work. He fit Jesse's idea of a Texas rancher. Stranding about eye to eye with Jesse, he was lean, his tan skin like a tight leather glove. The gray that peppered his black sideburns made him look old to Jesse, maybe as old as forty.

The dust whitening his jeans looked like it belonged there, and the sweat darkening his shirt and straw cowboy hat looked like hard work. Instead of the boots Jesse had expected on a rancher, he wore heavy-duty high-top work shoes.

Mister Braun turned to them. "How come you didn't put the trough in the shade?"

Dudley said, "Buddy said to put it right there."

Jesse wondered why he hadn't picked the shady spot. It would have been better than digging in the full sun. Water would stay cooler, too.

Mister Braun studied them and then scanned the area. "Where's your water?

Jesse said, "Don't have any."

"Damn. Buddy should never've left you out here without water." Mister Braun opened a cooler in the Jeep's truck-like rear end. Ice rustled when he pulled out two bottles of Coke, popped the tops off with an opener welded to the side of the Jeep, and passed them out. "I brought these as a treat, but you need 'em for more than just fun."

Jesse's Coke was ice-cold heaven. He chugged most of it, some dribbling down his chin, the rest causing a cold ache in his chest, but it felt so good going down in a rush. He said, "Thank you, sir."

Dudley burped. Jesse laughed. Mister Braun smiled with the first warmth Jesse had seen from him.

Mister Braun handed Jesse a thermos. "Better wash it down with this."

A long swallow of ice water completed Jesse's resurrection. He handed the thermos to Dudley and wondered if he was as sad a sight as his friend—clothes dirty and rumpled, shirttail half in, half out, sweaty, dirt on his face. They hadn't expected to work right away, so they'd arrived at the ranch in nice clothes to make a good impression. Jesse's sport shirt, khakis, and new penny loafers were now a mess.

Mister Braun said, "You boys ready for some supper?"

Dudley nodded. "I would kill for something to eat."

Jesse realized how empty his belly felt. "Me, too."

Mister Braun grinned and hopped into the Jeep, and they scrambled to join him. Dudley took the shotgun seat, and Jesse climbed into the back, which was sorta like a miniature pickup truck. Mister Braun roared off, and Jesse thought maybe there were some things to like about the boss.

There were a ton of things to like about Lola, too . . . not that Jesse would ever dare to do anything about it.

Then there was Buddy. And rattlesnakes humming a tune in the cactus.

Lola smoothed her new Coral Pink lipstick onto her lips, pressed them together, and then blotted with a tissue. She studied the look in her dresser mirror and liked it. Now if only her mother wouldn't get so weird about her wearing makeup. She rubbed a bunch off so it wouldn't be noticeable.

She grinned at how the shy summer boy, Jesse, couldn't keep his eyes off her after she gave him her "secret sexy thoughts" smile. His big friend was nice, but Jesse had what her friend Cindy called bedroom eyes. She checked her clock—it would be a while before they got back to the house.

Sweat made a run down her spine—she stood and paced, and then paged through the new *Western Horseman* magazine, but the ads just made her want stuff her parents would never buy, especially the fringed leather jacket.

She fanned her face with the magazine. Maybe a ride down to the river—it was always cooler under the cypress trees. She changed from her shorts into jeans and pulled on her boots. A little bit hungry, she headed for the kitchen.

Connie shucked corn at the kitchen sink, her gray maid uniform relieved by an apron ablaze with bright yellow daisies. She'd pulled her long black hair, threads of gray running through it, into a ponytail that swayed while she worked. It seemed like every other week Connie said that it was Lola who put the gray there and that she oughta pack up and go back to Mexico. Then she would smile and sometimes throw in a hug for good measure.

As Lola examined the oatmeal cookies Connie had baked for the new hands, searching for the perfect balance of raisins and cookie, Connie said, "*Señor* Braun I think is too hard on the *niños,* makin' them work the minute they get here."

"You always say that. You're such a softie."

Connie aimed a glare at Lola—and then added a grin that turned it fun. "So I should be tougher? On you too, maybe?"

Lola laughed. "I'm shakin' in my boots."

Connie grinned. "He could have start them tomorrow."

"Daddy has to know if they can cut it. Remember last year we had to send that crybaby home and work short-handed?"

"I don' think it was the working, I think it was Buddy."

She had a point. "Yeah. The way he's mean to the boys is dumb. They go home, and there's still just as much work."

"Buddy don' do no more."

Lola nodded. "That's for sure." She knew what he knew—he could put the extra load off on the wetbacks, who would never complain because they'd lose their jobs.

Connie rinsed the corn. "Are the *niños* nice?"

"One is kinda cute."

Connie looked around, and so did Lola. It was best to make sure they were alone when the talk concerned boys. Connie said, "Don't let the *Señora* hear you say that. You know what she tell you about the boys."

"I'll be careful."

Connie whispered, "Which is the cute one? I could only see one was big and one not-so-big."

"Not-so-big. Jesse. He's real shy." Lola selected a plump, perfect cookie. "I'm going for a ride." She left with an exaggerated swing of her hips. Looking back, she giggled when Connie shook her head and rolled her eyes.

When Lola reached the big red barn a couple-hundred yards downhill from the house, she stopped at the open doorway to say hello to Spot, the barn cat, and scratched the orange patch in his otherwise white fur. The barn was always a comfort to her—she probably spent as much time there as she did in her room at the house. The upper-level hayloft had been her playhouse as a kid, and it was still a good place to get away for a little privacy. But it would be an oven today.

Inside, Fibber, her little brown-and-white paint, stuck his head out of his stall and nickered. Even though he wasn't much over thirteen hands tall, he was a good size for her and fast as the dickens, which was why they made such a good barrel-racing team. The other two horses peeked out of their stalls and then went back to munching hay. She went to Fibber and rubbed the sensitive bump between his ears, a spot that would set a horse to purring if it could.

"How about a ride down to the river?"

Fibber pawed the earth, which she took for a yes and went to the tack room in the corner of the barn to fetch her saddle and bridle. As she reached to lift the saddle from its rack, the ranch's flatbed truck arrived.

Loaded with hay bales, it backed up to the barn doors and shut down. Romero, one of their two Mexican hands, got out of the driver's side. Heavyset and as old as her father, he frowned at her, his black mustache emphasizing his sour look.

He grabbed a bale and carried it toward the stack at the end of the barn. Romero had been friendly the summer before, but not now. She stuck her tongue out at the back of his sweat-stained blue denim shirt.

She smiled when Alejandro, not all that much older than her, rounded the other side of the truck, his lean body bare from the waist up, his coppery skin glistening with sweat. She loved his beautiful eyes, a brown that was as dark as night, and the musical sound of his name, Ah-lay-HAN-dro.

He returned her smile with one of his big, bright-white ones and came to her, his gaze roaming over her like a little kid eyeing a Popsicle on a July day. Excitement fluttered in her. She glanced at Romero; he was still headed toward the back.

She expected Alejandro to just sneak a quick peck on her Coral Pink lips, but he slipped his hands under her arms, lifted her off her feet, and carried her into the tack room, where he pulled her to him for a real kiss.

She liked it at first, but then he put his hand to her breast and squeezed. She pushed away. "No!"

"Ah, *mi corazon* . . ." He slipped his arm around her waist and forced her toward him.

She pushed against his chest, and then brown hands clamped onto his shoulders and jerked him back.

Romero bared his teeth and shoved Alejandro against a wall. "*Estupido!*"

Alejandro launched himself at Romero, swinging a punch that caught Romero on the shoulder and staggered him back against a saddle rack. Alejandro crouched, arms wide, eyes hot.

Romero pulled a straight razor from a pocket, flicked it open and dropped into a fighting stance.

Lola yelled, "Stop it!"

Neither man glanced her way. They circled.

"Stop or I'll tell my father!"

Long seconds passed, and then Romero straightened and glared at her. He jammed the razor into his pocket.

Alejandro came out of his crouch and took a step back.

Romero brushed past Alejandro. "You gon' git us kicked out." He strode to the truck, grabbed a hay bale, and carried it into the barn.

Alejandro smiled at her as though there'd been no trouble. He said "Tonight" and returned to his work.

She ran from the barn. Heart slamming, she forced herself to walk, and then stopped and looked back. They were unloading the truck in silence, but she could see the anger on Romero's face. She headed for home, thinking on what to do.

When Alejandro first came to the ranch, she'd thought she could have some fun with him. And she had, getting him all lathered up with sexy glances, lowering her gaze and then looking up through her lashes, and sneaking kisses. But the way he had grabbed her today hadn't been fun. She would tell him when they met later that if he didn't behave himself it was "*no mas*," no more.

She trudged up the driveway and had reached Buddy's trailer, a hundred yards to go to the house, when the Jeep's horn honked behind her. She stopped and her father pulled up beside her. Dudley was in the passenger seat and Jesse sat in the rear.

Her father said, "Want a lift?"

"Sure." Dudley swung a leg out to give up his seat, but she hopped into the back with Jesse. "Let's go." Her father took off in his usual hell-bent-for-leather fashion.

Jesse's face was sunburned as red as an apple. Buddy, the turd, had made 'em work in the sun without hats. She smiled at Jesse. "How're you doing?"

His answering grin was shy but warm. "Great." His gaze darted away and then came back. He grinned again. A really cute grin.

"Get along okay with Buddy?"

His eyes tightened, but he said, "Great." This time his gaze flicked away and stayed there, looking back at the barn.

Her father sent a glance at Jesse, his eyebrows raised.

She couldn't blame Jesse for not answering truthfully with the boss right there and it being his first day.

Lola found herself hoping it wouldn't be his last.

Jesse loved the rush of air in the back of the open Jeep as they drove up the crushed rock driveway toward the house, maybe a quarter mile from the highway. He spotted Lola in front of a small house trailer set fifty feet back from the driveway. A gleaming black '57 Chevy sat in front of the trailer. Jesse admired its fender skirts, dual exhausts, and spinner hubcaps.

Buddy had warned them. "That's my place. You go near it I'll kick your asses."

What a shame to waste such a cool car on such a prick.

A thrill pulsed through him when Lola got into the back. With the cooler in the cramped back of the Jeep, their knees touched now and again as they bounced up the driveway. He snuck peeks at her as they finished the ride to the house, and enjoyed a fantasy that the touches were not accidental on her part. Then she'd smile at him and he'd look away as if he hadn't been looking.

When they got to the parking area in front of the house, she hopped out, said "See y'all later," and headed across the lawn. Jesse admired the view until she disappeared inside.

Then he had to get his body out of the Jeep. Muscles had stiffened and he hung a foot up on the Jeep's tailgate and damn near fell on his face. He managed to turn the fall into a staggering dismount and hoped nobody had noticed.

No such luck. Mister Braun grinned at him and said, "You boys get your gear and I'll show you where you're bunking."

They limped to Dudley's Caddy and hauled their suitcases out of the back seat—Dudley didn't use the trunk much because his car had a custom-made continental kit, a metal shell that went over the spare tire and sat on the rear bumper. You had to unlatch it and swing it down to open the trunk; it wasn't a handy place to store the spare, but it sure looked terrific.

Mister Braun said, "Nice car."

Dudley's 1953 Cadillac Coupe deVille two-door hardtop was a hand-me-down from his dad. It had once belonged to Greer Garson, the movie star, who also lived in Dallas. The Caddy was long and silver-gray, with fishtail fins and dark gray fabric covering the top. Jesse had helped put lowering blocks and glass-pack mufflers on it. Boys would watch Dudley rumble by and talk about what a great car it was for getting girls.

Now that Jesse thought of it, Lola had given it a long look when they arrived.

As they followed Mister Braun across the lawn, Jesse admired again how the stone walls and cedar shake roof of the low ranch house made it seem like a part of the hilltop. He stopped in the shade of a big maple tree to look down the long view to the Guadalupe River far below. Like a blue thread, it wound toward Kerrville, a few miles downstream but hidden by hills.

A quarter-mile away, a circling hawk folded its wings and arrowed down, death on the way to a rabbit nibbling in a peaceful meadow.

Dudley called, "You coming?" Jesse ran to catch up.

Around back, Mister Braun pointed at a small, tree-shaded log cabin thirty yards behind the ranch house. "That's where you'll stay."

To the left of the cabin, a woman wearing a wide-brimmed sun hat hoed weeds in a garden that was mostly vegetables, including tomatoes and corn. Rose bushes bordered the front with blazing yellows and pinks and reds. A screened gazebo between the garden and the house looked like a nice place to cool off. A fenced dog run, complete with dog house but missing a dog, was on the other side of the gazebo. He gazed at a cottage that sat fifty feet beyond the gazebo and wondered who lived there.

Mister Braun called out, "Margaret!"

The woman waved a gloved hand. "How was it?"

"They got some work done."

"Good." She pulled off her gloves and strode to them.

Mister Braun said, "Boys, meet my wife, Margaret."

Miz Braun topped out half a head taller than her husband, and heavy shoulders gave her a look of strength. Red hair curled around her broad face, and a white two-inch scar cut through one eyebrow.

Mister Braun indicated Dudley. "This's Dudley Miller."

Grinning, she pumped Dudley's hand. "Pleased to meet you, Dud."

Jesse groaned inside. No doubt she thought she was being funny, but Dudley hated his name and couldn't stand being called "Dud." He was on the lookout for a good nickname, but nothing had stuck yet.

Dudley smiled anyway. "Howdy, ma'am. This's my friend, Jesse Carver."

After a friendly handshake and a smile, she said to Mister Braun, "You done for the day?"

"Yep." He smiled toward Jesse and Dudley. "I think I've squeezed about all I'll get out of 'em."

She nodded. "They look it. Guess I better get ready for supper." She smiled at him and Dudley. "See you there." She headed toward the house.

The path forked, and Mister Braun took the branch that led to the cabin. The other fork continued twenty yards to another small house with a chicken-wire fence attached. Inside the fence, a white rooster stood guard over a half dozen hens.

Excitement grew in Jesse as they approached the cabin. A place all their own. No grown-ups.

The screened door opened and Buddy stepped out, a broom in his hand. He was a burly guy, Jesse's height but a lot bigger in the chest and shoulders, with thick arms hanging out of rolled-up sleeves.

Mister Braun said, "Get 'em all?"

Buddy flicked a glance at Jesse and Dudley, and then he gave an easy grin. "Sure." He smiled a lot, but then so did sharks. Jesse was glad to see him head for the ranch house.

Mister Braun led them inside.

They stood in a room just big enough for a double bunk bed, a four-drawer dresser, two chairs at a small table, and a little space left over to walk around. A battered old radio sat on the table, and an easy-going breeze wafted through the screened door and out the single side window.

A doorway into a bathroom revealed an old-fashioned tub with feet; a metal bar suspended from the ceiling encircled it with a shower curtain. Jesse stepped to the door and looked in. The toilet had a seat but no lid, the sink had a medicine cabinet above it but the mirror was cracked.

Beautiful.

Dudley said to Mister Braun, "What was Buddy getting?""

"Oh, the black widows come back over the winter while the cabin's not used. Just a little spring cleaning. But you should still check your shoes for scorpions in the morning. Darn things are impossible to keep out."

Okay, mostly beautiful.

"You boys come up to the house when you're cleaned up."

After Mister Braun left, Jesse swapped gleeful looks with Dudley. This was like living their dream of going partners in a place of their own after they learned ranching at Sul Ross

College in west Texas. They'd been best friends forever, except for a couple weeks after Jesse chased Dudley off his place with a pellet rifle. He'd forgotten why.

They argued about who got the bottom bunk until Jesse noticed how thin the slats supporting the top mattress were. Thinking about the possibility of Dudley crashing down on him, he said, "You know, come to think of it, maybe the top bunk's better."

Suspiciously—just the way Jesse knew he'd react—Dudley said, "Why?"

Jesse sent his fingers scurrying like a spider up Dudley's arm and pinched him.

Dudley laughed, said "Screw you," and plopped down on the bottom bunk.

When they washed and threw on clean shirts, Jesse took special care with his hair, sweeping it back but not into dumb-looking ducktails. Not that he thought (hoped) anybody (Lola) would notice.

When Jesse opened the screened door at the back of the ranch house, a fat, fawn-colored Boxer dog, so wide it waddled, greeted him, wagging its stump of a tail so hard its entire rear end wiggled. He returned its doggy grin and gave it a scratch behind the ears.

As he and Dudley stepped into the kitchen, a short Mexican woman took a pan of biscuits from an oven. She had that shapeless shape older women sometimes get when their chests and belly and the rest are all about the same size, with a belt around their middles to tell you where they figured their waists were. In this case it was an apron with daisies on it.

Miz Braun grabbed the dog's choke chain and yanked hard. "Down, Poko!" Jesse hoped the chain didn't hurt as much as it looked like it did. The dog didn't seem to mind; she kept on grinning and wagging.

Dudley said, "She's a big one."

Miz Braun smiled. "Oh, she's due any day. We bred her to a champion down in San Antonio. She stays in the house now that she's so close." She scratched Poko behind her ears, which made her wriggle even harder. Miz Braun laughed. "C'mon, big mama." She led the dog through a door off the kitchen, closed it, and then gestured them toward the dining area and a big round table set with six places. "Take a seat, boys."

The dining area opened onto a living room. Somebody liked the same kind of early American furniture Jesse's mother favored, right down to a braided oval rug made with rings of different brown colors. It felt like home . . . not that feeling like home was a good thing.

Mister Braun already sat at the table, stirring his coffee, with Buddy in a chair to his left. Mr. Braun said, "Take a seat and dig in." Buddy nodded to them.

No Lola in sight.

Jesse and Dudley claimed seats opposite them. Heaping bowls and platters of food crowded the table: corn on the cob, mashed potatoes, fried chicken, dinner rolls, salad, and string beans. A flood rose in Jesse's mouth.

Mister Braun aimed a call at a hallway at the far end of the living room. "Supper!"

Lola made an entrance. She'd changed into light pink shorts and a sleeveless blouse that was the same color. The way it blended with her tan and her sun-streaked hair made Jesse think of a ripe peach. He was captivated by the sway of her hips. He lifted his gaze and found her watching him watch her, the corners of her mouth hinting at a grin.

Buddy stood and pulled out the chair next to him. Lola ambled like a lazy cat to the spot between Jesse and her dad and slid onto the chair.

Buddy sat. His eyes looked like knots. Miz Braun took the seat next to him.

Lola said hi and flashed a playful smile. Jesse thought of a pixie and wondered what mischief danced in her mind.

Buddy grabbed a fork and stabbed a drumstick on the platter hard enough to shake the table.

Lola said, "What's eatin' you?"

"Nothin'."

Mister Braun narrowed in on Buddy and stared, his gaze unmoving.

Miz Braun put her hand on Buddy's shoulder. She smiled big and said, "Did Axel tell you Buddy is my little brother?"

Dudley said, "No, ma'am." That explained why Buddy had the same red hair as Miz Braun and smiled big like she did—although his muddy-green eyes never seemed to have anything to do with his show of teeth.

The Mexican woman set a basket of biscuits and a bowl of honey on the table. Miz Braun said to her, "Connie, this is Jesse and Dudley, our new summer boys."

Connie's brown eyes were friendly. Her words were softly accented when she said, "I have cookies always fresh in the kitchen for you."

Dudley patted his belly. "Say thank you to Connie."

She smiled at him and returned to the kitchen as Miz Braun said, "You need something for the cabin, ask Connie. She'll take care of your laundry." Her voice hardened. "Connie, they got a basket out there to put their dirty clothes in?"

"Not yet, Miz Braun."

"Get one."

"Yes, ma'am."

"Sheets on the beds?"

"Yes, ma'am."

Mister Braun said, "Here's what *oughta* be eatin' Buddy."

It took Jesse a couple of seconds to make the leap from sheets to what should be bothering Buddy. It seemed Mister Braun liked to chew on a thought before he spit it out.

"He left these boys out there with no water."

Buddy said, "I forgot."

"Heat stroke comes too easy, and we got an obligation to take care of them."

Buddy snapped, "All right, all right!"

Mister Braun's voice stayed soft and level. "You don't talk that way to me." Jesse saw a flush rise on the back of his neck.

Buddy's eyes looked for a place to hide. "Yessir."

Miz Braun smiled at Dudley and Jesse. "Well, no harm done, right?" Above her smile was a look that made it clear she didn't want to hear otherwise. They shook their heads.

She glanced at Lola. "Is that lipstick, Dolores?"

Lola shot a look at her mother. "It's *Lola*, Mom."

Miz Braun's eyes narrowed.

Lola said, "My lips are just chapped by the sun."

"You know how I feel about makeup."

"Yes, ma'am. I do."

Lola looked into Jesse's eyes and grinned. "So, pass me the biscuits and tell me all about Dallas."

That tied Jesse's tongue completely up. Luckily, Dudley was a talker, so he went on about where they lived, in Casa Linda near White Rock Lake on the east side of Dallas. Jesse ate and nodded.

Lola leaned close and Jesse caught the clean smell of soap, a sweet hint of perfume, and something else he could only identify as "girl." Her hand brushed his, and he melted.

Buddy set his glass down hard and Jesse glanced his way. If Buddy's eyes had been rocks, Jesse would have had to duck.

Buddy held Jesse's gaze as he picked up a roll, curled his fingers around it and crushed it. When he opened his hand, the roll was a lump of dough on his palm.

After supper, affection triggered a smile in Lola when she watched her father begin his ritual. He finished his coffee and excused himself to settle into his easy chair in the living room. He would separate his newspaper into sections and read every last word, and then he'd stretch, yawn, and track her down for a good-night hug.

She caught Jesse looking at her and grinned when he jerked his gaze away and said, "Miz Braun, that was a great supper."

Her mother rose. "I'm glad you liked it. Tomorrow you come back for breakfast at six. We generally work Saturdays. On Sundays we rest, like the good Lord says." She left them for the living room, where she sat and opened a *Ladies Home Journal*. Connie hustled in and started clearing the table.

Jesse whispered to Dudley, "Six o'clock? On Saturday? Won't it be dark? What can you do in the dark?"

Dudley grinned. "How about eat breakfast?"

Lola laughed. Buddy stood and rubbed his distended belly. "Well, I'm goin' in to church." As if he were telling a dog to fetch, he added, "Come with me, Lola."

"Oh, gosh, Uncle Buddy, I've got to wash my hair." Which she had washed that morning, and knew it would be evident even to Buddy's bone brain.

Sure enough, he said, "Looks all right to me."

She widened her eyes into the expression that, she knew from practice in front of her mirror, portrayed calf-eyed innocence. "That's sweet of you to say so, but it's just filthy and itchy. Y'all go on. Besides, Father Murray doesn't like me going to other churches."

Buddy didn't stomp out, but he came close, shoulders hunched and fists tight like he wanted to throw a punch. She was glad she was done with him.

Her body seemed charged with electricity. Just to see what happened, she got up and strolled toward the back door. It was as though she were a human magnet, drawing both boys to their feet. Dudley followed, grabbing cookies from a plate on the counter as he passed. Jesse came along like a pull toy on a string. She led her little parade outside to the patio.

The sun was low in the sky and the air had cooled. A breeze lifted the sweat off her skin; there was a pleasure to it, like a weight being removed. She walked to the two-foot stone wall that bordered the patio. Dudley stopped beside her and Jesse went to Dudley's other side. She'd never seen anybody so shy; was she going to have to do everything?

Dudley handed out cookies and pointed at Connie's cottage. "What's that?"

"That's where Connie lives. She's been here since I was knee-high to nothing."

Faintly, the trumpets and guitars of Mexican music came from the direction of the hen house down the path from the cabin. Jesse laughed.

Dudley said, "What?"

Jesse grinned. "I never heard of playing mariachi music for chickens."

She giggled. "It's our wetbacks. That's their house." Then she thought of the fight between Alejandro and Romero, and she shivered.

Dudley said, "We don't see people like that where we live."

"You want to?"

"What?"

"See 'em. Come on." She stepped from the patio and they followed her down the path. The music grew louder as they drew closer to the chickens.

She paused beside the chicken-wire fence attached to a weathered wall of the house. Ralph the rooster, who would yell his head off come morning, cocked his head at them. She whispered, "We used to have more chickens for an egg business, but then we fixed up the hen house for people."

A cautioning finger to her lips, she led them to a deeply shadowed spot behind the house where two towering cedars intertwined branches to create a secret place with a view into a window. She made sure she stood next to Jesse.

They peered in. Clothes were strewn on battered kitchen chairs and a tattered love seat that had once been in her living room. It had been her favorite spot to curl up and read *Winnie-the-Pooh.* Alejandro sat on a chair; Romero lounged on a cot. Another cot was shoved against the opposite wall. They drank beer from longneck bottles.

She whispered, "The young one is Alejandro, the old guy is Romero. He's been with us before, but Alejandro is new."

A ballad began on the radio; Alejandro stood and slow-danced, his arms holding an imaginary partner. He sang words different from the radio. "*La niña está hermosa-a-a-a.*"

So he thought she was beautiful. She smiled.

Romero frowned. "*La niña* is trouble."

Lola stifled a laugh.

Alejandro tripped over his feet and fell onto Romero's lap, knocking Romero's beer out of his hand. Alejandro laughed.

Romero shoved, sending Alejandro sprawling on his back. Romero leaped to his feet and shouted, "*Bobo!*"

Jesse leaned close. "What?"

"Fool."

Alejandro scrambled to his feet and raised his beer bottle high, holding it by the neck. Dregs of beer dribbled down his arm and onto the floor. "*Chinga tu madré!*"

Lola flinched. "Fuck your mother" were fighting words.

Romero yelled right back. "*Cabrón!*" He pulled out his straight razor and flicked it open. The blade glittered. He slashed at Alejandro.

Alejandro jerked back. A line of blood appeared on his bare chest. He raised his bottle higher, like a tiny club.

Romero crouched, his razor ready.

If they'd been dogs their hackles would have stood like bristles on a brush.

Mariachi music played on.

Alejandro touched the cut and focused bleary eyes at the blood on his fingertip and then licked it. "Aw, shit."

He tossed his bottle into a wastebasket and went to the sink. He studied his wound in the mirror above it and then wet a washcloth and dabbed at the cut, muttering to himself.

Lola realized she was holding her breath and eased it out.

Romero slipped his razor back into his pocket and got a fresh beer, his expression hard.

Her insides all quivery, Lola looked at Jesse. His eyes were wide, maybe with the same fright she fought to control. Wanting no more, she reached for his hand to lead him away. She found it clenched into a fist, but his fingers sprang open at her touch, accepted her fingers, and closed gently.

His gaze met hers. There was fear—but excitement, too, and a calm strength. She felt . . . relieved. She tugged his hand and led him from the shadows. Dudley followed.

One thing was certain; she was done with Alejandro. Tonight. Then they'd stop fighting about her. Alejandro would do as she said.

He had to.

Jesse's thoughts ricocheted back and forth between the fight and the fact that Lola held his hand. By the time they got back to the path, he was pretty much focused on the sensation of her slender fingers wrapped by his.

She released him when her mother called from the house. "Dolor . . . Lola, you've got chores."

Lola shouted, "Coming." She turned to them. "Don't tell my dad about that, okay? They could lose their jobs."

Dudley said, "Okay."

Jesse glanced at the hen house. Romero had looked like he was ready to kill. "Do you think they'll, you know, be okay?"

She hesitated. "I think so. They need their jobs too much to do anyth—"

"Dolores!"

Her sigh was exactly like his when his mother was being a pain. She answered, "I'm coming." Under her breath, she added, "Christ!" She gave Jesse a worried look. "You won't tell?"

He couldn't deny those eyes anything. "Nope."

Lola's smile flashed. "I'll see y'all tomorrow."

He watched her walk away, wondering why she had taken his hand. The fight had scared her, sure, but maybe she had liked it when he'd—

He shook his head. Naw.

Dudley said "Come on, I'm dying for a smoke," and led the way to the cabin. Inside, Dudley fished out his Camels. He grinned; his parents didn't know he smoked and he had to sneak at home.

Jesse used the bathroom; when he came out, Dudley stood facing him, his shirt open to reveal his massive belly. A lit cigarette stuck out of the cavern that housed his tummy button. Dudley sucked his stomach in, oh'd his mouth and blew a smoke ring.

Jesse'd seen the trick before, but it looked so weird he had to laugh.

Dudley grinned and plucked the cigarette from his navel. "Want one?"

Jesse had always turned cigarettes down, but this time he figured, what the hell. He nodded and Dudley tossed him the pack and his Zippo. Jesse flicked a flame, lit up and puffed.

"You got to breathe it in."

Jesse inhaled deeply, the smoke struck deep in his lungs, and he doubled over with coughing.

When he could breathe again, Dudley said, "Just little ones at first."

Jesse wheezed, "Thanks for the warning."

Dudley sat on his bunk and blew a string of smoke rings, a talent Jesse envied. He tried but just got blobs. His mouth tasted like shit, and his head was light and spinny. He went to the bathroom and flushed the cigarette, and then brushed his teeth, examining his face in the cracked mirror for anything that would be of interest to Lola. Nothing.

Romero's fierce expression came back to him as he returned to the bedroom. "That was scary."

"Yeah. I thought he was going to kill him."

"You ever see a fight like that?"

"No. Don't want to again, either."

"You think we'll be working with them?"

Dudley stretched. "I guess. I don't know which is worse, razor-happy wetbacks or the almighty Buddy."

"Lola was scared."

"Hell, so was I."

Dudley pulled his suitcase from under his bunk and took out a sketch pad and drawing pencil. "I'm gonna do some brands." They had ongoing discussions about the design to be burned into the hides of their stock when they had a ranch. "How about the Bar DJ?"

"How about the Bar JD?"

Dudley laughed. "I'll do both."

Jesse opened his suitcase and took out Isaac Asimov's *Foundation.* Sitting at the table, he read while Dudley drew.

They lasted until shortly after the sun set at eight-thirty. Dudley closed his pad and yawned. "Stick a fork in me, I'm done." He shed his clothes down to his underwear, dropped them on the floor, and crawled into bed.

Jesse realized he had been staring at a page for minutes but not reading the words. "Me, too." After undressing, he turned out the light and climbed up to sink into his bunk.

A tangle of noises made by crickets and other bugs came through the screened door. His body relaxed into a limp mound of flesh populated by dull aches and the pleasure of relief. But his mind refused to be still. Moments from the evening flashed through like a lightning storm.

Flash, the gleam of Lola's smile.

Flash, the glitter of the razor blade.

Flash, the touch of her hand.

A snore rose from under him; Dudley could sleep any time, anywhere. Jesse rapped on the bed frame. "Hey!"

Dudley snorted and then turned on his side and quieted. After maybe a million sleepovers, Jesse knew how to deal with Dudley's noisy nose.

Jesse clamped his eyes shut, but it was as though a movie was showing on the insides of his eyelids, a fractured film of the day chopped into pieces and randomly assembled into a chaotic stream.

There was no way he was going to get any sleep. He slid to the floor, pulled on his jeans and T-shirt, and fished a small flashlight from his suitcase.

He eased the screen door open and shut. Outside, all was quiet in the noisy way of a country night: a toad croaked, cicadas chittered. The moon shed light enough, so he tucked the flashlight into a pocket. All day he'd wanted a look at the horses in the barn, so he set out for a visit.

He walked behind the garden and then past Connie's cottage. Light glowed from a curtained rear window; her voice, soft and low, hummed a melody. He rounded her place and approached the bedroom end of the ranch house. Two windows were lit, one facing the back yard and screened by bushes, one on the front corner. He smiled at the sound of Elvis coming from the rear window.

As he neared the front of the house, the light in the corner bedroom extinguished. He froze, hoping he hadn't been heard. He didn't want the Brauns thinking he was some kind of sneak, spying on them.

Bedsprings creaked. Jesse waited for silence and then slipped past the window.

When he hit the driveway, the crushed rock turned his noiseless footsteps into crunches. He stepped off and continued in the dust and sparse grass that bordered the drive. A cricket went quiet when he drew near its hiding place and then chirped again after he had passed.

Buddy's trailer came into view; it was dark, and the '57 Chevy was gone. Good; he didn't want any nighttime encounters with that guy. The barn loomed further down the drive, shadowy and mysterious.

The inside of the barn was as dark as the inside of a cow, so he flicked on the flashlight. An orange and white cat scurried up the stairs to the loft.

"Sorry, cat."

A little paint horse, Roman-nosed and not a whole lot bigger than a pony, poked its head out and eyed him. In the next stall stood a buckskin that looked to be a regular size, fourteen or fifteen hands tall at the withers. He liked the buckskin's handsome head, finely sculpted like an Arabian's.

The stall across the way held an ancient bay, its sway back curving like a hammock from its withers to its flanks. His light came across a sack of feed. He fetched a handful of oats and offered them to the buckskin. The horse nibbled eagerly, its chin whiskers tickling his palm.

The low rumble of an approaching car broke the silence and headlights illuminated the front of the barn. Jesse turned off the flashlight and slipped into the buckskin's stall. Light blazed into the barn, and the car pulled up and stopped at the front. He hunkered down in a spot that couldn't be seen from the corridor.

A car door opened and shut. Buddy's voice came. "Hey? Somebody there?"

Darn, he'd seen the flashlight. The buckskin stuck its head out the stall door.

"Hey, Dusty, you see a light?" Buddy's hand reached in and patted the horse. "Those little summer creeps screwing around in here?"

Buddy's hand disappeared. Footsteps faded. A car door slammed and the Chevy's lights left. Jesse stood, and then had to lean on the buckskin when his knees started to give way.

Jesse waited inside the barn and watched for Buddy's lights to go out. When the last window went dark, he headed for the cabin, his skin prickling as he passed the trailer.

At the ranch house, Lola's light was out and her music off.

A snore came from the Brauns' window. It wasn't much of a snore compared to Jesse's mother, a real wall-shaker when she'd been drinking. Which was all the time.

His mother. It felt so good to be away. As weary as he was from digging that damned hole, it was a breeze compared to the exhaustion he felt after a day of reining in his anger toward her. Or the defeat that came with one of their shouting matches about "the problem." He couldn't say "drunk" out loud, no—

A meaty slap from the back yard yanked his thoughts from his mother. He stopped and listened. Lola's fierce whisper cut the silence. "Keep your hands off me!"

Amusement flavored Alejandro's voice. "You hit hard for such a *pequeña niña*."

The voices came from the gazebo, fifteen feet from Jesse. He could see nothing. What was Lola doing with Alejandro?

"I'm not a little girl."

"Then come here."

Sounds of feet scuffing a floor ended with a masculine grunt and Lola's angry whisper. "I'll scream."

Fear for Lola stirred in Jesse. Alejandro had been pretty drunk earlier. Jesse felt like he should do something. But what?

Alejandro said, "You won't. Your parents would be very angry with you meeting me."

"I'll tell them you forced me—with a razor!"

The screened door on the gazebo slammed open and Alejandro's shape paused in the black of the doorway. "You little prick teaser!"

Jesse ducked behind a small cedar and crouched low, heart thudding in his chest so loudly it seemed they must hear it.

Alejandro's whisper was like a knife. "I'm not through with you, *Señorita*." The door banged shut and he walked into the dark.

Lola stepped from the gazebo and whispered after him, "You better leave me alone. My Daddy finds out, you're dead."

Relief washed through Jesse. It was over. Lola ran to her window, lifted the screen by the bottom edge and climbed. In seconds, she was inside. The night was as quiet as it had been.

Quieter.

The snoring from the Brauns' room had stopped.

A soft thump came from the front of the house.

Had the noise awakened the Brauns? Would they come looking and find him?

Moments later, Ricky Nelson sang from Lola's room about being a poor little fool for carefree devil eyes.

Glad for the music to cover his footsteps, he hurried to the cabin, undressed, and climbed into his bunk. His heart settled down, but his thoughts wouldn't. What was going on? Whatever it was, Lola was no kind of girl he'd ever known.

Events swirled in his mind: Romero and Alejandro like dogs at each other's throats, the voltage of Lola's touch, Alejandro's fury when he left Lola. It seemed to Jesse he'd never go to sleep.

Then the clang of Dudley's alarm clock dragged him from dreams of razors and carefree devil eyes.

It was dark when Dudley's alarm annoyed Jesse awake at five-thirty. He couldn't believe these people started the day at night. The rooster wasn't crowing. Even dumb clucks had sense enough to wait for the sun to rise.

His first scare of the day came when he swung his feet over the side of his bed. He started to slide off and then grabbed the rail to stop from landing on Dudley, who sat below, holding his head in his hands. Jesse was going to have to remember his bed was way off the floor.

Dudley moaned, "Isn't there some kind of law about cruel and unusual punishment?"

Jesse wanted to lie back down, but the thought of Mister Braun coming to wake them because they'd overslept kept him moving. He climbed down and dug jeans and a shirt out of his suitcase.

He pulled on his boots—black with red, white and blue eagles on the tops. No more shoes, this was a ranch! He stood—then remembered about checking for scorpions. He braced for a sting, but his toes felt nothing strange.

He thought he looked pretty darned cowboy.

It was a good thing neither of them shaved very much yet; they'd probably have cut their throats with hands drugged by sleep. Jesse's fuzz had been looking a little heavier lately, but

Dudley's baby face only had a couple of pale things resembling whiskers even though he was a year older.

Still groggy, they ambled to the main house in faint predawn light. Jesse's dim memories of his late-night walk to the barn were tangled with dreams, so he discarded it all and looked forward to the day.

The first thing he saw inside was Miz Braun at the stove, pouring something brown from a saucepan into a small pitcher. Connie was frying bacon, and the aroma set Jesse's mouth to watering. It occurred to him that he spent a lot of time salivating, either over food or Lola.

Mister Braun and Buddy were already at the table, which held stacks of pancakes, a box of Cheerios, bananas, and pitchers of orange juice and milk.

No sign of Lola.

Miz Braun approached Jesse, her mouth tight-lipped.

Jesse tried a smile. "Mornin', Miz Braun."

She doused his smile with a cold look and then handed him the pitcher—warm maple syrup by the smell of it. Her tone flat, she said, "Take this and get started." A four-slice toaster popped toast up and she went to take it out.

Where had that nice woman from yesterday gone? Jesse followed Dudley to the table.

Mister Braun sounded normal when he said, "Mornin'."

Dudley and Jesse chimed greetings back, hitting a nervous unison. Mister Braun chuckled.

Buddy lifted a surly look at them. Lot of grumpy people here in the morning.

Miz Braun set a plate piled high with bacon beside Jesse and took a seat. He took four strips, reached for the pancakes, and dug in. Nobody talked, just chewed and swallowed.

After a plateful of food and a bowlful of cereal had filled the hollow beneath his belt, he felt satisfied—then Connie brought a platter of scrambled eggs and sausage. The Brauns and Buddy took big helpings, and so did Dudley.

Jesse hesitated, and Mister Braun said, "Better have some. You'll need it."

Jesse had no trouble following his advice. After the previous day's work, he could see a need for a double breakfast.

He was full as a tick by the time Mister Braun drained his coffee cup and stood. It was light outside. The rooster crowed and Jesse held in a laugh that no one would have understood.

Mister Braun eyed Jesse and Dudley. "You boys got hats?"

They stood, shaking their heads no, Jesse feeling stupid because they hadn't thought of that.

Mister Braun glanced at Jesse's booted feet. "Work shoes?"

He got another no.

Mister Braun reached for Jesse's hand and looked at the blisters. "I guess it would be too much to think you thought to bring gloves."

Dudley said, "Sorry, sir."

Jesse raised his hand. "We could buy some."

"You'll have to."

Buddy chugged his orange juice, belched, and stood. "What do you want me to do with them this morning?"

"Nothin'. I'm going to show them around and then run them into town for work gear. You take Romero and what's his name and muck out the barn."

Jesse thought it couldn't have happened to a nicer guy.

"Daddy?" Lola crossed the living room, wearing a light blue robe over white baby doll pajamas. The robe was open, and each step showed a lot of Lola.

Miz Braun jumped up from her chair and blocked her daughter's way. Her voice was sharp. "Dolores!"

Her daughter corrected her. "Lola."

"*Dolores.* You will not display yourself like that."

Lola's face tightened, and it looked like she was going to say something. Then she bowed her head. "Yes, ma'am."

She pulled her robe together and stepped around her mother. Miz Braun's glare followed her.

Lola smiled at her father as if nothing had happened. "Daddy, are you going into town today? I need some things for my barrel-racing outfit."

Respect joined Jesse's feelings about Lola. Barrel racers rode full speed from one end of a rodeo arena to the other, weaving their horses around barrels so tightly it looked liked they ran parallel to the ground. A mistake could cost a broken leg for horse or rider.

Mister Braun said, "I'm takin' the boys to town in about an hour. You be ready." He looked to Jesse and Dudley. "You got any money?"

Jesse said, "In the cabin."

"Run get it and meet me at the Jeep."

When they trotted around to the front of the house, they found Mister Braun, Buddy at his side, talking to Romero and Alejandro in rapid Spanish. It was too fast for Jesse's year of high-school Spanish to catch. The Mexican hands nodded a lot. Buddy did not look pleased.

Mister Braun signaled Jesse and Dudley over.

"You'll be working with these men." He indicated Romero. "Jesse, Dudley, this is Romero."

Romero smiled and removed his dusty black cowboy hat. Sunlight flashed from a massive silver ring on his right hand, its blue stone carved into a hawk or something. "*Buenas dias.*"

He seemed like a nice guy. Jesse said, "*Buenas dias.*"

Romero's hat had a red feather tucked into a snakeskin hatband. Jesse wondered if he could find a hatband like that.

Romero's blue denim shirt was faded and worn, his jeans patched but clean. Jesse figured the slim bulge in his right pants pocket was the razor he'd pulled on Alejandro. It had worn a lighter blue outline of itself in the fabric the same way Jesse's comb had created its shape in his hip pocket.

Mister Braun said, "And this is Alejandro."

Alejandro gave them a big smile, nodded, and said, "*Como está?*" A knee showed through a hole in his worn jeans. He wore a gleaming white dress shirt open halfway to the waist, the razor cut a dark line across his chest. His white straw hat was sweat-darkened around the base of the crown. Because Jesse had thought of him as a man, it surprised him to see that Alejandro was a little smaller than he was. And maybe not much older, either. Romero, although thick and strong-looking, was also short.

Alejandro's nasty words to Lola in the night came back to Jesse, and dislike brewed in him.

Dudley answered him. "*Muy bien.*"

Mister Braun said, "Let's get to work." He headed for the Jeep and Jesse followed, Dudley a step behind; Buddy, Romero and Alejandro trudged down the driveway toward the barn.

Jesse glanced back at the house as they pulled away and saw Lola standing at the door, watching them. Her robe was open, one naked leg peeking out. Her mother appeared behind her and pulled her inside. When Jesse turned back, Dudley smiled and shook his head. Jesse figured his friend was laughing inside at how hopeless he was. He didn't care—he replayed images of smooth, tan thighs as the Jeep bounced down the drive.

As the driveway curved by a tree-shaded creek, Mister Braun pointed and said, "We've got a swimmin' hole there. It feels real good after a hot day's work."

After the Jeep rumbled over the cattle guard and onto the highway, Mister Braun gestured at both sides of the road. "We work all of this. I own about five thousand acres and we lease another five thousand from the government."

They cruised by Angora goats populating one hilly pasture, and then past fat-looking sheep dotting another. "We'll be shearing the sheep before it gets too much hotter."

They turned onto a dirt road, and a rooster-tail of dust rose behind them. Mr. Braun waved at land that was mostly grass with clumps of prickly pear and a few live oaks clustered here and there. "Our cattle graze here in the summer."

Dudley glanced back from the front seat. Jesse knew what he was thinking. One of these days they'd have cattle, too.

They passed a handful of cows grazing, and then came to a huge bull mounting a heifer. His tallywhacker was pink, easily a foot long. He had his front hooves on her back and was poking away, but his prick had missed and bent out to the side of her hind leg. The cow moved out from under him and the bull lumbered after her to try again. Dudley and Jesse guffawed, Mister Braun smiled.

Jesse caught Dudley's eye and winked. "I bet his name is Mister Completely."

Dudley snickered and Mister Braun turned a puzzled look his way. Dudley said, "You know, that old joke about a book called 'A Hole In the Bed' by Mister Completely." Dudley made "Mister" sound more like "Missed Her," and Mister Braun shook his head and chuckled.

They flew past three whitetail deer that bounded away and flushed a wild turkey from a bush at the side of the road.

Mister Braun stopped near a small wooden windmill. A pipe came from the ground at its base to feed a metal trough like the one Jesse and Dudley had dug the hole for, but no water spilled from the pipe. The windmill blades weren't turning. He drove to the pasture gate. "Somebody get the gate."

Dudley showed no inclination to move—no surprise—so Jesse jumped out, opened the gate, and closed it after Mister Braun drove through. He was determined to make Mister Braun think well of him, so he was happy to take on the duty.

As Mister Braun mounted the ladder on the windmill's side, Jesse saw that a board had broken loose and blocked the blades. Mister Braun called for Dudley to bring up a hammer from a toolbox in the back of the Jeep. Dudley climbed the hammer up, and then the boss pulled nails out of the board.

He shouted down to Jesse, "Straighten this," and tossed down a three-inch nail bent in the middle at almost a right angle. Jesse took a hammer from the toolbox and then stood thinking. How do you straighten a nail?

Mister Braun called down, "On the bumper."

Oh, sure. Jesse knelt in the dust, held one end of the nail against the Jeep's flat steel bumper, and tried to hammer the upright end down. He hit it, and the other end came up, no matter how hard he tried to hold it. Heat rose into his face, and it wasn't just from hammering.

Forever went by with no progress other than bashing his thumb. Mister Braun muttered "Damn" and climbed down.

He grabbed the hammer and nail. "Don't you know how to do anything?"

Right then Jesse didn't think so.

Mister Braun turned the nail so the bend was up and the ends down, pounded on the bend, and the nail was straight.

Jesse felt a half-inch tall.

After the boss nailed the board back into place, the windmill resumed creaking and groaning as it strained to pull water from the earth. Mister Braun drove in silence back to the ranch house.

At least, Jesse thought, he'd learned how to straighten a nail. What an idiot.

Lola waited on the front lawn, an inviting eyeful in white shorts and blouse with a red scarf tied around her waist like a sash. The white set off smooth tan skin that called to Jesse like honeysuckle to a bee.

She thanked Dudley when he surrendered his seat and moved to the back, but Jesse thought her smile was for him.

On the way out, Mister Braun stopped below the barn and honked, but nobody appeared. It was dead quiet.

He scowled, and then pointed to the flatbed truck parked near the barn and said to Jesse, "I don't want that truck settin' in the sun. Key should be in it, move it into the barn for now." He narrowed his eyes at Jesse. "You can do that, can't you?"

Even though Jesse didn't have his driver's license yet, he'd practiced driving with his mom's car on back streets. "Yessir." He jumped out and ran to the truck.

He climbed in and— Damn. It was a stick shift. With a three-foot floor gearshift. He had never driven a stick, although he knew about using a clutch from the old Volvo Dudley'd owned before the Caddy. There was no way he could tell Mister Braun there was another thing he couldn't do.

So he pushed in the clutch and grabbed the gearshift knob. He didn't have any idea which gear was where, so he pushed and pulled until it felt like it slid into a place it belonged. He started the truck and eased the clutch out, giving it gas slowly the way Dudley had his Volvo.

The engine died. He glanced at the Jeep. Even though he couldn't really see Mister Braun's face, he felt sure a frown was gathering there. Okay, so why—oh. The emergency brake was on. He disengaged the brake and the truck rolled backward.

He stomped on the brake and looked out the back window; a huge tractor lurked ten feet behind him. Now he had to put the clutch in, start the truck, and then take his foot off the brake and get the truck going without rolling into the tractor.

So he did it. Engine racing, the truck mercifully moved forward at a crawl. Jesse was pretty sure he had it in the wrong gear, but he wasn't about to stop and fish around for a better one that he didn't know where was. He steered through the wide barn doorway.

As he drove from dazzling sunlight into the dark interior, he was momentarily blind.

A white blur appeared, dead ahead. Somebody stretched out on the barn floor.

Jesse hit the brake, the truck jerked to a stop, and the engine died.

The wheels hadn't struck anything. All he could see now was a wooden shaft standing straight up in front of the truck's hood. Fear jammering in his mind, he yanked the emergency brake and jumped out, blurting an apology as he ran to the front of the truck.

"I'm sorry, I couldn't see . . ."

The somebody was Alejandro. On his back. A pitchfork stood upright, the tines buried deep in Alejandro's bare chest.

Blood pooled between his ribs. A red stream had run down his side and stained his open white shirt.

"Alejandro?"

He didn't move.

Jesse flinched back a step and then steadied himself. "Jesus Christ." He couldn't pull his stare away.

A fly landed on Alejandro's chest. It joined others gathered on the blood. There was a smell in the air like the taste of a penny.

The pitchfork had been driven into Alejandro with such force that he was pinned to the dirt floor. Alejandro's eyes were open wide with a look of surprise.

They promised to stare at Jesse forever.

It wasn't Jesse's nature to panic, but right then he was only one more thought away from the screaming meemies. A honk from the Jeep's horn wrenched him from his trance. He turned and ran out.

At the Jeep, puffing from his run, he said, "Mister Braun, there's something in the barn you need to see."

"What?"

"Uh, Alejandro is, uh, got hurt."

"Buddy's not there?"

"Nossir."

"Romero?"

"I didn't see anybody else."

Mister Braun stepped out of the Jeep. Lola started to climb out too, and Jesse told her, "You better stay here."

She stopped. "Why?"

"Uh, I don't think he'd want you there."

"Why not?"

Jesse couldn't tell her what lay on the barn floor. "I can't, I just, you shouldn't, uh . . ."

Mister Braun frowned at Jesse. "Stay here, honey. I'm sure this will just take a minute." She shrugged and sat back.

Dudley raised his eyebrows, but there was nothing Jesse could say.

Mister Braun walked toward the barn, Jesse at his side. When they were far enough away that Lola wouldn't hear, the boss said, "He hurt bad?"

"He looks . . . dead, sir."

Mister Braun stopped and stared at Jesse.

"Yessir."

Mister Braun took off running; Jesse caught up with him and led him around the truck. Mister Braun said, "Damn!" and knelt by the body. He felt for a pulse in Alejandro's neck although, when Jesse looked at the three pitchfork tines in his chest, one of them right where Jesse thought the heart was, it seemed like a useless thing to do.

Mister Braun stood and looked around the barn. He called out, "Buddy! Romero!"

There was no answer. He called again; still no answer.

A soft gasp came from behind them and they turned to find Lola there, her hand over her mouth. She sagged; Jesse jumped to her side and steadied her.

Her dad didn't fuss at her about coming, just stepped to her and turned her away. He put his arm around her and started walking; Jesse followed.

Mister Braun stopped at the mouth of the barn. "Jesse, stay here. Don't let anyone near him, and keep watch for Buddy and Romero. I'll send Dudley to help." He escorted Lola back to the Jeep and then Dudley came running up. When he started into the barn, Jesse said, "I wouldn't."

"I've gotta look." He went inside.

Jesse stayed where he was. He wasn't about to go back to where Alejandro lay dead. Dudley returned looking sick. They stood guard at the entrance. Jesse tried not to hear the buzz of flies behind them.

Mister Braun drove like a house afire to Buddy's trailer, jumped out and hammered on the door. Buddy came out, shirtless and in his sock feet. Mister Braun's voice was loud, but not enough to understand what he said. He pointed at the barn. Buddy shook his head and then pointed into his trailer. Mister Braun said something and Buddy ran inside.

Mister Braun hugged Lola, and then left her in the Jeep and trotted back toward the barn. Seconds later Buddy ran out, feet stuffed into shoes, pulling on a shirt the color of the bright blood on Alejandro's chest. He piled into the Jeep and raced toward the ranch house.

Flies buzzed.

Dudley said, "What do you think happened?"

"I can't help thinkin' about them fighting last night."

"Yeah, me too."

"Did you catch what it was about?" Dudley had a year more Spanish than Jesse.

"A girl." He gazed at the receding Jeep. "A pretty girl."

Oh, shit.

They went back to the silence of their thoughts and watched Mister Braun approach. When he got to them he said, "Buddy's going to call the police and then see if he can find Romero." He went inside and glared at the body and the pitchfork as if he could force them to yield answers. He called for Romero again, and then walked around the outside of the barn, calling for Romero. Dudley and Jesse stayed put.

Minutes crept past. The quiet was suffocating. Then a creak echoed deep in the barn. Jesse tensed, wondering if Romero would charge out, wielding his razor. Nothing happened, and he decided it was the heat making the wood expand.

The look of surprise in Alejandro's dead eyes haunted Jesse. It was just like—he couldn't keep the memory away—just like the astonishment in his father's expression when he lay dead on the sidewalk in front of their home.

Jesse's throat tightened—he forced his thoughts away from that. He stared at the landscape, making himself imagine what it would be like for him and Dudley to have their own place. There wouldn't be any wetbacks if he had anything to say about it.

A buzzard flew above and then circled high overhead. Did it sense what lay in the barn? Did death send out a notice that it had arrived?

The Braun's family car, a Chrysler sedan he'd seen parked next to the house, hurtled down the driveway from the house. The big car was all beige, inside and out, except for two spots of color—Buddy in his red shirt and something blue in the back seat.

Jesse thought it took some guts for Buddy to go looking for a killer.

Sheriff Carl Webb's deliberate moves reminded Jesse of John Wayne, a steady, unstoppable force. He was a bear-sized blond man, his mustache stained brown in the center by smoke from a constant stream of Pall Mall cigarettes. After the sheriff looked around the barn, careful to keep away from the body, he radioed for a photographer and the coroner.

While he was on the radio, a deputy arrived; Sheriff Webb set him to guard the area and then asked Mister Braun, Dudley and Jesse to accompany him to the house for an interview. Nobody said anything on the long walk up the driveway, the only sound the crunch-crunch of rocks.

Miz Braun opened the door just as they stepped up on the front porch. Her gaze darted around, never lighting anyplace long, avoiding people altogether. Her face was pale; in contrast, the scar across her eyebrow was a deep red. She still wore her gardening gloves, her hands clenching and unclenching as if they had minds of their own.

Inside, the sheriff went to her. "I know how upsetting this must be, Margaret." He patted her shoulder. "It'll be all right."

She nodded. It didn't look to Jesse like she believed the sheriff. He didn't either.

Everyone took seats in the living room while Miz Braun had Connie bring them iced tea. Connie's face was tight, and she kept her eyes aimed at the floor. Lola came in from the hallway to the bedrooms and sat on the window seat in the front bay window. Her eyes were red and puffy, and she looked frightened. Jesse understood that. Fear kept rising up every time he started to feel normal again.

He hadn't known how parched his throat was. The tea cooled and calmed him, a good thing because the sheriff started the questioning with him.

"Jesse, you found the body?"

"Yessir."

"Did you touch it?"

He shook his head. "I couldn't."

"Get close to it?"

"About six feet."

"See anybody else there?"

"No sir. I didn't hear anything, either."

The sheriff nodded as if that was a good thing to have added, and then turned his questions to Mister Braun, who told the history of the morning and his part in the discovery.

Buddy burst in the door, hot and sweaty. He went to Miz Braun and put a hand on her shoulder in a reassuring way. His gaze hopped around the room just like hers had.

Jesse had trouble looking people in the eye, too; he hadn't done anything wrong, but it felt like he had.

The sheriff turned to Buddy. "Where were you when the killing took place?"

"My trailer. I was working in the barn and got too hot, so I told the men to finish up the stalls they were cleaning and then take a break. I went to my trailer and laid down under the air conditioner. I didn't know what happened until Axel came bangin' on my door."

"And you don't know where the other man is?"

Buddy shook his head. "I just drove everywhere I knew to look. I haven't seen him since I left the barn."

"Where do they bunk?"

"Out back. I checked there first."

An image of Romero's razor slashing across Alejandro's chest popped into Jesse's head. Absorbed in watching the sheriff investigate, he hadn't thought to say anything. He didn't really want to, either. But he had to, didn't he?

"Uh, Sheriff, we saw them fighting."

All heads turned to him, Lola's the quickest, and he was sorry he'd opened his mouth.

The sheriff said, "Who?"

"Alejandro and Romero. That's how he got that cut on his chest. Romero's razor."

"When was this?"

"Last night. Me and, uh . . ." He glanced at Lola. "And Dudley were exploring after supper, and we looked in their window, and they had this fight, and then they stopped after Romero cut him with a razor."

Mister Braun glared. "Why didn't you tell me about this?"

"We, uh, forgot, sir." He put a wide-eyed look on his face. Dudley nodded.

Mister Braun frowned, but let it go. It hit Jesse that he *had* done something wrong. Maybe if he'd told about the fight, Alejandro would be alive.

The sheriff asked, "What were they fighting about?"

Jesse reined in an urge to look Lola's way. "I don't know. It was all Spanish that I couldn't understand."

Dudley added, "They were drinkin' beer."

The sheriff nodded as though that had particular meaning and then raised his eyebrows at Mister Braun.

Mister Braun shook his head. "I can't believe Romero did it. The man has worked for me for ten years, and I never saw him lose his temper."

Jesse hated to contradict Mister Braun, but he had to say, "He did last night, sir."

The sheriff stood. "I need to see where they lived."

Mister Braun rose and headed for the back door, the sheriff loosening his pistol in his holster as he followed. Buddy stood, but the sheriff told him to stay put.

Lola left for her room, looking like she was going to cry.

Jesse startled when the kitchen door jerked open twenty minutes later—it was just Mister Braun, followed by the sheriff. He was glad to have them back; the ticking of the living-room clock had him clenching his teeth with every tock.

The sheriff stopped in the kitchen where Miz Braun was adding sugar to her third glass of iced tea. "No sign of him, Margaret, and it looks like his things are gone. You didn't see him come or go?"

"No. I did hear the chickens stir a while back when I was working in the garden, but I didn't see what it was."

The sheriff gave Mister Braun a stern look. "I assume these men were not here legally."

Mister Braun sighed. "No, Carl, they weren't. Just like half the help in the county."

Sheriff Webb nodded. "I know, Axel, I ain't gonna get on you about it. It just makes it harder to trace the man. Any identifying marks or mannerisms?"

Mister Braun shook his head. "Just looks like a Mexican." He thought. "Oh, he wears this silver ring. Big, heavy thing. Got a turquoise eagle on it. Wears a black hat."

Jesse pictured the ring flashing in the sunlight.

The sheriff said, "I'll put out a bulletin on him. He's probably headed across country for the border, and it's a hundred fifty miles. We could get lucky."

"I hope so. Only a wetback was killed, but justice should be done."

It troubled Jesse to hear Alejandro called "only" a wetback as if that made him less of a person.

After the sheriff left, there was silence. Jesse gritted his teeth and wondered what to do. Mister Braun turned to him and Dudley. "If you boys want to go home, I'll sure understand, and I'll see to it."

Going home had never come to Jesse's mind.

Mister Braun said, "I'll be honest, I need you more than ever now. And I think everything will be all right here. The sheriff figures Romero's run for it, so I'm sure we're safe. I mean, it's just us here now. It's up to you."

Jesse didn't have to think about it. He loved the hills and the clean air. And not being home. He looked at Dudley and shook his head. "I want to stay."

Dudley said, "Me, too."

Jesse couldn't remember being the first to do something between him and Dudley.

Mister Braun's frown lightened. "Good." He took off his hat to run his fingers through his hair and Jesse noticed for the first time that the top half of his forehead was whiter than the rest of his sun-browned face. On another person it would have been comical; on Mister Braun it was just a fact.

"Let's take the rest of the day off. Tomorrow's Sunday, and there'll be no work. You're welcome to go to Mass with us. We leave at ten."

Jesse said, "Yessir."

Mister Braun put his hat on the rack by the front door and walked down the hall to the bedrooms, his back a little less straight, as if he bore a weight.

Jesse shifted from foot to foot. He glanced at Dudley. What now?

Miz Braun fussed with her tea, and then she snapped, "You need somethin' to do, I can scare up some work."

Jesse said, "Can I use the phone to call home? I should have checked in last night, but I forgot."

Dudley said, "Me, too."

As Jesse listened to the phone ring, he hoped his mother's voice would be sharp and clear. No such luck; as usual, she slurred her words. With Jesse gone there was nobody to find her vodka bottles and pour out the booze. He didn't see any sense in upsetting her with the murder, so he just told her, "Everything's fine, Mama."

"Miss you, honey."

Yeah, sure. "You, too, Mama. 'Bye."

Jesse hung up, knowing she'd fall asleep sitting on the couch that night, watching television, a drink in her hand. Her vodka was never far from her reach since his Dad died. She even had a holder that hung on the car door by the vent window, and she never went anywhere without a fresh drink. She'd had four accidents in the last four months, including one where she backed into the brick wall of a Safeway.

Dudley gave his folks a quick call, not telling them anything either. They'd have made him come home.

On the way out, Jesse noticed Connie attacking a pile of potatoes at the kitchen sink with a peeler, gouging at them so hard Jesse wondered if she wasn't going to peel off a finger or two. It occurred to him that the sheriff hadn't asked her a single question. It was almost as if she hadn't been there, or didn't count.

As Jesse led the way to their cabin, the hen house pulled at him. He wanted to pry into it, to see what was left behind. But not right away. Alejandro's eyes would be on him.

It was cool enough inside their cabin, thanks to the thick log walls and the shade of live oak trees. He sat on a chair and Dudley lay on his bunk. Silence settled.

Jesse thought back to the Alejandro he'd seen dancing in the hen house—young and laughing and so alive—now he was dead. With shame, Jesse remembered the dislike he'd felt toward Alejandro that morning.

What was Dudley thinking? "It was awful."

"Yeah." Dudley's voice was tight, like when you asked him how he was doing in a class he was having trouble with.

Jesse didn't want to talk about it either. "What do you want to do tomorrow morning, church or sleep?"

"Sleep."

"Yeah."

Dudley got up for a drink of water from the bathroom and then stood in the doorway. "Do you think we're nuts for staying?"

Jesse shook his head. "We just got here. We got nothing to do with those guys. And I want to work on a real ranch."

Dudley nodded. "Yeah. I mean, this is what we've been talking about."

"Besides, I wouldn't feel right about deserting Mister Braun. He needs us."

"Me neither."

Now that Jesse thought about it, he felt a lot safer than he had after seeing the Mexicans fight and Lola's late-night meeting with Alejandro. Things would be fine. "Hey, maybe Buddy'll let up now."

Dudley grinned and shook his head. "Once an asshole . . ."

Jesse joined him for the chorus. ". . . always an asshole."

Dudley turned on the radio, found a lone rock-and-roll station in a crowd of country music, and lay back in his bunk.

Jesse climbed into his bunk to lose himself in the psychohistory of the Foundation. Bless Isaac Asimov, he helped Jesse forget dead eyes.

For a time.

A persistent, soft knocking on Lola's bedroom door freed her from a dream of Alejandro's lifeless face. She cracked her eyes open and then scrunched them shut at the brightness of daylight. They hurt from crying. She groaned.

The knocking wouldn't stop.

"What?"

Her father's voice was gentle. "Time to get up for Mass, honey. C'mon."

Church? She was limp with exhaustion. "No-o-o-o. I can't. I can't."

"Get up, Dolores." A little firmer that time.

"Please?"

A pause. Oh, please.

"I'll think about it."

"Thank you, Daddy."

She tried to relax, but her stomach ached. Heaving sobs had gone on and on after she could no longer deny what she'd seen lying on the barn floor. Curling into a ball, she pulled the sheet over her head to shut out the world.

Her door was flung open so hard it banged against her dresser.

Now what?

Somebody yanked her sheet away.

"Get up." Her mother's voice had that stiff, you-better-do-it edge. "We all need Mass this morning."

Lola rolled over and pleaded, "Mommy . . ."

Her mother was on the way out the door.

Lola crawled out of bed. Choosing something to wear helped her keep at a distance haunting images of . . . of . . .

At her closet, she reached for her blue gingham skirt, thinking the white peasant blouse would look pretty with it.

Her parents were eating breakfast when she joined them. The sight of food sickened her—she stopped in the living room and collapsed into her father's easy chair.

Her father said, "You'll feel better with some food in you."

She placed a hand on her sore tummy. "I can't."

Her mother frowned. "You can," and her stare forced Lola to her feet and into the kitchen.

Connie poured corn flakes into a bowl and then held her arms wide. Lola stepped into them and sagged against motherly comfort. Connie cooed, "*Niña*," and patted Lola's back with the rhythm she'd seen Connie use to sooth a colicky baby.

Lola's mother called out, "That's enough, Connie."

Connie broke the embrace, sliced a banana on top of the corn flakes, poured milk in, and handed the bowl to Lola. "Try this."

Lola's favorite breakfast roused only nausea. She carried it to the table and slumped into a chair. Begging her father with her eyes, she said, "Can't I stay home? I feel so bad."

Her mother said, "Bad? About what? Good riddance to bad rubbish."

Lola burst from her chair, ran down the hall and slammed her door behind her. She threw herself onto her bed, rage and sorrow exploding in wracking sobs. It hurt; she gripped her belly and tried to stop.

The door opened behind her and her bed sagged when someone sat. A hand settled on her shoulder. She relaxed at her father's touch; it gave her what she needed to stop crying.

He said, "Will you go in to Wednesday-night Mass?"

She nodded.

"All right. You rest." He squeezed her shoulder with a miniature hug and left.

The door closed, but she could hear her mother in the hallway. "You spoil that girl. There's no reason she shouldn't go to church."

Her father's voice had a sharpness Lola seldom heard come from him. "Finding a murdered man in the barn seems like reason enough to me. Didn't you see her eyes? I think she cried most of the night."

"A waste, you ask me."

Minutes later, the front door slammed, followed by the crunchy sound of the car going down the driveway. Lola tried to sleep, but the thoughts that had kept her awake so late wouldn't leave her alone.

It was her fault Romero had killed Alejandro. She'd made Romero mad because of what she was doing with Alejandro, which wasn't fair because she'd only been trying to have fun. But they had fought because of her. And Alejandro was dead.

She was bad news.

The still heat in her room was suffocating. She had to move, to escape her thoughts. She rose and slipped out the front door to get away to the cool peace and quiet of her favorite place to be alone.

As she crossed the driveway, she saw a column of dust rising behind Buddy's car coming in from the highway. Out all night again, she figured. Thankfully, he turned off at his trailer. She hurried toward the creek, hoping he hadn't seen her.

Jesse woke up feeling good at first. Then an image of crimson blood pooled on Alejandro's chest crept into his mind. He pushed the thought away, focusing instead on the fact that it was Sunday and his sore muscles didn't have to do anything but lie there.

He peered over the edge of his bunk—Dudley sprawled on his back, mouth gaping, breathing loudly. No sense in waking him.

Jesse's belly let him know it was empty. He climbed down and dug into his suitcase for clean jeans and a crumpled paisley short-sleeve shirt. Maybe later he'd unpack and put his stuff in the dresser. He checked his loafers for scorpions and then slipped them on.

Connie was at the kitchen sink, washing dishes. The clock read ten after ten, so the Brauns had already left for church. She glanced his way and said, "You want breakfast?" She didn't seem as friendly as she had been before. But that made sense—his guard had been up ever since . . . since . . .

Jesse said yes, she got eggs from the refrigerator and cracked three into an iron skillet. Jesse thought about those eggs coming from the hens next to where he had watched Alejandro and Romero fight—he derailed that train of thought.

He watched Connie cook. It seemed like she was always in the kitchen. "When do you go to church?"

She shook her head. "The *Señora* doesn't like me to be at their church, and I have no way to get to Saint Mary's across town, so I make a little altar in my room and I pray there. I hope it is enough for God."

Jesse didn't pray, but he said, "I'm sure it is." He'd tried prayer as kid, first for toys, and then for the big one, his father's life. None had been answered.

He asked, "Have you heard any more about—you know."

There was a tremor in Connie's voice. "No."

He recognized her emotion—it was grief. It touched him. He went to her and put his hand on her shoulder. He didn't usually touch people unless he knew them well. His father had never given out hugs and his mother, well, the only thing she liked to get her hands on had ice cubes in it.

A shudder passed under his hand. "Are you okay?"

She sniffled. "Alejandro was my sister grandson."

"I'm sorry."

She shook her head. "It was me brought him here to work."

He blurted, "Are you a . . ." He stopped, but not soon enough. He cringed inside.

She turned and his hand slid from her shoulder. Tears ran down her cheeks, but a scowl tightened her eyes. "*Si*, I am a *wetback*." She didn't say the word so much as she spit it. "I have lived and worked here for twenty-two years, but I am not a Texan, I am not an American, I am a wetback!"

She turned away from him.

"I'm really sorry, Connie."

Her voice was like a punch. "My name is Consuelo."

How could trying to do right go so wrong? "I'm sorry. I thought it was Connie."

"That is what the *Señora* do to my name."

She jammed a slice of bread in the toaster, slammed the lever down, and attacked the eggs with a fork. The fork blurred when she beat the eggs.

Jesse wanted to leave, but that would only make it worse. He said again, "I'm sorry."

She banged the skillet onto a burner, lit the fire, and stared out the window.

The toast popped up.

He took a plate from a cabinet, got the toast and then butter from the refrigerator. He turned to find her watching him.

Consuelo released a long, shaky sigh. "No, I am the one who is sorry." She offered a smile that trembled just a little. "You are a good boy, none of it is your fault." She took the skillet from the flame, beckoned him to her, and slid the scrambled eggs onto his plate. "Milk or orange juice?"

He asked for both.

When she brought them, he said, "*Gracias*, Consuelo."

She patted him on the arm. He felt simultaneously embarrassed and good.

Dudley hadn't made an appearance by the time Jesse finished breakfast, so he decided to find the swimming place Mister Braun had pointed out.

"Consuelo, how do you get to the swimming hole?"

She pointed toward the front of the house. "There's a path by the creek. Go downhill."

He went out the front door, crossed the lawn and parking area, and headed for a line of trees that had to be where the creek was. Just as he reached the trees that bordered the creek, he heard faint whistling. It sounded like "Coming 'Round the Mountain." Looking back, he saw Buddy trudging up the driveway. Probably going to breakfast. Buddy took a long swig from a brown bottle. Jesse wouldn't have minded a Coke; it was already hot.

He ducked into the trees and found a cool blessing of shade. The stream was only a few inches deep in places, so clear that the rocky bed was as easy to see as if there were no water. Minnows looked like they were swimming in air.

Wandering downstream, Jesse came upon a weeping willow. Its long, drooping branches made him think of Lash LaRue, a cowboy comic-book hero he had liked when he was little and whose weapon of choice was a bullwhip. Jesse pulled off a whip-like branch, stripped it of leaves, and lashed at bushes and rocks as he walked.

A mockingbird sweetened the quiet with its melody. Jesse spotted the bird in an oak, its feathers gray and white against leaf green. The bright red of a cardinal flitted from tree to tree. He smiled as he walked and listened and watched.

He came upon a path alongside the stream and followed it.

Soon, the creek widened into a pond; downstream, a low dam plugged a narrow part of the creek.

When he stepped past a tree onto a stone patio bordering the pond, he discovered Lola sitting on a wooden bench a few feet away, her back to him. She was dressed up in a white blouse with puffy sleeves and a full skirt with petticoats. Her blouse had slipped low on one bare shoulder.

She startled at the sound of his steps and twisted toward him. She was even prettier in a dress. "Sorry."

She relaxed. "That's all right."

"I thought you'd gone to church." He wanted to sit next to her and he wanted to run away.

She plucked at her skirt. "I needed to be alone."

She wanted to be alone and he'd busted in on her. "Sorry." So far, this was a really sorry day. He backed away.

"Stop!"

He did. She said, "You were about to step into the pond."

Jesse looked around and, sure enough, his next step would have been a wet one. What a dope. He couldn't do anything right. "Uh, thanks."

She gave him a small, tentative smile. "Before you came, I was feeling a touch *too* alone."

She put her hand on the bench beside her and looked up into his eyes. He was drawn as irresistibly as a yo yo spinning up a string.

Her eyes were red the way his got when he cried.

He wished he hadn't bothered her.

He was glad he had.

Wings fluttered above him. He glanced up to see the mockingbird land next to a clump of mistletoe high above their heads. He wondered if the mistletoe entitled him to a kiss—not that he had the nerve to claim it.

When he dropped his gaze, it met hers. He had a feeling she knew what he'd been thinking. And that she didn't mind.

Her petticoats rustled when she scooted over, and Jesse sat beside her. A soft breeze rustled leaves. The mockingbird warbled songs it had collected from other birds.

She said, "I dreamed about it." She lowered her head. "He looked so . . . so . . ."

Alejandro's dead face came to Jesse's mind. "Empty."

She echoed him. "Empty."

He sometimes filled in words people were searching for. Dudley teased him about being some kind of telepath. He wished he were so he could know what Lola was thinking. About him.

Silence took over. Jesse wished he had Dudley's gift for always having something to say. He had to settle for searching the pond for signs of fish.

He flinched at the sound of Buddy's voice behind them. His whole body tensed.

"Well, looky here." Buddy walked onto the patio, a bottle of Pearl beer in his hand. He stumbled on a stone, righted himself and came to an unsteady stop next to Jesse. The stale odor of beer breath cascaded down; Buddy chugged the dregs and tossed the bottle into the pond.

Lola said, "Daddy'll get you for that."

"Me?" He laughed. "Not me."

He stepped behind Jesse, grabbed his right arm, bent it behind his back in a hammerlock, and lifted. The pain forced Jesse to his feet.

Buddy said, "Hey, it looks like I caught city boy here sneakin' a beer and throwin' the bottle in our pool. Too bad, kid." He looked to Lola. "You know how your daddy feels about the hands drinking."

Jesse struggled and Buddy yanked up. Jesse couldn't stifle a moan. He stood very still, tiptoeing to relieve the pressure.

Lola saw how Jesse hurt, but he clenched his teeth and

said nothing. Her grief and guilt fused into anger. She jumped up and pounded Buddy's arm. "You let him go!"

His big hand struck like a snake and swallowed her fist. He grinned as he squeezed and twisted, bringing tears to her eyes. "Like you let go of me, you little bitch?"

She yanked her hand away. Searching for something to hit him with, she saw Dudley sneaking up behind Buddy.

The mockingbird flew away and for a moment the woods were so silent she could hear Buddy's heavy breathing.

Dudley took another step closer. His foot cracked a twig.

Buddy started a turn toward the sound, so she swung her fist and connected with his shoulder. His fist shot out and struck her forearm; she staggered back and gripped the pain.

Dudley's big arm circled Buddy's neck, pulled tight and wrenched his head back. "Hey, Buddy ol' buddy, how about letting my friend go?"

Buddy yanked up on Jesse's arm, Jesse yelped. Buddy said, "You want your friend to have a broken arm?"

Dudley lifted Buddy until his toes barely touched the ground. "I was you I wouldn't be talking about breaking things. I think you oughta let him go."

Buddy held out, which didn't surprise Lola—he was as stubborn as he was mean.

Dudley lifted, Buddy's feet left the ground. Buddy dangled for a moment, his face reddening, and then he released Jesse.

Jesse staggered away and turned to face his attacker, rubbing his shoulder.

Buddy flailed his arms and kicked; Dudley tightened his hold. Buddy pulled at Dudley's arm, but couldn't budge it. He got a foot on the bench to take some pressure off his neck.

Lola asked Jesse, "Are you all right?"

He nodded, avoiding her eyes. Why?

Dudley said to Jesse, "He hurt you?"

"Some."

Dudley's face grew grim. "You know, I been wondering if you really can make somebody pass out with a choke hold." He tightened his arm.

The whites of Buddy's eyes showed. He tried to twist away.

Dudley yanked. "Be still."

Buddy quieted.

Jesse said, "Be careful, now. You know how that guy at school killed a kid doing that."

Alarmed, Lola looked at Jesse. The corner of his mouth twitched up, and then firmed. She turned back to Dudley.

Dudley winked.

A grin wanted to bubble up; she squelched it.

Dudley said, "Yeah, but I think I can do it. Only one way to find out." He tightened his hold.

Buddy's voice was hoarse and strained. "Don't."

"You'll be leaving Jesse alone?"

Buddy croaked, "Yeah."

"I don't know. What do you think, Jess?"

Jesse took his time answering. Buddy looked panicky. At last, Jesse said, "Let him go."

Dudley straightened his arm and Buddy dropped to his knees, sucking in deep breaths of air.

Lola said, "Serves you right."

Buddy used the bench to push himself to his feet and face the boys. He swayed, rubbing his throat. "You little assholes are through. Get to the house and call your mammas. I want you off this ranch by tomorrow."

Oh, no! She glanced at Jesse and saw a sick look that reflected her reaction. Well, Buddy wasn't the boss here. "Who do you think's going to be off this ranch when Daddy hears about you being drunk as a skunk on Sunday morning?"

Buddy aimed a mean look at her. "You ain't going to tell him."

"I will."

"I'll tell him different."

"I think you know who he'll believe."

Buddy glared at her, but she gave as good as she got. He wasn't so drunk he didn't know she was right. He turned to Jesse and Dudley. "You bastards are gonna regret this."

He looked at Lola. "You, too." He walked away, his hand still at his throat.

⁂

Shame flooded Jesse. He must've looked like the biggest chickenshit in Texas. He didn't want to see the disgust bound to be on Lola's face. He said to Dudley, "Thanks, man."

"You'd have done it for me." Dudley shook his head. "That guy's scary. And strong. He nearly got away from me."

Jesse needed to leave. He asked Dudley, "You eat yet?"

"Naw. Connie told me you were going down here and I wanted to see what you were doing." He rubbed his big belly and grinned. "But I'm damn hungry now. You coming?"

"Yeah."

Out of the corner of his eye, Jesse saw Lola rub her arm where Buddy's fist had caught her. He risked a look her way. "You okay?"

"Yeah." She was frowning.

She clearly didn't want to talk to a—a gutless wonder. He followed Dudley up the path.

⁂

What had she done to make Jesse go so cold all of a sudden? As she searched for a reason, she spotted the beer bottle in the pond. Buddy was going to have to fish that out before her father saw it. She savored their victory. These summer boys didn't scare so easy, did they, Buddy ol' buddy?

She wished Jesse had stayed. He'd been sensitive and caring when he thought he had intruded on her, and brave when Buddy tortured him. He was tough and sweet in ways she'd never seen in a boy. And she was certain he liked her.

But she'd brought him trouble. It was like a mummy's curse, where everybody who opened the tomb died. Romero and Alejandro had fought because of her, and now one of them was dead. Jesse was just being nice to her, and Buddy had jumped him.

What if she actually was a curse? If she decided to like Jesse—who was she trying to fool, she was already past the decision point—would something really bad happen to him?

It wasn't fair. She only wanted someone to love her. Tears puddled in her eyes. She scolded herself for being such a bucket of eyewash. She thought of racing through pastures and woods on Fibber, wind on her face—a long ride would help. She ran to the house to change. She would ride where trouble couldn't find her.

For a time.

"Umph!" Jesse startled himself awake. He'd been back home, nine years old, his mother weeping in her bedroom, his father's murder only hours old. The dream faded, along with the old anger, but they left a sad feeling behind.

"What?" Dudley's sleepy voice brought him back to the present. It was still dark.

"Bad dream."

"Me, too. I dreamed about Alejandro lying there dead, then Romero sneaking around outside our cabin."

Jesse shivered at the thought. "What time is it?"

"Three-something."

Jesse flopped on his stomach and searched for a happy thought to take him back to sleep. He settled on Lola's legs, and that got him to dawn with no more unrest.

That morning launched a week of dawn-to-dark labor, with the only exception a quick Sears trip first thing Monday to finish the shopping canceled by Alejandro's death. Jesse and Dudley bought hats, gloves, and work shoes—Jesse thought the shoes were pretty cool because they had steel toe caps under the leather.

With the ranch short two hands, they were, as Dudley complained, busier than a coyote in a chicken coop. Jesse and

Dudley worked with Mister Braun to put in a barbed wire fence across a section of pasture, Buddy got stuck with most of the manual labor Alejandro and Romero had done, and Lola looked after the livestock in the barn and mucked out stalls on top of her regular chores. With fatigue came deep sleep and the end of nighttime hauntings.

The shock of Alejandro's death and the puzzle of Romero's disappearance dwindled to a background unease for Jesse, but it didn't seem that way for Miz Braun. Her face was tight all the time, but he couldn't decide if she was scared or angry. It took a week for Buddy's gaze to stop skittering around and look people in the eyes. Miz Braun did lock all the doors at night, and told Jesse and Dudley to do the same. They did, for a while, but Jesse stopped because every time he did it he had to think of the reason why. Dudley stopped checking the door about the same time, though they never talked about it.

Lola was quiet, her expression sad or tense, Jesse couldn't tell which. He caught her gaze on him now and then, but he didn't want to think about why, not with the way he'd turned into the boy of Jello when Buddy had hammerlocked him. Jesse couldn't think of anything he could have done about that, but it plagued him that he should have done something to fight back.

When Lola joined them for breakfast Friday morning, she dragged in, head down—Jesse missed the pixie look that had lit her face whenever she set out to tease.

Mister Braun encouraged her with a smile. "Hi, Sugar."

Her lips twitched in a feeble imitation of a grin, and then she said, "Daddy, can I go into town tonight and see Cindy?"

"Sure. Just remind me when we're done toasting cactus."

Jesse's eyebrows rose. Toasting cactus?

Mister Braun smiled at him and explained, sort of. "With this drought we lose a lot of grazing, so we feed the cattle prickly pear." He returned to his scrambled eggs as if that was all that needed to be said.

Jesse had to ask. "What about the needles?"

"That's why we toast it."

Jesse grinned. "What do we do then, butter it?"

Lola broke out the first real smile Jesse had seen on her all week. Maybe he wasn't a total idiot, after all. Mister Braun chuckled and switched to asking Consuelo what she was packing in a picnic basket for lunch. Baloney sandwiches. Jesse didn't like baloney much, and he was glad to see Consuelo include fresh chocolate chip cookies, an excellent antidote for the taste of baloney.

After breakfast, they installed wooden sides on the flatbed truck. Mister Braun brought a contraption from the barn that was made up of two metal tanks with straps and a black rubber hose attached. It made Jesse think of an aqualung, but there was no mask. The hose led from the tanks to a pistol grip with a trigger; a metal tube extended from the grip to end in a flared nozzle. The whole thing reeked of something scorched. Mister Braun stowed it in the back of the truck next to the picnic basket.

Buddy threw in machetes and pitchforks and told Dudley and Jesse to ride in the back. He joined Mister Braun in the cab, and away they bounced.

Jesse studied the pitchforks, but he couldn't see blood on any of the tines. "You think one of these killed Alejandro?"

Dudley gave him a look that reminded him of the one he'd gotten from Mister Braun the day Jesse couldn't straighten that stupid nail. "Naw. The sheriff prob'ly took it for evidence."

Well, yeah. That was dumb.

Mister Braun drove to a rocky hill well populated by cactus. He parked next to a clump that was a good six feet tall and twelve across. A jillion needles prickled from hundreds of flat green ovals; Jesse didn't see how a cow would ever eat it.

After they'd hopped down from the truck, Mister Braun opened a valve atop one of the tanks and then slung them on his back. "You boys stand back."

He dug a Zippo from his jeans and lit a small flame at the end of a tiny pipe at the mouth of the nozzle, like the pilot light for a kitchen-stove burner. Mister Braun stepped up to the cactus, pulled the trigger and, with a hiss and a whoosh, a six-foot jet of flame blasted out of the nozzle. Jesse jumped. Buddy snickered. Mister Braun did it again, and that time the flame was ten feet long. Although Jesse was a few yards away, heat brushed his face. The stench of burned fuel oil drifted on the breeze.

Mister Braun worked his way around the cactus, shooting bursts of flame into it. The fire licked the cactus and singed the needles off, but seldom scorched the leathery green skin.

Once he had circled the clump and the needles were gone, Buddy handed Jesse and Dudley machetes. "Chop it up into chunks we can load onto the truck."

The three of them chopped while Mister Braun moved on to de-needle another clump. When Mister Braun faced away from them, Buddy would point with his machete and say things like "Come on, city boy, get your fat ass in gear."

The nasty edge in Buddy's voice and a mean squint about his eyes made Jesse skittish about turning his back on him. Jesse didn't think for a minute Buddy would let his defeat at the pond go unanswered.

When they'd chopped the cactus into manageable clumps, they switched to pitchforks and tossed the pear onto the truck. As Jesse and Dudley loaded, Buddy stood idle until Mister Braun turned his way. Only then did he scoop up cactus and pitch it onto the truck bed. Jesse had to marvel at his uncanny knack for going into action at just the right moment.

By mid-morning they had pretty much filled the truck, leaving just enough room for Dudley and Jesse to stand at the end. Mister Braun drove them to a pasture, and they shoveled the cactus out with the pitchforks.

The cows had seen this before. They gathered around the truck and eagerly dug into their cactus brunch. They munched and drooled green slobber.

Mr. Braun took them back to the cactus farm and they started the process again. When the sun was high, Mister Braun called a halt and took the picnic basket to the shade of a live oak tree to hand out the baloney sandwiches. Consuelo had also packed apples and a big thermos of iced tea. She didn't put sugar or lemon in the tea the way Jesse liked it, but he was learning to drink the stuff straight. It tasted more grown-up like that anyway.

They munched, just like the cows had, not saying much. Then the sound of the Jeep wormed its way into the quiet.

Miz Braun drove up. She seemed hesitant, not her usual forceful self, when she said to Mister Braun, "Sheriff Webb is at the house, and he wants to talk with you."

"What about?"

"He wants to know who Romero's contacts were. I told him you'd know more about that."

"All right. Hard to believe they haven't found him."

Mister Braun took the rest of his sandwich and his iced tea with him. "Buddy, after you're done eating, chop up that last clump and get it loaded. If you finish before I get back, move the truck and the gear to another patch. But I don't want anybody using the flamethrower while I'm gone."

"Yessir."

Mister Braun looked hard at Buddy. "I mean it."

The look was countered by round-eyed innocence. "Yessir, I know that."

The Brauns drove off and Jesse returned to his munching. Then Buddy shot him a sharky grin, and he wasn't as content as he had been.

After lunch had settled a bit, baloney and chocolate chips at war in Jesse's belly, he and Dudley were back to chopping cactus when Jesse heard a whoosh and felt a blast of heat. He turned, and there stood Buddy, the flamethrower strapped to his back and the nozzle aimed at them.

Jesse yelled, "Hey!"

Buddy smiled. "Hey, what, city prick?" He shot a tongue of flame that licked Jesse's shoes.

Jesse hopped back and shouted, "Stop that!"

"Who's gonna make me?"

Dudley moved next to Jesse. "Come on, Buddy, that thing's dangerous."

"No shit? Maybe even more dangerous than a choke hold?" He fired another burst that sent them stumbling backward over chopped cactus. Buddy kept pace.

Jesse shouted, "Split up!" He ran to the left and Dudley took off to the right.

Buddy stayed with Jesse, firing short bursts. The flame missed, but it scared Jesse. He backed away and Dudley paralleled them, keeping his distance.

Buddy was having a high old time. "You're gonna wish you'd called your mammas and packed your butts out of here like I told you."

Dudley yelled, "Asshole!"

Buddy laughed.

"Chickenshit asshole!"

Buddy wheeled and shot a flame that brushed Dudley.

Dudley yelled and jumped back, Buddy pursued, Dudley turned and ran.

Jesse searched for a weapon, but there was nothing but cactus and rocks. Rocks! He stood in a field littered with rocks the size of eggs.

Jesse grabbed two stones and heaved one at Buddy. It missed but, like most Texas boys, he'd grown up to be a good rock-thrower, and his second throw hit Buddy on the shoulder. Buddy bellowed and turned on Jesse, his eyes wide and crazy. He advanced, shooting flame and dodging rocks.

Jesse yelled, "Dudley!"

Dudley turned in time to see one of Jesse's rocks catch Buddy on the leg. He yelled, "Yeah!" and joined the barrage.

A Dudley rock thudded into Buddy's back. Buddy yowled and swung the flamethrower at Dudley.

Jesse's next throw smashed into Buddy's shoulder blade before he could fire.

Buddy turned back and Dudley clanged a stone off a tank as Buddy had to duck his head to avoid a throw from Jesse. He retreated toward the truck.

They pelted the son of a bitch and didn't stop throwing until he was out of flame range. They all stopped, panting.

Dudley yelled, "You're fuckin' crazy!"

Buddy lunged forward and shot a flame at them—Jesse took Buddy's hat off with a rock, Buddy wincing as though the rock had bounced off bone. He stopped and rubbed his head. "You little shit."

The three stood, poised, stalemated. War had been declared, and the first battle was a draw.

Buddy said, in a low and threatening voice, "I want you gone, one way or another."

Jesse said, "It's not you who decides."

Buddy opened his mouth as if to say more, then suddenly slipped the tanks off his back and ran to put them beside the truck. He grabbed a machete and set to chopping. Then Jesse heard the Jeep. He and Dudley ran for their machetes and got to work seconds before the Jeep rounded the hill.

Miz Braun dropped her husband off. The scent of fuel oil was in the air; Mister Braun sniffed and looked questions at them, but Jesse kept chopping. You didn't rat on people, not even a rat.

Mister Braun walked to the flamethrower, held his fingers near the nozzle, and then aimed a glare at Buddy. "I thought I said nobody was to use this."

Buddy said, "Yessir, but I wasn't really using it, I was just showin' them how it worked."

Mister Braun shook his head they way people do when they're suffering a fool. "Next time, Buddy, don't use it means don't use it."

Jesse shot a quick grin at Dudley and got a wink in return.

They toasted cactus and fed cows all day. The flamethrower made work hot enough to raise a sweat on the Devil, and Mister Braun called a halt early, about five o'clock by the sun.

"That's enough. Let's feed this load and head for the pond."

When they unloaded the tools at the barn, a pitchfork "slipped" from Buddy's hand and a tine drove into the toe of Jesse's shoe, piercing the leather and bouncing off the steel cap beneath. Buddy said, "Oops."

Jesse decided he'd better never be alone with Buddy.

Halfway through supper, Lola noticed her father's eyes ease shut and then he'd force them back open—toasting cactus always took a lot out of him. He would want to go to bed early, and that meant no ride to town. Darn. The pressure building in her to get out of the house would blow her brain right out of her head if she didn't escape for a few hours! She'd planned a movie with Cindy—Cindy had broken up with Bruce, and they needed a good cry together.

When supper ended, her father settled in the living room with the newspaper while Connie cleared the table. Her mother disappeared down the hall toward the bedrooms, which was fine with Lola. She wouldn't ask her for a ride if somebody put a knife to her throat.

Buddy looked meaningfully at her. "Guess I'll be goin' in to church."

Okay, there was a way to town. But Buddy would want something in exchange that she wasn't going to give. She gave him the biggest, widest, fakest smile she could. "Y'all have fun." She'd never seen anyone spend as much time looking pissed off as Buddy did. It didn't seem like life could be much fun for him. He left.

Dudley and Jesse headed for the plate of cookies on the kitchen counter. She gazed at Jesse, liking his looks more all the time. Hmm. Would Cindy like Dudley? She called, "Hey, Dudley, what kind of cookies?"

"Peanut butter. You want one?"

"Sure."

He brought her a cookie, and she tiptoed to whisper her idea into his ear. He grinned, nodded, and went back to Jesse. She nibbled her cookie and watched to see what Jesse would do. This just had to work.

Dudley said, "Hey, Jess, want to go to a movie tonight?"

Jesse smiled; she liked the way his brown eyes crinkled at the corners. "Sure. Let's check the paper for what's on."

Mission accomplished. Lola skipped to her father and plopped into his lap, making him move his newspaper out of the way. He smiled. "Now, what do you want, Princess?"

Jesse and Dudley arrived just as she said, "You said I could go see Cindy tonight."

He sighed. "Oh, yeah. How late do you want to be?"

"A movie."

He shook his head. "By the time it's over, I'll be dead to the world."

She pouted. "But, Daddy . . ."

Dudley spoke up. "We could give you a ride. We're goin' in for a show."

She made her eyes extra wide and put her hands together as if praying. "Please, Daddy?"

He grinned and then looked sternly at Dudley. "You a good driver?"

"Made it here from Dallas."

Lola said, "Okay?"

"You'll be back not a minute later than ten."

"Eleven?"

He smiled. "Ten-thirty."

"Yessir."

Lola gave her daddy a hug, hopped off his lap and said to

the boys, "I gotta change and call Cindy. Meet you out front in a half hour?"

Dudley said, "A half hour it is."

Jesse and Dudley showered, changed into good clothes, brushed their teeth, slicked their hair back, and met Lola out front. He'd thought she was pretty before, but now . . .

She was a vision in a pale yellow sundress, scooped low with little skinny straps over the shoulders. A breeze pressed the thin fabric against her, revealing the soft shapes under it. Jesse knew he was staring, but he couldn't help it.

The golden glow from the low sun attached itself to her. The light through her dress revealed the slender curves of her legs. Heart-shaped earrings dangled and lipstick painted a pretty picture of her lips.

Jesse opened the car door for her. As she passed in front of him to get in, oh so near, he said, "You . . ."

She stopped and turned her eyes up him, only inches away. His words about how pretty she looked choked on a tidal wave of shyness.

"Yeah?"

"Uh, nothin'."

She smiled and got in.

Way to go, nitwit.

He took his spot next to Lola on the Caddy's wide front seat and wished he had a brain in his head.

On the drive to town, Jesse sorta listened as Lola bubbled about her best friend Cindy who she knew they'd like because she had a great personality, but he mostly basked in her closeness. It was a relief to have a reason to gaze at her without having to sneak peeks.

Then Dudley took a curve fast and her warm thigh pressed against Jesse. A kid could dream, couldn't he?

After they crossed the bridge over the Guadalupe River into town, Lola directed them north on Water Street, then through a residential maze to Cindy's house. It was an ordinary brick house on an ordinary street.

When Lola got out, she didn't say thanks for the ride, and she left her purse on the seat when she ran to the house.

Dudley leaned back with a cat-ate-the-canary grin decorating his round face.

Jesse said, "What's happening?"

"You'll see."

Terror clutched Jesse's innards. "This isn't some kind of blind date, is it?"

"You'll see."

"You double-crossing son of a bitch."

Dudley laughed. "It'll be good for you."

That pissed Jesse off. Not that he had any experience with blind dates, but he'd heard that a girl with "a great personality" was a sure sign a moose was about to trot out the door.

The girl who came out wasn't a moose, but she was tall, Jesse'd bet eye-to-eye with him. Tall girls made Jesse feel even more inadequate. She was plumpish, but had a pretty face and blond hair pulled back in a ponytail. She was dressed up like Lola, in a blue flowery thing with a full skirt. They chattered at each other as they walked to the car.

Throwing a killing look at Dudley's grinning face, Jesse pulled the back of his seat forward so the girls could climb into the rear.

Lola laughed. "Jesse, get in the back."

Oh.

He did, and slid over to the far side of the car. Lola leaned into the front. His heart raced. What the hell was he going to do with Cindy? Talk about cactus and cows?

Then Lola got her purse and climbed into the back with him! Her dress flipped halfway up her thighs when she got in.

She saw him look.

He blushed.

She smiled.

Introductions were made all around. Dudley said, "So what do you want to see?"

Lola said, "*Cat on a Hot Tin Roof.* Paul Newman's in it."

Cindy cooed, "Oooo, those blue eyes."

Lola leaned toward Jesse and smiled. "Okay with you?"

Her nearness consumed any brainpower he had left and he nodded, a gnat in a hurricane.

Dudley said, "Okay, where do I go?"

Lola didn't hesitate. "The drive-in."

Oh, God.

Cindy gave Dudley directions and then turned to face Lola and Jesse as Dudley drove. After small talk about how hot it was, her blue eyes grew round and wide when she asked Jesse, "What was it like when you found the body?"

He flashed on the scene in the barn. Alejandro's blank gaze stared up at him. He shuddered. He'd managed to stop thinking about it, and now he'd have to start all over.

Lola said, "Don't be talkin' about that, I'm here for fun!"

"Did they find the other guy yet?"

Lola whacked Cindy on the arm. "You deaf? We're not talking about that. Ever."

Dudley pointed ahead. "Is that it?"

The drive-in was a quarter mile ahead. Lola lunged forward and tapped Dudley's shoulder. "Quick, pull off into that street and stop."

Dudley obliged.

Eyes asparkle, Lola said, "Let's sneak some of us in."

Jesse and Dudley did that all the time back home. Once they'd crammed four into Dudley's trunk. Not that they couldn't pay, it was just for the fun of getting away with it. The drive-in made a fortune off them at the snack bar, anyway.

The hardest part was keeping quiet while the driver bought a ticket. Jesse's friend Chuck loved to goose the person in front of him, setting off smothered giggles that hurt to hold in.

Dudley said, "The trunk'll hold all of y'all, but it would look weird to drive in alone."

Cindy opened the car door and then scooted next to him. "I'll ride with you."

Lola pushed the front seat forward and got out, giving Jesse a look at the backs of her legs and the shape of her bottom. "Come on, Jesse."

He understood then what a fish felt like when it was being reeled in. He followed her while Dudley got out and opened the trunk. Unlatching the continental kit was a bother, but that wasn't about to stop Lola from having her fun.

Jesse climbed in first and then Dudley helped Lola in. She lay in front of Jesse with plenty of room to spare. Once the trunk closed, she scooted back in the utter darkness and spooned herself against him. Dudley took off with a squeal of tires and Jesse had to reach over her to brace himself, although he couldn't avoid being pressed deliciously against her.

She wriggled her bottom against his, ah, lap. He hoped she couldn't feel the boner that took about a second to arise in his Levis.

Dudley shouted, "Be quiet, we're going in."

Then came a period in heaven and hell, heaven being molded to Lola's warm curves, hell being not knowing what to do with his arm, his hand, or his hard-on. He suspected he also fairly glowed in the dark, blushing with the idea that she could feel the lump in his pants. How could she not? What did she think?

Jesse gave up cogitation altogether and lay there, inhaling the sweet scent of girl wafting from the back of her neck.

Once inside the drive-in, Dudley stopped by the back

fence to let them out and then drove over the miniature hills and valleys of rows to an empty spot by a speaker. After he hooked it on the door, they piled out to go to the snack bar.

Except for the boots and cowboy hats, it was just like going to the drive-in at home in Dallas. Boys strutted in clumps of two or three, dragging their heels on the asphalt, just like him and Dudley. It was the custom at Woodrow Wilson High to put taps on your heels so they didn't wear down so fast. Class changes sounded like a Fred Astaire convention.

Jesse hoped no one noticed that he wore loafers instead of boots. Why hadn't he worn his boots?

As he and Lola waited in the popcorn line while Dudley and Cindy got Cokes, two boys strolled up to Lola. They were both bigger and older than Jesse. Their clothes were dirty, the heels on their work shoes were run down, and it had been too long since they had washed. Jesse felt like a soft, white marshmallow next to them.

The skinny blond one wrapped his arms around Lola from behind, pinning her arms to her sides. "Hey, how about a little, Do-lor-es?"

She struggled to free herself. "Let me go, Leroy."

"I hear you like it."

Her gaze went to Jesse. It looked hurt.

Anger rushed in. Jesse said, "Let her go."

Leroy laughed.

Lola cried, "Leroy!" Her voice quivered.

Jesse grabbed Leroy's wrist and yanked him away from her with enough force to turn him sideways. "Stop it."

The thankful look in Lola's eyes was worth the beating Jesse figured he was about to get.

Leroy's grin turned mean. "You little son of a bitch." He took a step toward Jesse, lifting his fists waist high.

Jesse backed up a step. His anger took a run for it. He didn't want to fight.

Leroy smiled at Jesse's retreat and jabbed a finger hard into his chest.

It hurt. Jesse fell back another step.

Leroy said, "Who are you, punk? One of those idiots old Braun brings in to work for free with his greasers?" He grinned. "Maybe you're a white greaser."

Lola said, "Leave him alone, Leroy."

"He asked for this."

He punched Jesse's chest with his finger again.

Jesse's temper started to rise, but it had a long way to go to get to where he would think it was a good idea to fight. "Leave us alone."

Leroy's finger readied for another poke, Jesse's brain rummaged fruitlessly for what to do, and then a man's voice came from behind. "What's happening here?"

Leroy put a wide-eyed look on his face, the same "who me?" expression Jesse used when he was caught at something he shouldn't be doing. He didn't think it really fooled adults—they'd once done the same thing.

Leroy said, "Nothin', sir. Just jokin' around."

The man stepped beside Jesse. His name badge said Roger Schultz, Manager. "Maybe you'd have more fun joking around somewhere else."

Leroy shrugged. "Sure." He leaned close to Jesse. His breath didn't smell any better than the rest of him. "You better hope you never see me again, boy."

The boys swaggered away. Jesse felt hollow inside, and his knees were saggy. He leaned on the counter and watched popcorn spill from the popper. He didn't want to see in Lola's eyes what she thought of his chicken-like behavior.

She laid her fingers on his forearm and slid them down to take his hand. She leaned close and whispered, her breath warm against his neck. "Aren't you a surprise."

He still felt shaky inside, but the reason was different, and the hollow feeling turned into a trembly kind of excitement. He looked down at her, and she smiled. Wow!

Lola returned to the car abuzz with anticipation. What other things were there to discover about this boy? He was her first real summer boy; she'd been too young last season. Then over the winter she'd done some fast growing up, thanks to Buddy. She snuck glances at Jesse, who'd pasted himself to the far side of the car as they watched the first show, the Three Stooges. It felt so good to laugh for a change.

Dudley put his arm across the back of the front seat and Cindy scooted next to him. At least that was working out. Lola looked to Jesse, but he stared at the movie, his arms close to his sides. What he was thinking about? When was he going to put *his* arm across the back of the seat? She'd liked his arm around her in the trunk. She smiled when she remembered the bulge she'd felt grow against her bottom. His warm breath on the back of her neck had sent a delicious shiver through her.

Cat on a Hot Tin Roof started. She was a big fan of Burl Ives as a singer; he was new to her as an actor, but he was the perfect Big Daddy.

Jesse seemed to be caught up in the movie, craning his neck to see around Dudley and Cindy's heads, which inched closer and closer. Lola gazed at him, studying his face. He had nice lips. She wondered what it would be like to kiss him.

His ignoring her was becoming irritating. And boring. She slipped her flats off, stretched her legs across the seat and plopped her bare feet onto his lap. He looked down at them as though a scorpion had landed there.

She said, "It's hot."

"Yeah."

She pulled her skirt up high on her thighs. His eyes traveled up her bare legs. She grinned, but he just looked scared and turned back to the movie.

He was funny to watch. He had no place to put his hands except on her legs, which he clearly didn't want to do. He folded his arms across his chest and focused on the movie.

But his gaze kept dropping down and then sliding up her legs, her bare skin aglow in the soft light from the movie screen. Aha, progress.

She was jealous when Dudley planted his first kiss on Cindy. Come on, Jesse, do something.

That ever-eager attachment to Jesse's lap had arisen again. He hoped she wouldn't notice; it was right under her ankle.

When Elizabeth Taylor, dressed only in her slip, yelled at Paul Newman, Lola swapped ends, laying her head in his lap with her feet on the other side of the car.

Oh, God.

He couldn't fold his arms any more because his elbow would poke her in the face. So he put one arm along the window behind her head and the other gingerly, very gingerly, across her. His hand fit into the curve of her waist, just above her hip. She was warm. And soft.

Her face turned up to his and she whispered, "Hi."

He steeled himself and looked. In the flickering movie light, she was the most beautiful creature he'd ever seen. And he didn't know what to do. The only girl-kissing he'd ever done was on the cheek of his cousin Emily, who liked him but said his eyes were scary, like he could see into her. So he said, "Hi," back at her and tried to watch the movie. Trouble was, he didn't seem to be able to think about the movie.

She frowned, then lifted up, draped one arm around his neck, and snuggled her face under his chin. He knew it was time to kiss her. But he'd die if he screwed it up.

She leaned her head back and looked up at him.

He tilted his head and put his lips against hers like they did in movies. The scent and taste of her dizzied him.

The tip of her tongue ran across his lips and prodded, softly, warmly. He parted his lips, her tongue darted in and then out. His naturally followed hers and she moaned so low that only he could have heard it. Their kiss deepened, their tongues got acquainted.

The kiss lasted until Elizabeth and Paul finished their quarrel, then Jesse and Lola surfaced briefly for air and dove back in. He took to it like peanut butter takes to jelly.

His arms went around her and hugged her close. She came willingly, the hard cones of her bra pressing into him. His hands explored her slender back down to her waist, sometimes venturing to the flare of her hip, but no further. He kissed her lips . . . the corner of her mouth . . . her cheek . . . she lifted her chin and he delved into the hollow at the base of her throat with his lips and tongue. She tasted as good as she had smelled when they were in the trunk of the car.

They necked the rest of the movie away, their kisses long and hot. As if he'd been starved, he couldn't get enough of the taste of her. The universe shrank down to hungry mouths. By the time the movie ended, they were damp with sweat and breathing heavily. And Jesse was no longer the kid he'd been a few hours earlier.

The lights came up and cars all around started. Dudley looked at them in the mirror. "Y'all enjoy the movie?"

Jesse said, "Yeah. It was a lot more exciting than I thought it would be."

Lola giggled.

Dudley guffawed and drove out. Lola pulled Jesse's head down for another kiss.

Lola hated it when the movie ended; her body was aroused and wet. Every caress had sent a surge of pleasure that made her wish he'd go further with his hand, down between her legs where it felt so good. She couldn't help but think about the hard part of him pressing against her in the trunk of the car. She snuggled next to him, and he put his arm around her and pulled her closer. She tilted her head up got kissed. Mmm.

They arrived at Cindy's house, and Dudley walked her to the door. They stood in shadows and kissed.

Lola and Jesse moved to the front seat. She turned on the dome light and looked at her watch, then leaned across Jesse and whisper-shouted out the window, "We've got to go!"

She gazed into Jesse's brown eyes. She closed hers and put her lips to his. So-o-o-o sweet.

Dudley trotted to the car. "Hey, break it up." They rumbled away, going easy at first so the noise of his car's pipes wouldn't upset Cindy's parents. Once back on Water Street, though, he let the Caddy roar. She loved the heavy, throaty sound of it.

As they approached the bridge over the Guadalupe, she thought of Buddy at church, just down the next street. "You oughta see Buddy and his holy rollers."

Dudley said, "Yeah?"

"It's a scream." She couldn't resist. "Take a left."

Jesse said, "Don't you have to get back?"

"We got time if Dudley knows how to use that gas pedal."

Dudley said, "Ha!" and floored it. They burned rubber around the corner, and she was shoved against Jesse by the force of the turn. Oh, yeah. They came to a low brick building with a cross on the front and she directed Dudley into the parking lot. Tires crunched over gravel, he stopped and put the Caddy into park.

Lola said, "Listen."

Voices cried and yelled and sang, a babble coming from an open window in an otherwise blank wall.

She shoved at Jesse. "Get out." Dudley got out too.

They climbed into the bed of a pickup truck backed up under the window and peeked inside.

The building looked like it had once been a store of some kind; it was now a big, empty box with a beige linoleum floor. Rows of metal folding chairs faced a lectern. Half the congregation sat, many with their eyes closed, swaying back and forth, singing. The other half, scattered through the chairs and filling the aisle, stood and waved their arms or danced. A plump woman quivered on the floor.

Dudley said, "I can't understand what they're saying."

She whispered, "They're speaking in tongues. They believe it's God talking through them."

Jesse said, "I always thought God spoke English."

She giggled. Then she spotted Buddy and pointed, "There he is." Buddy stood in front, his head back, mouth flapping, eyes rolled up, and hands shaking high in the air.

It pissed her off to think about what he had done with his hands last winter, and what that had led to. He could shake all he wanted to, but he had sins he'd never be shut of. She smiled. She, on the other hand, just had to go to confession and she was clean.

Jesse whispered, "Look at that snake!" Next to Buddy, a skinny guy with a scraggly beard hoisted a huge rattlesnake. It writhed and wrapped around his arm.

A preacher at the lectern yelled at his congregation. Lola could only make out a few words, like "Jesus" and "damned."

She held her watch up to the light from the window. "I gotta get home."

They climbed down and got into the Caddy, its big V8 idling with a low rumble. Lola thought of the nasty way Buddy had treated Jesse. She grinned. "Let's give ol' Buddy a visitation from the Lord."

She stretched her foot out and jammed the gas pedal all the way down. The big engine blasted the side of the building with thunder. She yanked her foot off the gas, the pipes racked down, and the back pressure set off bangs like gunshots. The pipes quieted and they heard screams.

She laughed and yelled, "Go, Dudley, go!"

He whooped, slammed the car into drive and floored it, the wheels spun, and Dudley hit the building with gravel and sound as they tore away, hooting and laughing.

When they turned off the highway at the ranch, Jesse snickered again at the mental picture of Buddy flapping his mouth. His laughter triggered another round of giggles from Lola and Dudley. She shushed them and whispered to Dudley to go slow so the car wouldn't wake her parents. She was only about five minutes late, but she said her mother sometimes got real weird about missing her deadlines. One time she'd been grounded a month for being fifteen minutes late coming home from a church social.

They pulled into the parking area. Lola said, "Listen, it's okay to say we went to the same movie, except not to *Cat On a Hot Tin Roof* 'cause they might find out it was at the drive-in. Let's say we saw *Fort Dobbs* at the downtown show. Daddy likes Brian Keith and Westerns."

She gave Jesse a long kiss. Aware that Dudley was watching, Jesse flushed with embarrassment and pride.

Back in the cabin, Dudley looked at Jesse like he knew something. "Well, you have a good time?"

Jesse shrugged. "It was all right."

Dudley laughed and punched Jesse's arm. "All right? I thought y'all were going to swallow each other."

"Yeah? How much of the movie did you and Cindy see?"

Dudley cupped his left hand. "Not much, I admit."

Jesse's eyes widened. "You did?"

Dudley grinned. "Yeah. You?"

"None of your beeswax."

Dudley winked, went into the bathroom, and shut the door. Time went by. Chokin' his chicken, Jesse thought. Jesse settled into reliving the evening.

His reverie shattered when the screened door banged open and Buddy charged in, his eyes flared wide and his face flushed red.

"You bastards!" He grabbed Jesse by the shirt, lifted him from the chair, and slammed a fist into Jesse's belly, right on the diaphragm. Jesse doubled over, trying to suck in air, but nothing happened. He couldn't breathe in or out.

The bathroom door opened, Buddy let go of Jesse and spun on Dudley. He yelled, "It was you, you son of a bitch!"

Dudley held his hands up. "Me? What did I do?"

"You godless asshole, it was you at my church!"

He shoved Dudley's chest and sent him staggering back into the bathroom to fall into the tub, tearing the shower curtain down on top of him.

Jesse got enough breath back to gasp, "No."

Buddy grabbed Jesse's shirt with both fists and lifted him. "You lying piece of shit."

Dudley struggled out of the tub and came into the room. "It couldn't have been."

Buddy's narrowed gaze shifted from one to the other. "That was your car I heard, you sacrilegious bastards."

Jesse said, "We were at the drive-in, and we don't even know the name of your church."

That was true.

Doubt entered Buddy's expression. "But it sounded just like your car."

Dudley shook his head.

Buddy shoved Jesse away and aimed a fist at Dudley. "I better not find out it was. If I do, you'll pay for what happened to Brother Harley."

Jesse couldn't help but ask, "What happened to, uh, Brother Harley?"

"The noise scared his rattler. Harley's in the hospital."

Jesse flinched. Oh, shit.

"They're pumping him full of that anti-snake stuff."

Dudley said, "Damn."

"If you did it, God will get you." Buddy gave each of them a glare and banged out the door.

Jesse was shaken, and not just from Buddy's punch. He sat down hard on a chair. "Goddam."

"Yeah."

"I feel bad."

"Yeah."

Jesse stared out the door at the darkness. "What'll we do if the guy dies?"

"What'll Buddy do if he finds out we did it?"

"How could he find out?"

Jesse and Dudley turned to each other and Dudley said the word in Jesse's mind. "Lola."

Jesse said, "She'll tease him about it."

"And we'll be dead meat."

"I gotta tell her."

"Watch out for that guy."

Jesse waited ten minutes for Buddy to get good and gone, and then left the cabin. He made his way around the back of Consuelo's cottage. Her windows were dark.

The bedroom end of the main house was also dark. Snoring sawed the night from the Braun's window. Miz Braun's sleepy voice slurred, "Axel, you're snoring." After a couple of snorts, the noise stopped.

Jesse eased through the bushes in front of Lola's window; a hint of perfume drifted from her room. He scratched on her window screen. Nothing. He scratched again.

A white oval suddenly appeared before him and scared a chill up his spine. It was her face. She whispered, "What're you doin' here?"

"I gotta tell you somethin'."

"Stand back." Unlatching the hook at the bottom of the frame, she pushed the screen out. A bare foot appeared, and then a bare leg, and then the bottoms of baby-doll pajamas.

"Help me."

He reached up under the screen and took her waist. His fingers sank into warm flesh. He lifted, she brought her other leg out and slid to the ground.

She turned in his embrace, tiptoed, wrapped her arms around his neck, pressed herself to him and found his lips with hers. The sensation of her body against his seared the reason he'd come to see her from his mind. Her small, soft breasts, no longer hard, bra-covered lumps, flattened against him. He felt her nakedness under the flimsy pajama top.

Lola opened her mouth, his tongue dove in, and he was instantly hard. Just when he was afraid she would notice, she ground herself against it. A warm rush spread from his prick and flooded his brain.

She broke away, leaned back, and smiled. “Is that what you wanted to tell me?”

For a split second he couldn’t think why he’d come. Then he stepped back from her, wilting. “No. Something bad happened at Buddy’s church.”

Her smile faded. “Because of us?”

“Yeah.”

She glanced at her open window. “We can’t talk here.” She took his hand and led him to the gazebo. He winced when the screened door squeaked.

Inside was a picnic table with two benches; he sat next to her on a bench. The rusty screens obscured the outside, and he felt cut off from the rest of the world. He held her hands. “Remember the guy with the rattlesnake?”

“Yeah.”

“When we racked Dudley’s pipes, it bit him.”

“Oh, God.”

Jesse hurried to add, “They’re giving him antivenom.”

Tears pooled in her eyes. “That’s so awful.”

He pulled her close, and she nestled her head on his shoulder. “It’ll be okay.”

They sat that way for a while. His mind turned to her body, radiating heat, so nearly naked. Her next words pulled him up short.

She sniffled. “What if he dies?”

“I don’t know.”

“How did you find out about it?”

“Buddy came to the cabin and accused us.”

She pulled away and put a hand to her mouth. “Oh, no!”

“We told him we didn’t do it, that we didn’t even know where his church is.”

“Does he know about me being there?”

“No. And you can’t ever let him.”

“No.” She turned her head away and stared at the dark.

"That poor man."

Jesse reached for her, but she pushed him away.

"You'd better get away from me. I'm cursed."

"Cursed?"

"Bad things happen because of me."

"Like what?"

A long silence. A sob. "That man. And Alejandro."

"Alejandro? What . . ."

She turned to him, her eyes wide with fright. "You should leave now. And stay away from me." She stood.

He grabbed her hand and pulled her back down. "What are you talking about?"

Her voice quivered, "The night before he was killed, I met him here."

He knew that.

"Just to talk. And when we left, I thought I heard someone in the bushes, but I couldn't see anybody."

He couldn't tell her he'd been spying on her, even if it was unintentional.

She turned her gaze to the house for a long moment, then looked back to Jesse, fear on her face. "Somebody could be out there right now, watching us."

Her fright was so large, and she so small, all he could do was pull her to him and wrap his arms around her. She pushed at him to escape, but he firmed his grip and she stopped resisting. "There's nobody there. Listen."

An owl hooted in the distance. A coyote yipped.

She shivered.

"Maybe you'd better get back to your room."

She nodded. He got up and led her, now nervous about every shadow. But there was no one, at least no one that let themselves be seen or heard.

At her window, she said, "Listen, you've got to stay away from me."

Jesse studied her face, the curve of her lips. "I don't want to. I . . . I think I—"

She silenced him with fingertips to his lips before he could tell her he loved her. She whispered, "Shhh." She gave him a small smile. "All right. But we'll have to be careful to make sure nobody knows."

Happily, he nodded, gathered her to him for a long, kiss, and then helped her back through the screen.

As he slipped out of the bushes he thought he heard the soft rustle of clothing, but it could have been the breeze brushing against leaves. He froze in place and listened hard. No more sounds came, and he hurried back to the cabin.

Monday morning, it wasn't more than two minutes after the alarm had yanked Jesse awake when somebody banged on the screened door. He hoped it wasn't Mister Braun—they'd been late for breakfast Saturday because Dudley's clock was running slow, and he darn sure didn't want to be late again. He raised up and squinted out the screen door.

Lola stood there, her face alight with an excited smile. "Poko's having her puppies! Y'all come see!"

From below, Dudley muttered a sarcastic "Yippee."

Lola hopped like a little kid at a State Fair cotton candy booth. "Come on!"

Time with Lola was not to be passed up; Jesse threw his sheet off and started to swing his legs over the edge of the bed, then realized he was only wearing underwear. "I gotta get dressed."

Her impish grin appeared. "What's stopping you?"

He blushed. "Would you mind . . .?"

She laughed and stepped out of view. He climbed down, pulled on his jeans, socked his feet and stuffed them into his work shoes. He froze for a long moment when he realized he'd forgotten to check for scorpions. Nothing stung, so he grabbed a shirt and headed for the door, shoelaces flapping. He left Dudley sitting on his bunk, yawning.

Lola ran ahead. "Come on!"

Jesse followed, pulling on his shirt. A fast walk was all he could muster, his eyes on flashing brown legs set off by white shorts. On top, she was ready for a day that was already warm; a skimpy blue knit top precariously suspended by thin straps over bare shoulders.

She disappeared through the kitchen door and was nowhere to be seen by the time he straggled in. Her voice came from the left. "In here!"

Jesse went through a doorway he hadn't paid much attention to. It opened into a utility room. He noticed Miz Braun's sun hat on a peg by the doorway, above a small shelf that held her gardening gloves. Along one wall were a washer, a dryer, and a steel double sink. Against the opposite wall sat a big freezer that looked just like one he'd seen a body stored in on *Twilight Zone.*

Jesse regretted thinking about bodies and pushed away an image of Alejandro lying in the dirt. He wondered if that picture would ever be laid to rest in his mind. Maybe after they caught Romero.

"Here!" Lola stood next to Miz Braun at the end of the room, waving him in. A big grin created a dimple in Lola's cheek. He wanted to kiss it.

In the corner, Poko lay on bedding made of newspaper torn into narrow strips. Four little lumps with tails squirmed near her belly, three of them the same light-brown, fawn color as Poko, the other a brindle with a striped pattern of black and fawn. Their eyes were clamped shut, and they looked like blind mice. As Jesse stood next to Lola, another puppy emerged from Poko's rear end.

Lola said, "Oh, a white one!"

He'd never seen a white Boxer. It had one brown spot on its side. A wet-looking film covered the puppy; Poko shifted and licked the newborn until the film was gone. Jesse'd never seen anything being born before. It aroused both disgust and wonder. Like the pup's brothers and sisters, its eyes were shut as if it didn't want to see its new world. It had floppy ears instead of the pointy, stand-up shape of their mother's, and its tail was long, not the stub Jesse usually saw on Boxer dogs.

"How come their tails are so long?"

Miz Braun said, "We bob their tails and crop their ears when they're older."

The pups wriggled on their bellies, pushing with their stubby little legs out to their sides like they were doing a breaststroke, straining to get to Poko's teats. Once a tiny mouth found one, it fastened on and started sucking.

Lola knelt and placed the white pup at a teat. She looked happily up at her mother. "Mom, can I have this one?"

Miz Braun didn't answer.

Jesse glanced at her.

She frowned. "There'd better not be any more of those. Not with the stud fee we paid." Her tone had a hard edge.

He asked Miz Braun, "How many puppies will she have?"

"There's usually eight to twelve a litter."

Mister Braun spoke from the doorway behind him. "Breakfast's on the table."

Miz Braun said, "Got a white one."

Jesse turned to go and saw Mister Braun frown.

Lola chirped, "I think we should name it Spook."

The Brauns exchanged a look that Jesse couldn't interpret, and then Mister Braun said, "We got things to do." He turned and walked back to breakfast, and Jesse followed.

Bite by prodigious bite, Dudley was already moving a serious stack of pancakes from his plate into his mouth. It surprised Jesse that Buddy wasn't there; whatever else he was, he was good at showing up for food.

As Jesse forked sausages onto his plate and rolled them up in pancakes to cover with a flood of maple syrup, Mister

Braun announced, "We're going down to the river today to cut a cypress for the den paneling."

Dudley asked, "Just us?"

"Buddy'll be there. He left at five to drive the big tractor to the river."

Dudley cracked, "Yeah, I'll bet he just loved that."

Jesse had admired the big red tractor, its rear wheels almost as tall as him. He imagined rumbling down the highway in the early morning. "I would."

The conversation rambled around how to keep a cypress from falling into the river when they cut it down. Just as they finished eating, Lola rushed in. "Thirteen! Thirteen puppies!"

Her dad said, "Any more white ones?"

"Nope. My little Spook's the only one."

"Good."

Jesse wondered what the problem with white puppies was but, before he could ask, Mister Braun stood and headed for the door. "Let's roll, boys."

Lola gave Jesse a wink and blew a kiss. Dudley saw it, and Jesse thought Consuelo did too, but he didn't care. He left with a fat grin on his face and visions of hot kisses filling what was left of his mind.

Riding in the cab of the flatbed truck to the river, Jesse watched how Mr. Braun shifted the gears. He'd never make that mistake again.

The Guadalupe River was shallow, but Mister Braun told them it didn't dry up, so there were good stands of cypress trees along it. He drove to a wide part of the river with low, flat banks.

Buddy waited on the tractor, his face like a storm cloud. Mister Braun parked and then strode to the river and pointed at a tall, straight cypress. "This's the one I want. Buddy, you turn the tractor around and back up to about fifty feet from the tree. Boys, you bring the rope."

He went to the truck and took out the chain saw and a gas can while Jesse dragged an inches-thick coil of rope from the truck bed. Its weight surprised him and he dropped it. Dudley grinned, picked it up, and they both carried it.

Mister Braun waited by the tree for them. When they plopped the coil down, he grabbed one end and climbed up slicker'n a whistle. He tied the rope around the trunk about twenty feet up and then took the other end to the tractor, where he tied it to a steel bar on the rear.

Buddy was over at the river, skipping stones. It didn't seem like he was one to be close to where work was happening if he could help it.

"Buddy," Mister Braun shouted, "get over here."

Buddy trudged in their direction. Mister Braun said, "We don't have all day."

Buddy trotted.

"All right, get the tractor started up and put tension on that rope. I'm going to cut so the tree'll fall sideways, but it could twist and I don't want it going into the river."

He looked at Jesse and Dudley. "You boys just stand back."

Buddy took up slack on the rope with the tractor until Mister Braun said, "That's good."

Mister Braun started the chain saw and cut a deep notch low on one side of the tree. Then he went to the other side. He had to shout over the saw's racket. "Buddy, be ready. If it starts to go toward the river, you pull it back."

Buddy yelled "Right," gunned the tractor engine, and grinned down at them, high in the catbird seat.

Mister Braun cut at a down angle from above and opposite the first notch. Soon there was a crack and the tree started a slow-motion fall.

But this tree had it in mind not to cooperate. It twisted and tilted toward the river. Mister Braun yelled, "Buddy!"

Buddy put the tractor in gear and gave it gas. The engine roared and the tractor edged forward a few inches.

But the tree was determined to go for a swim. The tractor came to a stop, and then started to roll backwards.

Buddy gave it more gas, the huge rear tires dug in, and the tractor halted.

The tree pulled, the tractor pulled, it was a stalemate. The soil was sandy, and the tractor's rear wheels dug down.

The tractor's front wheels lifted a few inches off the ground. Buddy goosed the engine and they settled back down. The tractor engine roared—there wasn't a muffler, like on a car, just an exhaust pipe sticking up.

The front wheels lifted again. The tree was on the move now, pulling on the tractor. But the rear wheels were in holes almost two feet deep. Buddy kept the gas down. The rear wheels spun and dug, the front wheels lifted higher.

Mister Braun ran towards the tractor, waving his arms and yelling. Jesse couldn't hear what he said, though, with the tractor engine blasting his ears.

The tractor looked to Jesse like it was going to go over backwards. But Buddy sat there, shoving the throttle all the way open.

The rear wheels dug deeper, the front ones lifted, and Mister Braun ran, but he was still thirty feet away.

Jesse ran to the tractor and yanked on Buddy's pants leg. "It's going over!"

Buddy kicked his hand away.

"You've got to get off!"

Buddy paid no attention.

Jesse climbed up on a brace and yelled in Buddy's ear. "It's going over!" He could feel it tilt, and he wanted to jump off.

Buddy ignored him.

Jesse climbed up behind him and pulled at his shoulders. Buddy batted at him with one hand, but Jesse dodged. Jesse risked a glance back; the tree strained against the rope, headed for the river. Unable to climb out of the holes it had dug, the tractor *couldn't* move forward.

Its nose rose more. Buddy swung at Jesse again and Jesse grabbed Buddy's fist and twisted his arm into a hammerlock.

Jesse lifted and Buddy cried out. Jesse kept at it and Buddy rose to his feet. He yelled, "Let me go, you son of a bitch!"

When Jesse had him to his feet, he shoved as hard as he could and sent him head first off one side of the tractor. When his weight left, the nose of the tractor seemed to leap up. Jesse jumped the other way just as the front of the tractor rose up and over.

The tree splashed into the river, pulling the tractor over to crash upside down. The engine died at last, and the silence was huge.

Dudley ran to Jesse and helped him up. "Are you all right?"

Except for being out of breath and shaking, Jesse was, so he nodded.

He looked to where Buddy should have fallen just in time to see him running at him. Buddy tackled Jesse around the waist and drove him to the ground on his back. "You little bastard!" Jesse'd never seen such fury in anyone's eyes.

Buddy pinned him down with one hand on his chest and raised the other in a big fist; Jesse crossed his arms over his face and tried to twist free.

As Buddy's fist came down, Mister Braun's brown hand caught it. Time seemed to stop, and then Mister Braun heaved and threw Buddy backwards, off of Jesse.

Jesse scrambled up, and Buddy sprang to his feet. He said, "I almost had it!"

Mister Braun stepped in front of him. "Go down by the river and cool off."

Buddy lunged at Jesse, Mister Braun caught his shoulders, spun him around and shoved. Buddy stumbled a few feet toward the river and stopped. He glared at Mister Braun for a long minute, and then stomped away.

Mister Braun turned to Jesse. His gaze probed, and Jesse felt compelled to explain. His voice broke when he said, "I didn't think it would stop going over." He pointed at the deep ruts. "The wheels ..."

"You could have been hurt."

"I guess."

"So why'd you do it?"

It had been instinct, it seemed to him. The best answer he could come up with was, "I couldn't just stand there."

Mister Braun nodded. "There's a real good chance you saved Buddy's life." Then he shook his head at the upside-down tractor and the tree stretching out into the river. "Let's get to work. I still want to get this up to the sawmill today."

Two hours later, Jesse sat on one side of the four logs the cypress tree had become after having its top and branches cut off, with Dudley on the other. Mister Braun drove the flatbed truck up a winding road into the hills.

Buddy rode in the cab with Mr. Braun, and through the rear window Jesse could see the boss talking at Buddy with a look on his face he wouldn't want aimed at him. Buddy just stared straight ahead.

The sawmill road had been paved for a time after they left the highway, but it soon turned into a rocky, rutted, one-lane dirt track through the trees. It occasionally cut across a steep slope where Jesse couldn't see the ground on one side of the truck, just a scary fall down.

The sawmill turned out to be a shack built of weathered gray lumber. Next to it were stacks of logs and rough-sawn lumber, and a wooden platform with a huge, saw-toothed disk sticking up through a hole. A wooden trough long enough to hold trees led to the saw blade.

Mr. Braun parked and came around to the back of the truck. "We'll just unload the logs today. I want them to set a couple of weeks before we saw."

He took down the wooden stakes along one side of the truck and started rolling a log toward the side near the trough. Dudley got out of the way, and Jesse helped roll.

Buddy stayed in the truck.

When the log reached the edge of the truck bed, Jesse hopped down and stood ready at one end. The boss looked him in the eye as if questioning his ability to handle it. He looked him right back. For a second, anyway. Then he looked away. But he put his hands on the log.

Mr. Braun pointed. "We just need to get it over there." Over there was the trough, a good ten feet from the truck. Dudley hopped down to watch.

They eased the log off the truck bed. God, was it heavy. But Jesse thought he could handle it. If the weight didn't pull his arms out of his shoulders first.

They sidled toward the trough with short sideways steps.

Dudley said, "You guys look like you need a little help." It turned out his idea of helping was to do the grunting for them so they wouldn't have to. He let out a long, loud one. "Unnnnnnnnhhhhhh!"

The boss and Jesse grinned at the same time.

"Arrrrrggggghhhhh! Muurrrrrgggggg!"

Jesse giggled and the boss smiled. They stopped and broke into laughter, unable to move.

The truck door opened and slammed shut. Buddy came around and watched, his face like the taste of a lemon.

Still laughing, Mister Braun said, "Come on. Let's get rid of this thing before we drop it."

With a couple of grunts of their own, they hurried the log to the trough and dumped it just in time. Jesse didn't have an ounce of strength left in his arms.

They collapsed against the log and let the laughter come. Jesse shook a useless fist at Dudley. "Thanks for the help, big guy. You nearly killed us."

The boss sobered, but his eyes, usually so serious, had a twinkle in them. "Good job, Jess. Just three more."

After they'd muscled the other three logs to the trough, Mister Braun said, "You boys want to take a quick look around? Then we can head home for lunch."

Jesse went to the saw blade. It was a good five feet in diameter, a massive steel disk with long, sharp teeth. Thick planks piled nearby were rough, not smooth boards like he was used to seeing from a lumber yard. He ran his fingers over grooves where saw teeth had ripped through the wood.

The truck started up, and underneath the sound he heard another small engine start, kind of like a lawn mower.

He leaned across the blade to see the system of pulleys and belts that drove it. The belts led to a big electric motor bolted to a concrete slab.

Suddenly the belts lurched into action, and the blade inches from his shoulder whirred into motion, hissing as it spun faster, moving his way.

Two hands grabbed Jesse's arm and yanked him back. He fell against Dudley. He straightened Jesse and said, "Damn. You okay?"

He was. "Thanks." They gazed at the whirring blade. "I now know what people mean by scared shitless."

Buddy stood next to a switch on the shack wall, staring directly at Jesse. Beside him a small generator motor putted. He shrugged. "Sorry. I didn't see you there."

He couldn't have missed seeing them. He flicked the switch and the blade whined down.

The truck door burst open and Mister Braun boiled out. He ran at Buddy, who put on an innocent face, his hands held out wide. "Hey, I didn't—"

The boss grabbed his shirt with one hand and slapped his face with the other. "You little fool!" He slapped him backhanded and then shoved. Buddy staggered back and slammed into the shack.

The boss put his hand on Buddy's chest and pinned him against the wall. "That's how you pay back somebody who saved your useless ass?"

Buddy glanced at Jesse and back at Mister Braun. "He didn't. I'da been okay, I had it under control."

Mister Braun seemed to search for words, anger screaming from his body and face. He raised his other hand. Buddy lifted his hands to protect his face.

After a long, long moment, the boss stepped back. His silent fury said more than words. He went to Jesse. "Are you all right?"

"Yessir. He probably didn't mean—"

"He did, and you know it."

Jesse nodded. Yeah, he knew it.

"Let's go. Jesse, you and Dudley ride with me."

With Buddy banished to the truck bed, they went home. The Boss took the road down faster than he had on the way up, his face grim and tight. Through the back window, Jesse saw Buddy holding on as best he could. A couple of big bumps sent them bouncing off the seat and Buddy nearly off the truck. Mister Braun never looked back to see whether or not Miz Braun's little brother was still there.

After dropping Buddy off at his trailer at noon, they drove to the ranch house. When Mister Braun opened the front door, Lola ran to him, crying. "She's going to kill it!"

Jesse had never seen such fright on a face.

Mister Braun put a hand on her shoulder. "I'm sorry, honey." He started to embrace her, but she pulled away.

"Stop her! It's just a baby. It can't hurt anybody."

Shaking his head, his face stern, he said, "Gotta be done." He stepped past her and went into the kitchen where he began washing up.

She turned to Jesse. "Do something! She's going to kill little Spook!"

"Who?"

"My mother!"

"Why?"

Lola clenched her fists and wailed, "I don't know." She grabbed his hand and towed him toward the utility room. Dudley followed.

Inside, Miz Braun was filling a sink with water. She held the white puppy in one hand.

Jesse said, "'Scuse, me, ma'am?"

She glanced at Lola with cold eyes, then looked at him, but didn't say anything.

"You're going to kill that puppy?"

She nodded at the water deepening in the sink. "Yep."

"Uh, why?"

She stared at him as if wondering whether or not to deal with this dummy, and then said, in a matter-of-fact tone, "Have to. These are purebred dogs, and we can't have any white ones. It can't be registered with the American Kennel Club, and it can't be allowed to breed." She looked at the pup. "It's a waste."

Now Jesse knew why he had never seen a white Boxer.

She turned the water off. The puppy struggled as she lowered it toward the sink.

Lola cried out, "Mommy! Don't!"

Miz Braun couldn't do that—could she? How could she? "You can't!"

She glared at him. "I can't?"

Words were hard to find. "It doesn't seem—right."

"It's what we do. It's my dog. I can."

"Yes, but . . ."

He thought he saw a change flicker in her eyes. "You don't want me to kill it?"

He shook his head. "No, ma'am."

Miz Braun held his gaze. "Come here."

He stepped to her side.

"Take it." She held the puppy out.

She laid it in his hand. It was warm and frail, barely filling his palm. Its tiny nose twitched. He guessed it was hungry. Too scared to smile at the puppy, he stroked it with a fingertip.

Lola said, "Oh, thank you, Mommy."

Miz Braun pointed to the sink. "Hold it under until it stops moving."

Lola moaned. "No!"

What? She couldn't mean it. Her stone-cold face said that she did. Jesse looked around. Dudley seemed frozen in place. Mister Braun stood in the doorway. Jesse appealed to him with his eyes.

Mister Braun didn't grant a reprieve. It was all up to Jesse.

Miz Braun said, "You do it, or you're on the next train out of here. You came here to work, and this is part of your job." Her authority was immense. She was bigger and stronger than Jesse in every way. "You will do what I tell you."

A sick feeling in his stomach, he looked down at the water.

Lola moaned, "Jesse!"

Miz Braun said, "Now."

He looked to Mr. Braun again. The boss's face was sad, but his eyes said *you have to.*

Jesse lowered the puppy under the water. He couldn't watch, but he felt it squirm, strongly at first, then weakly, then it stopped.

Lola screamed "Monsters" and shoved past Dudley and her father; her sobs slammed at Jesse's heart.

Miz Braun gripped his forearm and lifted. "You're done."

She pried the puppy from his fingers. It appeared the same, wet like when it was born, eyes squinched shut. But it would never wag that little tail. Jesse looked into Miz Braun's face and found no emotion there. She wrapped the body with newspaper; it was just trash now.

Sick at heart, Jesse brushed past Dudley and Mister Braun.

Mister Braun said, "You better eat, we got work to do this afternoon."

Jesse stopped at the door and looked at him. "I can't."

Mister Braun studied him for a moment and then nodded. Jesse left the house and ran toward the cabin. But the hen house behind it reminded him of more death.

He veered and ran for the woods. He came to the creek and turned toward the pond, tears filling his eyes. As he wiped at them, he tripped over a fallen branch and sprawled, ripping the skin on one palm. He never felt it. Scrambling up, he ran until he came to the swimming hole. He sat on the bench and put his head in his hands. He cried for the puppy and the loss of its life.

He cried with shame for the weakling who had killed it.

His tears eventually stopped. He tried to think, but his mind spun with birth and death, hate and love, and Lola's cry of "Monsters."

Footsteps approached from behind. He wiped at his eyes and sat up. His side was so cramped from bawling like a big baby it hurt to straighten.

Consuelo appeared. She carried a sandwich and chips on a plate, and a bottle of Coke. She sat on the bench and put the food between them, then looked at his face, which he quickly turned away. He didn't want her to see he'd been crying.

Her voice was low and gentle. "How you doing?"

"Okay."

She sat in silence for a while. "I told Lola you had to do it, but she was not ready to listen."

He wondered, as he had for the last couple of hours, if he'd really had to. What would have happened if he'd refused? Would he actually have been sent home? Was "doing his job" worth the puppy's life? Although it had been doomed anyway—Miz Braun would have killed it. He searched for answers that weren't there.

"How could Miz Braun . . ." He couldn't say it.

"Terrible things have happen to her. They make her . . . be hard."

"That's no excuse."

After a long moment, she stood. "I must go back. The food is for you."

"I can't eat."

"Well, I leave it. *Señor* Braun say tell you that he see you in the morning."

"Okay."

She put a hand on his shoulder. Her touch was warm and light. "You tried stopping her. God will love you for that."

Jesse shrugged. If there was a God. And if there was, why would He let things like that happen? Or, if you went along with what some people believed, *cause* it to happen. Seemed to him a God like that was worse than no God at all.

Consuelo patted his shoulder. "You had to do it. The *Señora* is very strong. I would have."

Inside his head he thanked her for saying that. He nodded. She left.

The aroma of tuna fish sandwich worked its way into his nose. Despite himself, his mouth watered. He couldn't help it; he downed it all.

Then his shame rose again, and he hoped there wasn't a heaven so his father couldn't look down and see the terrible thing he'd done.

Lola spent the afternoon in her room, storming from grief to fury and back again. She hated her mother. And Jesse. She felt imprisoned, helpless. She tried to figure out how to run away from this evil place, but she didn't even know where to start.

She couldn't stop seeing the look on her mother's face as she forced Jesse to put the puppy under the water. Her eyes had been flat and dead, like the snakes in the San Antonio zoo, eyeing her through the glass as if she were prey.

Thinking of that, her feelings about Jesse changed. She'd crumbled under her mother's rule more than once; how was he to do any better? And he'd tried. Her father hadn't done anything. She wanted to hate him, too, but couldn't. Jesse had tried to stand up to her mother, and that was more than anybody else had done. And she'd called him a monster. She wiped her eyes, blew her nose, and decided to find him.

In the kitchen, she asked Connie, "You seen Jesse?"

"I take him food down to the pond, but that was hours ago." Brow furrowed, Connie studied her face.

Lola said, "I'm okay."

Connie smiled and opened the oven. "I save supper for you." The aroma of fried chicken made Lola's mouth water.

Lola was surprised it was so late. And that she was so hungry. "You've got a customer."

Connie smiled. "Good." She made up a plate and put it on the kitchen counter. When Lola hopped onto a stool to eat, Connie hugged her. Her eyes sad, she said, "I am sorry about the puppy, *Niña*."

Lola leaned her head against Connie's shoulder and relished the comfort of her embrace. "I feel bad about Jesse."

Connie released her and went to put away the food. "That poor *niño*." While Lola gobbled her meal, Connie told her about finding him at the pond.

It was dusk when Lola walked to the cabin in search of Jesse. But only Dudley was there, listening to the radio and sketching. "Where's Jesse?"

"I haven't seen him since, well, you know."

"Yeah."

She went back to the path, peering into the descending darkness. Jesse appeared, his head down.

Lola said, "Hi."

His head jerked up. Light from the cabin window revealed his surprise. She said, "Your eyes are all red."

He avoided her gaze. "I get these allergies."

She smiled. "Yeah."

They stood in silence. She could almost feel shame radiating from him. She wanted to ease his mind. "I guess you had to do it."

"I don't know. Maybe not. I don't know."

"I know my mother. You did."

He shrugged.

She stepped close and took his hand.

His eyes came back to her, wide and confused-looking.

He must think she hated him. She raised her other hand to his face. Standing on tiptoe, she kissed his cheek and found the taste of tears. Her mouth so near that her lips brushed his skin, she whispered, "Salty."

She lowered her head to his chest and slid her arms around his waist. Gingerly, as if he feared she would pull away, he wrapped her in an embrace. It felt good, as warm as Connie's, but stronger.

She said, "I'm sorry."

"Me, too."

They stood, silent, his warmth and strength a comfort.

Then his stomach gurgled. She realized it had been hours since Connie had taken him that sandwich.

It gurgled again.

Lola giggled.

He did too.

She placed her hand against his belly. "We had fried chicken for supper. There's plenty left over."

He shook his head. "I can't go in there yet."

"I'll get you some."

The song on the cabin radio changed. The Danleers sang,

"One summer night, I kissed your lips
one summer night, I held you close,
you and I, under the moon of love."

She looked up. Sure enough, there was a full moon. It was an omen. She gave him a kiss. "Meet me at Dudley's car."

Before he could say yes or no, she trotted up the path. She paused at the patio and looked back; he was headed for the parking area beside the house, walking with his head up. She dashed inside to get food for her man, a new kind of happiness coloring her thoughts.

Jesse slid off the front fender of the Cadillac when Lola hurried up. The moonlight was so bright he could see her smile.

She handed him a plate of fried chicken and potato salad. She held up two cookies. "Dessert." She hopped up on the fender and nibbled at a cookie.

He attacked the food.

An owl questioned the night.

It didn't take long to clean the plate and satisfy the hunger in his belly. He looked at Lola, her eyes liquid and dark in the moonlight. She hummed *One Summer Night.*

A different hunger rose. He set the plate on the ground and stood before her. She parted her knees and he stepped between them. He put his hands on her waist and they gazed into each other's eyes. They drew together for a gentle kiss.

She slid slowly off the fender and down against his front. Their mouths opened, their tongues made love.

Finally they broke for air. He wallowed in the inner heat that aroused his body. Then a cool touch of air brushed the back of his neck and a chill slithered down his backbone.

They were so exposed. He twisted and looked toward the house. The bright moonlight showed nothing. Deep shadows by the house and beneath trees were black hiding places. Although he had no reason to feel watched, he did.

Lola said, "Let's sit in the car."

The dome light was blindingly bright for the seconds it took to slip into the Caddy's front seat. They rolled the windows down and listened.

Bugs buzzed, the owl wondered who again, otherwise the night was silent.

Possessed by an uncertain bravery, he reached for Lola—and she moved to meet him. His awareness dwindled to lips, tongues, the feel of her slender body under his hands.

As if his left hand had a mind of its own, it stroked across her back to her side—and then around to her breast. Actually, to the firm cone of her bra, which didn't feel like anything other than a lump of cloth. He was too excited to care.

She not only didn't object, she widened her mouth. Their kiss deepened. His hand moved to her waist, slipped under her knit top, and caressed her skin.

It seemed like he had several minds operating at the same time. One thought of nothing but kissing. Another relished the touches his hand was finding. Another seemed to see them from above, wrapped in each other's arms. Another belonged to a kid who couldn't believe this was happening.

His hand stole upward, along her ribs, and slipped over the cup of her bra. He hesitated—she made no objection—and he dipped inside. Her breast was smaller than the cup, barely enough to fill his hand. But his hand didn't care, and neither did that part of his mind.

Her breast was soft and warm. His fingertips explored. They came to her nipple, which was hard.

She moaned, low and sweet. The sound sent a hot chill up his spine and through his prick.

Breaking their kiss, she leaned back. Her eyes were closed, her lips curved up. She placed her hand on the back of his neck, her chin lifted and, with the gentlest of pressures, she pulled his head downward.

He kissed the soft side of her neck and then glided into the hollow above her collarbone.

Kissing his way to her bare shoulder and then south, his lips sought her breast, his fingers pulling the bra cup down. His tongue found her nipple and circled it.

Since she'd been introduced to sex last winter, Lola had never felt such desire. There had been curiosity on her side, and then it had become what *he* wanted, not she, with no love to it.

Tonight she wanted more; her desire had gone beyond kissing and she craved release. She pushed Jesse's shoulders and straightened him. "Move back." The unfocused look of passion on his face changed to puzzlement, but he moved.

She slid back to lean in the corner formed by the car seat and the door. She parted her legs and slid the left one between his right side and the seat back. She held her arms out, and he returned and pressed his body to her.

She thrust against the ridge of his prick beneath his jeans; a thrill rushed through her. He was quick to match his rhythm to hers. They kissed, and their bodies moved together—a blossom of sensation rose with sweet, sharp intensity, and she surrendered to it.

Short moans came from him. She held him tightly as he thrust and then shuddered. He relaxed against her. The moment had lasted for an eternity and not long enough. Echoes of pleasure rippled through her.

Lola floated in time for a while, then Jesse stirred and shifted to the other side, behind the steering wheel. She straightened her clothes and slid next to him. His arm went around her and they sat in silence, letting the breeze cool them.

He turned his lips to her ear. He kissed it and whispered, "I love you."

She snuggled closer.

Jesse's mind wandered through the day. First the tractor flipping, then the saw blade about to rip into him, then the puppy, and now this. Compared to this day, the roller coaster at the Texas State Fair was a lazy stroll down a flat road.

Her father's voice called, "Lola?"

A current of guilt jolted through him, shocking his arm from around her shoulders.

They peered into the darkness, but no one was visible. They weren't caught. Yet.

Mister Braun called again. "Dolores?" It sounded like he was on the patio, out of sight.

She crushed a quick kiss onto Jesse's lips and started to climb out the passenger side window.

He whispered, "Hey, there's a door."

"Yeah. And a light that shines when it opens."

He enjoyed watching her slender body wriggle out the window. She peeked back and whispered, "See you tomorrow." Raising her voice, she trotted toward the house and shouted, "Coming!"

In no hurry to leave, he slumped in the seat. He'd never felt so good, heart and soul, clean through. He gazed at the full moon. Its face seemed kindly, smiling down on a boy whose life had taken a sudden turn for the great.

Dudley glanced up from a book when Jesse entered the cabin. "Where you been?"

"Just sittin'"

"You okay?"

Jesse shrugged. "Yeah."

Dudley put his book down and grinned. "Lola find you?"

"Yeah."

Leading the witness, Dudley said, "Yeahhhh?"

Jesse climbed up to his bunk. "She got me some food. It was . . ." He flashed on the taste of her breast. ". . . delicious."

"Annnnnd?"

"And none of your business."

"Watchin' you and Lola is making me horny. I need to get into town and see Cindy."

"What do you mean, watching us?"

"You know, you with your tongue hanging out, her wiggling that cute little ass."

Jesse leaned over the edge of the bunk and glared down. "Don't you say things like that about her."

Dudley held his hands up in mock terror. "Okay, okay, just don't hit me."

Jesse smiled. "Yeah, you're peein' in your pants."

"She does have a cute little ass."

Jesse laughed and flopped back. He couldn't argue with the truth of that.

Dudley said, "Miz Braun came here looking for her."

Oh, shit. Trying to keep his voice light, Jesse said, "What did you tell her?"

"The truth. I didn't know where either of you were. And I still don't."

"Well, let's keep it that way."

"You're not talking?"

"Nope."

Jesse lay staring up at the ceiling. The white puppy haunted him. "Dudley?"

"Yeah?"

"You believe in the afterlife?"

"You mean heaven and hell and all that?"

"Yeah."

"I guess so. My parents do. What about you?"

"I don't know. I have my doubts."

"Weird thing to be thinking about."

"It's that puppy. I was just hoping it's in a better place, if there is one."

There was silence for a while. Then Dudley said, without an ounce of sarcasm in his voice, "I'm sure it is, pardner. A helluva lot better."

Lola lay on her bed, trying to read her latest issue of *Mad Magazine*, but even Will Elder's nutty art couldn't distract her—she was still aroused and needed to *move*. She decided to visit Fibber and tell him all about the evening.

Her father was reading his newspaper and her mother her magazine when she passed through the living room. They raised quizzical glances and she answered, "Goin' down to the barn."

Her mother said, "That better be all."

What was it with her mother? Where had the smiles, and the hugs, and talking about dresses gone?

Striding down the drive, shoes crunching in the gravel, she sang *One Summer Night* to the moon, remembering love-making with Jesse.

She passed Buddy's trailer—it was lit up, his car parked in front. She'd left the trailer behind when she heard the door open and slam shut. She kept walking, hoping to hear his car start, which would probably mean a beer run to town.

Instead, she heard gravel crunch as he trotted to catch up with her. Shit.

"Hey, little girl, where you going?"

She stopped and he caught up. "I was going down to visit Fibber, but now I think I'll go back to the house."

She turned to leave, but Buddy grabbed her arm. She glared up at him. "Let go."

He leaned in close. His breath stank of beer. "I smell it on you. You been screwing that kid."

She struggled to pull her arm from his grip, but he was too strong. "You're crazy."

"You can do it with him, you can do it with me."

He pulled her toward his trailer, she planted her feet, they slid in the gravel as he towed her. "I'll scream."

That stopped him. But he didn't release her.

He tried a smile. "Why are you playing so hard to get? It wasn't that way this winter."

"You started it."

"You didn't stop it."

"I was a kid, and I was curious."

"You liked it."

"I liked what it felt like, but I don't like it with you."

"Come on, it's nothin'."

"It's wrong."

Moonlight showed anger gathering on his face. "You treat me right tonight and I won't hurt your little boyfriend."

She yanked her arm, caught him by surprise, and pulled

free. "You do anything and my parents will hear all about what you did to me."

"You ain't tellin' them nothin'. The shit'll be just as deep for you as for me."

"I'll take that chance. I might get a spanking, but what Daddy'll do to you'll be a whole lot worse."

Buddy seemed to deflate, then he blustered, "Watch yourself, girl. This place'll be mine one day."

"Don't hold your breath, Uncle Buddy."

"Your mama thinks it will."

"I don't know why she makes you out to be so special, Buddy Pritchert, but Daddy would sell rather than turn it over to you."

He laughed. "So you're going to run this ranch?"

"Damn right I am. And I can tell you who's not going to be my foreman."

He raised his hand, she flinched back. He loomed, so much larger than she, powerful, angry. A fluttery feeling flooded her belly. He could do whatever he wanted, there was no stopping him. His open hand curled into a fist. Then she thought of Jesse's determined resistance to Buddy's bullying. She straightened and raised her chin. "Go ahead. See what happens."

His fist jerked back as if to launch a blow. Then he stood, poised, straining. His face was so twisted, so full of—the meaning of what she saw jolted her. "Why do you hate me?"

The question surprised him. He lowered his arm and shoved her staggering back. "I'm not done with you." He stomped toward his trailer.

She wrapped her arms around herself and shivered. She hadn't been wrong. Down deep, Buddy hated her. But she'd never done anything to him.

She ran back to the house. In her room with the radio on low, she lay on her bed, called up the memory of Jesse's kisses on her breast, and wondered about the next time.

Gray clouds gave Tuesday morning an unfriendly look, but Jesse had all kinds of sunshine coming from inside. He woke early and had showered and dressed and was out of the cabin before Dudley's alarm sounded. He headed for the main house, looking forward to his first glimpse of Lola and hoping Consuelo had started cooking.

He sang Gene Vincent's *Be-Bop-A-Lula* to himself, but in his head it came out as be-bop-a-Lola. Yeah, she was, as Gene liked to sing, his baby love.

As he reached the screened door to the kitchen, he heard Miz Braun say, "I think we should send Jesse home."

He stopped, his hand inches from the doorknob.

Mister Braun said, "Pass the sugar." A spoon clinked in a cup. "Why? He's a damn good worker."

Maybe there was hope.

"I don't like the way he looks at Dolores."

Uh-oh.

Mister Braun sighed. "He doesn't look at her any different than any teenage boy does. I see the stares she gets in town. She's a pretty girl."

"And I don't like the way she looks at him."

"Well, he's a nice-looking boy."

"Where were they last night? I couldn't find her, and he

wasn't in the cabin when I checked there."

"Probably off somewhere with his tail between his legs over what you did to him with that pup. That was a nasty business."

Tail between his legs. Jesse hated it, but Mister Braun was right about that.

"He had no call to talk to me that way."

A coffee cup struck a saucer with a brittle click.

"And where did Dolores say she was out walking when you called her in?"

"I didn't ask. She was pretty upset over losing that pup. And she seemed to feel a lot better after her walk."

"Well, how do we know what she was really doing?"

She meant what *they* were really doing.

"She said walking."

Another clink of cup on saucer.

She said, "I still say he ought to go."

"Margaret, we're too short-handed."

"Get another wetback. There's a ton of 'em."

"Not with the sheriff all over us."

"That boy is trouble, you mark my words." A chair scraped, and footsteps faded into the house.

Mister Braun sighed.

Jesse went back to the cabin to wait for Dudley to get up. He escaped scary thoughts of being sent home by getting lost in the adventures of his favorite Western characters, Louis L'Amour's Sacketts. He often wished he could be like them, strong and determined to do the right thing, no matter what. Master of his own destiny. Maybe some day. But right now he was a flea under Miz Braun's thumb.

Buddy and Mister Braun were having coffee when Jesse and Dudley arrived for breakfast. No sign of Miz Braun, which was not a bad thing. Unfortunately, no sign of Lola, either. As they settled in, a knock came at the front door. Consuelo scurried to answer it, and admitted Sheriff Webb.

Mister Braun rose to greet him. "Mornin', Carl. Coffee?"

The sheriff took a chair. "Just a half cup."

As Consuelo fetched coffee, Mister Braun asked, "What brings you by?"

"Hoping maybe somebody's remembered something about the morning of the killing since I was here. I been wondering about things."

"Like what?"

"Well, the coroner says the victim was struck on the back of the head with enough force to have stunned him. Probably he was knocked down first and then somebody took the pitchfork and . . ." He lifted his arms high. "Well, you saw it. The doc thinks whoever did it was in an insane rage."

The sheriff pulled a small note pad from his shirt pocket and consulted it. "Now, Axel, you said you'd never seen this Romero lose his temper."

"That's right."

He turned to Jesse. "But you say he did."

"Yessir."

"How? I mean, was he wild? What?"

Jesse thought about it. "No, he was . . . he was mad, but he was calm, too." He glanced at Dudley for confirmation.

Dudley nodded. "Kind of a cold hot."

"Did he try to hit Alejandro?"

Jesse said, "No, just used his razor."

The sheriff shook his head and made a note.

Mister Braun asked, "You thinking somebody else did it?"

"Not exactly." The sheriff sipped his coffee. "It all seems to fit, but the way he was killed . . ."

"You find any clues in the barn?"

"Not much. No luck on fingerprints. Not that there weren't any, but the prints on that pitchfork were ones you'd expect. You, Buddy, Margaret, Lola, and both wetbacks. Can't prove a thing with fingerprints."

Mister Braun said, "So we need to find Romero."

The sheriff nodded. "We may get lucky. Got a call from the State Patrol down by McAllen saying they picked up a man matching his description just this side of the border from Reynosa, where you told me his sister lives."

"That would be a relief."

"They're gonna mail a photo. A few days, we'll see." The sheriff drained his cup. "Better go. Al Patterson's missing some cows. Probably a hole in the fence, but you know Al."

Consuelo placed a plate of hot cinnamon rolls on the table, their spicy-sweet aroma filling the air. The sheriff lingered.

Mister Braun chuckled. "Be obliged if you'd help us out with these, Carl."

"My duty is to serve, Axel." He plucked the largest roll from the plate and bit happily into it on his way out.

They ate in silence, Buddy's scowl radiating hostility at Jesse. When they'd finished, Mister Braun drained his coffee cup and stood. "Buddy, Jesse, I want you two to come over here." He indicated a space in front of him. Jesse stood and stepped forward. Buddy took his time getting there.

Mister Braun said, "I don't know what the problem is between you two, but it's going to stop here and now."

Since the only problem Jesse had with Buddy was being picked on, he was perfectly willing to stop. "Yessir."

Buddy took longer about it, but he finally nodded.

Mister Braun eyed Jesse and then Buddy. "Shake hands on it."

It was something Jesse's father would have done. Jesse stuck his hand out.

Buddy shook hands, although his grin was on the sharky side when he said, "No problem."

Then he squeezed until Jesse was about to yelp with pain.

For the next four days, Jesse saw the world through a haze of love and made stupid mistakes that had Mister Braun frowning at him.

On Tuesday he dropped a hundred-pound burlap sack of oats, which burst and wasted feed all over the barn floor.

Wednesday he left a pasture gate open and had to spend an hour rounding up sheep that had followed their appetites to greener pastures.

On Thursday he sloshed a bucket of water all over Mister Braun's shoes.

On Friday he sloshed water on Miz Braun's shoes.

He worked hard to compensate, and life was good. But not perfect. He saw little of Lola, and kissed her only in his memories. Her mother found things for her to do whenever an hour looked like it would turn up idle.

Thanks to Poko, they did steal in a few minutes together before breakfast every morning. The dog and her litter had been moved to the dog run, and Lola's job was to feed the mother first thing. Jesse got up early and met her there to help. Since they could be seen from the house, they couldn't do much more than feed the dog and play with the puppies—but she'd brush him with a hip as she passed by, or their hands would touch and linger as she handed him a puppy.

Friday, a surprise came with suppertime. Mister Braun announced, "We're takin' Saturday off. I, for one, am tired."

Lola said, "Can we do somethin' fun?"

He smiled at her with a soft Daddy look that said the answer would be yes. "What do you have in mind, honey?"

"Let's go to the lake." She turned to Dudley and Jesse. "You water-ski, don't you?"

Oh, great, another thing Jesse couldn't do. But he smiled. "Ah, not yet."

Dudley said, "Me neither."

Lola's leg twined around Jesse's under the table. She watched his eyes, looking for his reaction. He swallowed hard.

She leaned closer. "That's okay. We'll show you how."

Her hand slid onto his thigh. His voice broke when he said, "Great," and it wasn't the only thing reacting. He pushed her hand away; Miz Braun was staring at them.

Buddy chimed in, "It's supposed to be a hundred tomorrow. That cool water would feel awful good."

Mister Braun made a mock stern face at Lola. "Lotta work gettin' everything ready."

"I'll do it! I'll make a picnic lunch and everything."

Mister Braun smiled. "I don't know—I like somethin' besides peanut butter and jelly." What he really said was yes.

Miz Braun, who hadn't lightened up much, said, "Connie'll fix the lunch. You can get the towels and drinks ready."

Lola popped from her chair. "I gotta find my swimming suit." She started to skip away and then changed to a fast walk. When Jesse turned back from watching her wonderful wiggle, Buddy was staring at him, his eyes like knuckles on a fist.

Mister Braun stood. "You boys have swimming trunks?"

Jesse and Dudley chorused, "Yessir."

"Guess that's it. You can sleep in if you want, but be ready to go by nine. Take us an hour and a half to get there."

Being ready to go by nine o'clock was not Jesse's idea of "sleeping in." On the other hand, it beat five-thirty all to hell. Jesse was tired these days, but not so tired as their first week. In fact, after two weeks of hard labor, he was feeling pretty good. Work agreed with him.

But he had his doubts about water-skiing.

Saturday morning came bright and hot. Jesse'd had trouble getting to sleep, his head busy with scenes of him repeatedly falling off of water skis that alternated with visions of Lola in a bathing suit.

The vision that said hello at breakfast exceeded all anticipation. Lola wore one of her father's shirts over, he guessed, her bathing suit. It was a guess because he couldn't see anything but tanned legs, her neck and head, and her arms where the sleeves were turned up to her elbows. The effect was to make her seem to be naked underneath the shirt, which caused a growing interest below his belt.

The wicked little smile Lola gave Jesse after he got his eyes back into his face told him she knew full well the effect she had. Miz Braun frowned at her, but didn't say anything. Lola didn't seem to feel her disapproval, or she didn't care, or she liked being provocative. He wished he had that kind of nerve, but he'd rather not be noticed. People notice you, they see things they don't like.

Miz Braun turned to him, and her squinty gaze said she didn't like what she saw, for sure. He resolved to keep his attention away from Lola when her mother was around.

Fat chance.

After breakfast, Consuelo and Miz Braun packed a cooler and a big picnic basket. Mister Braun tossed Buddy the Chrysler keys and sent him and Jesse to get the boat.

Buddy backed the car up to a shed the size of a one-car garage that sat twenty feet out from the barn. Inside was a gas can, a stack of old tires, water skis leaning against a wall, and a blue and white motorboat on a trailer.

The boat's sleek lines provoked thoughts of speed. Jesse's expectations for the day lifted. He'd never been in a speedboat, but he'd seen them on White Rock Lake. The boat was sure to be fun, and water-skiing hadn't looked all that difficult. You just had to hold onto a rope and stand up.

On water.

At twenty miles an hour.

Yeah, nothin' to it.

They hooked up the trailer and slipped skis and the gas can under the boat's canvas cover. When they got into the car to go back to the ranch house, Buddy eyed him. "You never water-skied?"

"Nope."

One of Buddy's patented sharky grins spread wide. "Well, then, I'm just gonna have to make sure you have a good time."

On the ride to Canyon Lake, Jesse got stuck with the middle of the back seat, straddling the drive-shaft hump and sandwiched between Buddy and Dudley. Hot and uncomfortable, he distracted himself by gazing at Lola's neck, directly in front of him, placing imaginary kisses there and imagining her turning around to return the favor.

Then Miz Braun caught him grinning. Hoping she couldn't read minds the way parents seemed able to do, he shifted to studying the car floor.

His gaze wandered across a red feather, maybe two inches long. He picked it up. Hey, maybe he could use it in his hatband. He put it in his shirt pocket.

Buddy glanced his way. "What's that?"

"Nothing." Jesse went back to contemplating Lola, careful to keep an eye out for a turn of her mother's head.

Canyon Lake was a crystal blue gem in a setting of green and yellow-gold hills. Mister Braun drove to a boat ramp, where Dudley and Jesse removed the boat's canvas cover and Miz Braun and Lola loaded the cooler and picnic basket into the boat.

Lola took off her shirt while Mister Braun backed the trailer into the water. Sadly, she wasn't naked underneath. A black, one-piece bathing suit covered the important parts of her slim little body, but her bare legs and shoulders were sufficient to send Jesse into his usual spin. She waded in to help Buddy float the boat off the trailer.

Jesse shed his shirt and sneakers and dove in, Dudley right behind him. The water was cool, and Jesse surfaced refreshed. The three of them splashed each other and laughed until Mister Braun arrived, grinned, and ordered them into the boat. He and Buddy helped Miz Braun in and a day of sun, skis, and snakes began.

Mister Braun drove the boat the same way he did the Jeep—full speed ahead. A wake unfolded across the water, and cattails at the outlet of a small creek gave a friendly wave as the wake rocked them.

They toured the shore and then slowed to an idle in the middle of the lake. Mister Braun asked, "Who wants to ski?"

Lola and Buddy shouted, "Me!"

Dudley pointed at Lola and Buddy. "Them."

Jesse tried to make himself invisible by looking away—he didn't want failure to cloud his day.

"Ladies first," said the Cap'n, and Lola buckled an orange life belt around her middle, tossed skis into the water, and jumped in after them. Buddy snapped a tow rope onto a chrome ring mounted on the stern.

Supported by the life belt, Lola leaned back in the water and put her feet into the foot holders on the skis. When her ski tips poked up from the water in front of her, Buddy tossed her the rope, which had a bar at the end. Positioning the rope between her skis, she gripped the bar and grinned.

Mister Braun idled away until the rope was played out and the slack taken up.

Lola shouted, "Go!"

The boat lunged forward.

She seemed to pop out of the water. She glided smoothly behind them, then leaned and slid out wide to the side. When she crossed back, she launched a low jump when she hit the wake. Miz Braun smiled and applauded.

After ten minutes of graceful skiing, Lola tripped over a wave and went in headfirst. Mister Braun cut the throttle and circled back beside her. She bobbed in the lake like a water nymph and laughed. "Whooeeee!"

He smiled. "Had enough?"

"No!"

"Well, come on in anyway, it's somebody else's turn now."

Miz Braun clapped her hands together. "You are so graceful on those skis, honey."

Jesse helped her into the boat; her hands were cool from the water and her eyes bright. Her plunge into the water had pushed her swimming suit low in front—Jesse eyed the swell of her breasts.

Her mother reached back, hooked a finger in the top of Lola's suit, and yanked up. "Cover yourself!"

After they retrieved Lola's skis, Buddy tossed in a slalom ski and jumped in after it. The slalom ski was extra-wide and had holders for both feet. Using just one ski seemed impossible to Jesse—it turned out to be easy for Buddy. He came out of the water smoothly, and skied with sureness and control. Jesse grudgingly admitted that Buddy was good. He looked happy, the first time Jesse could recall seeing him that way.

Buddy swung wide and zoomed back toward the wake, launched himself high when he hit it, and turned a circle in the air. He wobbled on the landing, but stayed up.

Miz Braun beamed at Mister Braun. "That boy is a marvel, isn't he?"

Mister Braun smiled and nodded.

Behind her mother's back, Lola pantomimed sticking a finger down her throat and gagging. Jesse and Dudley laughed.

After a quarter hour of Buddy's tricks, Mister Braun said to his wife, "We better get you in, hon."

Her skin was splotched with red and her expression reminded Jesse of the way he felt when he had stomach flu.

She looked out at Buddy. "Let him go a little more."

Mister Braun said, "You know how sick you are when you get too much sun."

She sighed. "All right."

He throttled down and Buddy sank into the water. Buddy yelled, "Hey!"

Mister Braun circled around to him. "Margaret's got to go in. But you can take the boat back out." Buddy nodded with uncharacteristic grace and climbed in.

Mister Braun took them to a patch of sandy beach on a grassy slope bordered by live oak trees. When he neared the shore, Jesse was glad to see a chance to do something besides sit—he jumped out and pulled the boat forward to beach it.

Lola handed Jesse the picnic basket, and Buddy hopped out with the cooler. Mister Braun helped Miz Braun to the shade, carefully spread a blanket for her, and then returned to the boat.

"Buddy, you and Lola go ahead and take the boys for a run, then it'll be time for lunch."

As Buddy started the motor, Mister Braun told him, "I don't want to see anything dangerous out there."

"Yessir."

Mister Braun shoved the boat out and Buddy backed it away. When the boat was pointed out into the lake, he gave it full throttle. Lola grinned into the wind from the other front seat. Speed thrills.

Buddy idled to a stop a hundred yards out. "Who's first?"

Lola said, "Come on, Jesse."

Jesse looked for rescue. "Dudley, do you . . ."

Dudley didn't let him finish. "After you."

Jesse said, "Great." About as great as a sharp stick in the eye. Lola tossed skis into the water while he buckled on the life belt. Dreading what was to come, he jumped in.

This was not going to be fun.

It took a handful of tries to get his feet into the skis. He'd get one on and, while he wrestled with the other, the first ski would twist and float off his foot. All eyes were on him—it was like the time he'd tried to straighten the nail on the Jeep bumper, only worse.

At last, both ski tips poked above the water in front of him. Lola tossed him the tow rope, he got it between the skis, and Buddy pulled away to take up slack. Emotions streamed through Jesse. Fear. Excitement. Fear. Pleasure. Fear.

The boat surged ahead. Jesse hadn't anticipated the force of the pull, and his feet went to each side while his top was pulled forward. He got a mouthful of water and the skis fell off. As he paddled to round up the skis, Buddy brayed and Lola tried to hide giggles. Dudley clamped his mouth shut, but then had to let a laugh explode.

Determination built up in Jesse. On the second try he kept his feet together—and they shot up in front of him, landing him on his back.

Attempt number three, same result.

On four he made it to his feet, only to plunge headfirst and nearly lose his trunks when he hit the water.

On the fifth try he rose shakily to his feet and stayed there. He was water-skiing!

Lola yelled, "Heyyyyy Jesseeeee!"

This was going to be fun!

He leaned and slid across the water. His skis rode up and over the wake and into the choppier water outside the path carved by the boat. Soon he was confidently gliding back and forth across the wake. He waved to go faster. Dudley saw him and yelled at Buddy. The boat plunged ahead.

It seemed as though he stood on the surface of the water while it raced underneath him. Wind pinned his hair back, the sun shone warm on his face and bright on the water.

When they passed by the Brauns at the picnic spot, Jesse swung close to the shore to show off. Mister Braun waved. Miz Braun kept reading her book. Buddy turned suddenly out into the lake. Centrifugal force whipped Jesse straight for the cattails by the creek inlet. He gritted his teeth as he plowed into the reeds, hoping they didn't conceal a waiting log.

Black ribbons wriggled away from his path as he smashed through. Cattails lashed him, the boat's wake hit the bank and splashed across his legs.

He held on, and held on—and cleared the reeds. He was feeling pretty good about himself when he realized that the black ribbons had been snakes. And that something was on his ankle. He looked down—a water moccasin, hooked just above his foot, mouth wide, thrashed wildly.

Reflex took over. He jerked his foot up and shook it. The ski fell off.

The snake wrapped around his leg.

He kicked and felt a prick when the snake's head slapped against his leg. He gave one more wild kick and the snake dropped away.

He was falling. He let go of the tow rope and hit the water, his other ski flying. He plunged head over heels toward the bottom, struck soft mud, tucked his feet under him and shoved—he rocketed up and shot into the air.

He was happy to see the boat speeding his way, then Lola pointed behind him and shrieked, "Snake!"

Jesse whirled—a snake was ten feet away, swimming on a collision course. He stroked away from it as hard as he could. The bulky life belt around his middle slowed him, and he wondered how fast a snake could swim.

Lola yelled at Buddy, "Hurry."

Buddy goosed the boat and it slid between Jesse and the oncoming serpent.

Dudley and Lola hauled Jesse out, and he collapsed into a seat, out of breath. He could only puff and shrug when Dudley asked, "You all right?"

Lola turned on Buddy. "You idiot! There were water moccasins in there!"

He raised his eyebrows. "How was I to know? Hey, it was just a joke."

Then his gaze flicked at Jesse, and the tiniest of grins lifted one corner of his mouth. Buddy had darned well known there would be water moccasins in those reeds. Buddy busied himself with steering the boat to the skis so Dudley could pick them up.

A spot on Jesse's leg burned. He discovered a red lump the size of a golf ball on his calf. He poked—it hurt.

Lola peered at the swelling. "Did a snake get you?"

"I guess so. One hitched a ride."

She turned to Buddy. "You get us to shore right now."

Buddy frowned. "Now, that's not my fault, and I don't want any whiney city boys sayin' so."

Jesse looked Buddy dead in the eye. Somehow Jesse no longer feared him, even though Buddy had proved to be dangerous. Maybe it was the cowardly nature of what he'd done. Jesse felt like he was in control now. He shrugged. "Accidents happen."

Buddy's expression turned to surprise, then puzzlement. He gunned the boat shoreward.

Lola became motherly. "You lie down and rest." She took his life belt off and put it under his head, then held his hand and looked worried. Jesse didn't hurt all that much, but it seemed like a moan was called for, so he eased a small one out.

Lola said, "Oh!" She moved his head into her lap and stroked his hair, "You'll be all right."

He began to think he had something to thank the snakes for, both the ones in the cattails and the one driving the boat.

Mister Braun gave Buddy a hard look when he heard the story—Buddy raised his eyebrows and spread his arms wide in a what-could-I-do gesture.

Miz Braun actually said it. "What could he do?"

Buddy added, "Hey, I just missed a turn a little."

Mister Braun said, "And you could have killed Jesse."

A protest came from Buddy. "I didn't—"

Mister Braun cut him off. "I don't think you'll be driving the boat again this summer." Buddy's face took on that knotted look.

Miz Braun frowned at Mister Braun. "Aren't you being too harsh, Axel?"

Jesse said, "It was me. I lost control of where I was going."

Buddy's expression downshifted to a dim look of confusion. Jesse enjoyed Buddy's consternation.

Mister Braun sighed. "All right." He knelt and studied the swelling. "This could have been real nasty. The water cleaned it, and I think it's as bad as it's going to get. You'll be back to work by Monday."

He looked into Jesse's eyes, and Jesse saw warmth there. Mister Braun smiled. "You were lucky."

"Yessir." Jesse grinned at Lola. "You should have seen the look on that snake's face."

Laughter popped out of them, and the tension evaporated.

Miz Braun had unpacked sandwiches and potato chips and cookies and Cokes. Jesse quickly ended the existence of a roast beef sandwich, several handfuls of chips, a Coke, and three chocolate chip cookies.

Buddy ate next to Jesse. Between bites, he leaned close. "You skied okay today for a first-timer."

The way he said it sounded like "Thanks."

After they were stuffed, they spread blankets and lay back to surrender to the sun. Feeling bold, Jesse put his towel next to Lola. Buddy claimed space on her other side.

By lying with his back to Miz Braun, Jesse was free to travel his gaze down the smooth lines of Lola's legs to toenails painted a bright red. Then back up, to pause at the swell of her belly and that part of her that had pushed against him so urgently. He felt a stirring in his trunks. His gaze grazed on, over the mounds of her breasts to the hollow of her throat, ripe for a kiss. Then to her lips, her closed eyes—and Buddy, just across from him.

The sweet and sour in his life, one beside the other. One caused an aching lump on his ankle, the other an eager lump in his swimming trunks.

16

When they got home from Canyon Lake a little before sundown, Jesse shed his trunks in the cabin and put on dry underwear and jeans, but his shirt was okay. The snake bite had subsided to a throbbing ache, and he was eager to get back into *Foundation*—during the week he'd been too tired to do much reading. Dudley sat at the table and drew cartoon monsters in his sketch pad.

Dudley said, "Hey, look." He'd drawn a snake with bulging, crossed eyes and curly hair a lot like Buddy's.

Jesse laughed. "Now where have I seen that before?"

"What is it with that guy?"

"I don't know. He's been nasty since the day we got here."

Dudley added a drop of venom coming from the Buddy snake's fangs. "Yeah, but he mostly gets after you."

"You're bigger."

"I kinda think it has something to do with Lola."

Jesse found his book and tossed it onto his bunk. "Why?"

"He gets worse when she's around."

"Maybe he'll back off now. Those snakes today got Mister Braun to looking at him pretty hard."

Dudley grinned. "I wouldn't want the boss looking at me that way."

"Me neither."

The cabin was hot, so Jesse took off his shirt and tossed it toward the clothes basket in the corner. The red feather fluttered from the pocket.

He retrieved it from the floor—it was bent. "Damn." Still, it might work. He straightened it, got his hat, and tucked the feather in the band. He held it out for Dudley to see. "What do you think?"

Dudley glanced up from a sketch of a cow. "Neat. Kinda crooked, though." He frowned. "It reminds me . . . Romero? Where'd you get it?"

"Floor of the car." A faint memory tugged at Jesse, something about the Braun's car the day Alejandro died. Jesse shook his head. Hell, he'd been trying to forget that day.

Dudley said, "Is it Romero's?"

"How could it be?"

"Be creepy if it was."

Now wearing the feather on his hat didn't feel right. He tucked it under his shirts in the bottom dresser drawer and climbed to his bunk to read.

Lola closed her bedroom door when she got home, dropped her wet towel on the floor, and turned on her radio. Buddy Knox sang about every man needing a party doll to run her fingers through his hair.

She wished for Jesse's pretty brown hair, along with the rest of him, as she stood before her full-length mirror and pulled her bathing suit down below her breasts. They weren't much, but they were coming along. Jesse liked them. Thinking of his lips on her skin, taking off her bathing suit became a dance, with her mirror as audience.

Swaying to Buddy singing about wanting to make love to his party doll, she was inching the suit down her thighs when the door opened. She turned to protest.

Her mother's expression shifted from surprise to rage.

"You little slut!"

"I have a right to do what I want in my room!"

Her mother hissed, "You have no rights, the way you paraded yourself in front of those boys today."

Lola hadn't done anything like that. "You're crazy!"

Her mother lunged forward and slapped her. "Get some clothes on!"

Tears swamped Lola's eyes, but she'd be damned if she'd cry. She stepped out of her bathing suit and threw on a robe.

Her mother rubbed the scar that cut across her eyebrow. "And don't think I didn't know about you and that skinny little greaser."

Oh, God, she knew about Alejandro? "I didn't . . ."

"Don't lie to me!" She aimed a finger at Lola. "You will not, I repeat, NOT go near either of those boys, especially Jesse. I haven't gotten your father to get rid of him yet, but I will. I will." She strode from the room, slamming the door after her.

Somehow Lola had gotten Jesse in trouble again. All she wanted was somebody to love. It wasn't fair. She paced, wanting to defy her mother and go to Jesse. But she was afraid she'd bring her curse down on him.

Her room was hot. She was sticky with sweat. She threw her robe on the floor and went to her closet. A silk shirt she'd swiped from Buddy caught her eye—it would feel good against her bare skin. As she slipped into it, she decided she had to see Jesse. Praying she would bring no more harm to him, she climbed out her window.

The light was fading into sunset when a tap sounded at the cabin door. Jesse leaned over the edge of the bunk and saw Lola. He grinned. "Come in."

Another man's shirt, this one a silky blue western style with pearl snap buttons, covered everything but her legs.

Her expression was subdued; she smiled, but it was tentative. She glanced at Dudley and then said, her voice soft, hesitant, "How are you doing?"

Jesse swung his legs over the edge of the bunk. "Okay."

"Can you walk?"

"Sure."

"How about now?"

He'd crawl to be with her if that was what it took. He slid down and tried his bum leg. It hurt, but he could handle it.

He slipped his loafers on and she led the way out. Dudley wiggled his eyebrows and tossed in a pucker for good measure. Jesse gave him the finger and a grin.

When she turned down the path toward the hen house, Jesse said, "Where are we going?"

"Where we can get some privacy." Her eyes were wide and worried, and he held back his questions.

The sun was almost gone when they slipped into the place Alejandro and Romero had lived. Jesse tensed, but their ghosts weren't there. Consuelo must have moved Alejandro's stuff out. The cots were stripped, the room was clean, a shelf near the sink held fresh towels and washcloths.

Lola turned to him. "Jesse, I been thinkin' about the trouble I cause you." Tears welled in her eyes.

He took her hands. She cast her gaze down. He said, "You haven't caused me any trouble."

She looked into his eyes. "I have! I'm a curse. First to Alejandro, and now you. I'm no good, I make bad things happen."

"What you've made happen to me is as far from bad as you can get."

She shook her head. "Buddy's mean to you because of me. Those snakes . . ." She shuddered.

He lifted her chin and gave her a tender kiss. "Buddy is just a shithead."

She stared into his eyes; hers seemed to plead with him.

"You are no curse. You are a blessing, and I love you."

Her expression softened. She wrapped her arms tight around his neck, her body pressed against him, her face nuzzled into the hollow of his shoulder. She trembled. "Oh, Jesse, I need you to love me."

Jesse pressed her tightly against him. "I do. I will."

She sniffled, and then relaxed against him. Time stopped. He stroked the curve of her back. The heat of her against his chest spread a warmth through him. Slowly, time resumed. He grasped her shoulders and gently pushed until her head tilted back. He found her lips. They kissed deeply.

She broke away and stepped back. Holding his gaze with hers, she pulled apart the top snap on her shirt. When the second snap went, bare skin gleamed between her breasts. The third and fourth snaps parted, and her naked belly was exposed. She finished, revealing a wispy triangle of hair at the "v" between her thighs.

She stood, her flesh a pale glow in the last of the sunlight.

He reached for her and slid his hands under her shirt, she pressed her breasts against his bare chest. His hands explored. Their kiss was furious.

She broke the kiss and led him to a cot. He slipped the shirt from her shoulders and gazed at her body, just visible in the thin light. He was spellbound by her slim beauty, the curves of her waist and hips, the grace of her.

She stepped to him. As their lips met, her fingers tugged at the snap on his jeans. He took over and quickly had his jeans and underwear off.

He stood naked and erect before her, and she smiled. He kissed her neck, his hands sliding down to her hips. He kissed his way to her breasts. It seemed natural to suck gently on her nipples. Her hands stroked his hair and his shoulders.

His fingertips explored across her belly and down to between her legs. She thrust against his hand. She was hot, and wet. He straightened. Her fingers wrapped around his prick and he thought he'd go right then.

Lola whispered, "Love me."

She lay on the cot, opened her legs, and held her arms wide. He lowered himself to her, not needing to know what to do; his body was in control and his mind was along for the ride. She guided his prick to the warm place between her legs. She lifted her hips and silky heat enveloped him. A rush of pleasure became a current that spread up his spine. He lowered his body to hers and they kissed, pressed against one another, he deep inside her.

She pushed against him, he responded with a thrust. They moved together, finding a rhythm. Molten pleasure concentrated in the base of his prick and edged upward. As it grew toward explosion, his mind clamored with a fear of getting her pregnant. He couldn't let go inside her.

He forced himself to pull out. Bliss shot from him, and then through him. She moved against him for a few more seconds and then stopped.

They lay together, their breathing slowed. Tingles of pleasure sent shivers up his spine. He raised up on his elbows and looked at her. Her eyes were closed, a small smile curved her lips. He kissed them.

"Hey, Miss Curse, how you feeling now?"

She grinned. "Four kinds of wonderful."

Then, faintly, came her mother's call. "Dolores!"

Lola said, "Oh, shit."

They smothered crazy laughter with their hands. He rose and became aware of the mess he'd left on her belly. He remembered the washcloths and fetched one.

Giving her a cloth, he turned away, rounded up his clothes and dressed. His modesty had charged back in, and he was embarrassed for her to see his body. But when he picked up her shirt and handed it to her, she stood with no concern and slipped it on. He began to harden again as she snapped the shirt closed.

Miz Braun's voice came again. "Dolores? Where are you?"

Lola ran out the door and up the path ahead of him, moonlight showing her bare legs. The shirt tail flipped up to reveal her naked bottom. His prick would never calm down.

Miz Braun shouted, "Dolores!"

"Playing with the puppies!"

"It's dark. Get in the house."

"Coming."

She stopped and Jesse gathered her to him for a last kiss, his body only too aware of what lay one thin layer of cloth away. She had to push him away. She giggled. "Greedy." She ran up the path. He watched until he could see her no more.

Greedy, yeah. And amazed. And thankful. He stood in the dark, the night air lifting sweat from his body. A grin stretched across his face, a happy shout formed in his mind. He kept it inside and added it to the joy washing through him like a big smile.

A new emotion filled him—it was like all the affection he'd ever felt combined with all the desire he'd ever had and then multiplied. He'd thought what he'd felt for Lola before had been love, but that had been kid stuff. This was what a man felt for a woman.

He stood for long minutes, basking in his feelings, reliving the touch of her and the liquid warmth of being inside her.

When he returned to the cabin, Dudley was reading in his bunk. "Where'd y'all go?"

"Just walking. Talking. You know."

"Man, those shirts she wears. Sure looked like she was naked underneath."

"Yeah, it did, didn't it?"

Monday morning, Lola's mother complained of a migraine and left her breakfast unfinished. Lola thought her mother deserved a headache after all the pain she caused.

With her gone, Lola was free to ask, "Daddy, can one of the boys help me set up a barrel run next to the barn this morning? Me and Fibber need to start training for the rodeo."

She warned Dudley off with a look—he just grinned—and pretended no special interest when Jesse volunteered.

Mister Braun shook his head. "We're digging sandstone for the new fireplace today, and we've got an hour's drive to the quarry over in Fredericksburg."

"But, Daddy . . ."

He grinned. "But I was thinkin' of having another cup of coffee first."

She jumped to her feet and hauled on Jesse's arm. "C'mon! Time's a-wastin'."

It didn't take long for Jesse to work up a good sweat rolling three fifty-five gallon steel drums to the field behind the barn. Lola paced off a triangle with a base of ninety feet and two sides of a hundred and five feet.

Her manner was like her father's, direct and no-nonsense, which made it a pleasure to work beside her. When they finished, though, she put on a deep Southern accent and curtsied. "I sure do thank you, kind sir."

He bowed. "My pleasure, young lady."

She smiled and leaned forward with a kiss on her lips, then drew back. "You never know who's looking."

Sure enough, the truck's horn sounded and he had to run.

Heat waves were already rising from the quarry when Jesse walked into it, a pick over his shoulder. By afternoon the rock was uncomfortably hot even through gloves. The next day, Tuesday, after they hauled the last load of rock to the house and stacked it into a low wall alongside the parking area, Jesse and Dudley submerged in the pond for an hour to recover.

Wednesday was a dusty day of rounding up forty sheep scattered throughout a twenty-acre pasture and herding them to the big corral beside the barn. The softness and depth of their wool amazed Jesse; his fingers sank all the way in before touching skin.

Mister Braun had Jesse take one sheep to a pen to be slaughtered; screw worms had eaten away half of its face, down to white bone, and were still at work. The sheep didn't seem to feel anything, but the putrid smell of death was strong.

On Thursday, the traveling sheep shearer drove up in his pickup full of tools. He, Mister Braun, and Buddy sheared the sheep while Dudley and Jesse gathered the wool and sacked it.

When the shearing was done, Jesse and Dudley spent hours inspecting naked sheep for the red of blood from nicks caused by clippers, then daubing black, tar-like medicine on them to prevent screw worm infestation.

Friday was back to the sandstone quarry because Miz Braun decided she wanted a two-sided fireplace. Swinging a sledgehammer in a rock pit under a sun that had the temperature up to a hundred and one, Jesse thought of a labor gang in a prison movie.

He saw little of Lola that week. She was entered in barrel racing in the Pecos July Fourth Rodeo two weeks away, and she spent most of her time on workouts with her horse. On top of that, her mother kept her busy with chores until she could hardly drag herself to her room at night. Jesse knew how she felt.

On Saturday afternoon, as he and Dudley trudged to the ranch house from the barn to see if anything else needed doing, they waved to Lola as she tore around her barrels, but she never looked their way. Day after day, they'd seen her running her horse through the triangle of barrels.

They found Mister Braun in the kitchen, filling a thermos with iced tea. He looked over their red faces and shirts wet with sweat and smiled. "That ought to be enough for the day. Buddy's already taken off for town."

Dudley said, "Whew!"

"Would one of you mind running this tea down to Lola? I know she doesn't have the sense to stop and drink something."

Dudley snatched up the thermos. "I'm on my way." He hurried out the front door, Jesse on his heels.

Out on the lawn, Jesse said, "What the hell do you think you're doing?"

Dudley had the teasing grin Jesse knew so irritatingly well. "A favor for the boss."

"Do yourself a favor and give me that." Jesse reached for the thermos, but Dudley held it high, out of his reach.

Dudley said, "I'm trying to help you, man—I'd hate to see you get any hotter. Might be bad for your health."

"Speaking of health, yours is going to decline suddenly if you don't give me that."

"That a threat?"

"A promise."

"Well, damn, maybe I'd best get somebody else to do this little chore."

"Lucky I happened by."

Dudley laughed and handed the thermos over; Jesse walked to Lola, a grin on his face, somehow no longer weary. She galloped to him when he shouted, "Hey, you want some ice tea?" White sweat lather streaked the horse's neck and flanks, but he wasn't breathing hard and seemed ready to go for another run.

She swung a leg over the saddle horn and slid off. "Yeah. You can just pour it over my head."

That kicked off thoughts of a drenched Lola and the resulting need to get her out of wet clothes. Lola wore jeans and boots, a sleeveless blouse dark with sweat down her chest and sides, and a turquoise cowboy hat with the tip of an ostrich feather in the band. Her face dripped sweat, and she lifted her hat to wipe her forehead with her hand.

She couldn't have looked better to Jesse.

He poured a thermos cap full of tea. She drank it down and held it out for more. "Thanks."

Lord, he wanted to touch her. He poured another cup. "It was your daddy's idea."

"I'll have to thank him for sending you." She downed her tea. "Will you time a run for me?"

He capped the thermos. "Sure. I'm done for the day."

"I just want to see where we are." She pulled a stopwatch from her pocket and handed it to him. "Come on."

She mounted and Jesse followed her to a line she'd drawn in the dirt. She pointed to two large rocks forty feet ahead. Another thirty feet further was the base of the triangle of steel drums. "Those rocks are the timing line. Start the watch when I go between them, and stop when I come back through."

When Jesse reached the rocks, he checked to see that the stopwatch was set on zero, then called out, "Go!"

She kicked Fibber in the ribs, lashed his rump with her reins, and yelled, "Hyaa!"

The little horse took off like she'd whacked him with a cactus. The idea was to hit the timing line at full speed and go flat out from there. It looked like she did just that. He clicked the stopwatch when they dashed past.

Lola and Fibber whipped around the right-hand barrel at full speed, the horse leaning at a forty-five degree angle. It was a wonder his hooves didn't skid out from under him. They crossed to the other corner of the base and looped around the barrel. With a slap of the reins and another kick, Lola sent her horse toward the far barrel at the top of the triangle.

The way Fibber moved out, his neck extended, reaching with every stride, Jesse suspected the horse didn't feel like he was carrying anything, little as she was. Yet she had the strength to hold him tight through turns.

Fibber cut it so close around the far barrel a stirrup brushed it and started it tipping. Cool as could be, Lola put a hand out to steady the barrel while they rounded it. Damn, she could ride.

Leaving the barrel wobbling but upright, she leaned low over Fibber's neck and shouted, "Go! Go!"

So taken was Jesse with the fierce girl charging at him that he almost forgot to click the watch when they passed.

She pulled Fibber in, slid off, and patted his neck while he blew, catching his breath. "Good horse. That's my boy."

Jesse jogged to her and handed over the stopwatch. She whooped, "Fifteen three! We're gettin' there!"

"Another run?"

"Naw. I'm cooked. Want to give me a hand?"

He laughed. "I'll give you any part of me you want."

"I just might take you up on that."

In the barn, Lola unsaddled Fibber, replaced his bridle with a halter, snapped on a lead and took him out to the corral. Jesse set the thermos beside the tack room and followed. He lounged in the shade while she walked the horse to cool him. Then he realized they were pretty much hidden behind the barn, so he stopped her. "Hey, let me do that and you cool yourself down over here."

She handed him the lead and then grinned. "It's not easy to stay cool around you."

His cheeks got hot, and he was sure they got red. All he could think of to say was, "Uh, c'mon, Fibber."

He led the horse in a circle around the corral until Lola said, "That oughta do it."

Inside the barn, she got a currycomb and started brushing him. Jesse grabbed another currycomb and worked the other side, smoothing the horse's coat and getting rid of the lather.

When they were done, Lola took Fibber to his stall. Jesse scooped up a handful of oats from a sack and visited the buckskin. The horse stuck his head out and greedily nibbled.

"Remember me, boy?"

Lola joined him. "That's Dusty. He likes you."

"He is kinda the color of dust, isn't he?"

"Yeah, but we call him Dusty 'cause he likes to throw in a buck when he runs, and if you're not expecting it, well, a bunch of folks have come back dusty after they rode him."

"He's pretty, though."

"Good cow horse, too. Saw him once pick up a runaway calf with his teeth and throw him back toward the herd." She picked up Fibber's saddle blanket and bridle. "Would you mind bringing my saddle to the tack room?"

"Sure." The single-rig saddle was a handsome thing, black leather with white ties and floral engraving on the leather.

The tack room was a square space defined by two walls of planks nailed to a framework of studs that ran out from a corner of the barn. Tools hung on the outside of the wall—machetes, axes, shovels, pitchforks, and an old-fashioned scythe.

Jesse still couldn't look at a pitchfork without a chill scrambling up his backbone.

The flamethrower rig sat in the corner formed by the front wall of the barn and the tack room wall. The walls reached as high as the loft floor ten feet up, but there was no actual ceiling. Jesse's gaze roamed up—a portion of the loft floor covered half the space but left a five-foot gap overhead. A plank door that could be locked with a padlock and a hasp closed off the room.

In the tack room, he set the saddle on a stand while Lola draped the blanket over a rack and hung the bridle on a peg.

Then she closed the door and unbuttoned the top button of her blouse. "Sure is hot."

"Yeah."

She unbuttoned a second button. "A person could have a heat stroke if a person didn't take precautions."

She had a reckless look in her eyes.

But this was the middle of the day. Anybody could come in. As she put her fingers on the third button, he said, "Ah, don't you think that's a touch dangerous?"

"Nobody can see in here, Buddy's gone, Daddy's through for the day and I know he'll just sit on the patio and drink ice tea, and Mom never comes down to the barn."

He looked around. There was no window in the room. "Dudley won't, either. Too close to work."

She chuckled and undid the third button. He held up a hand to stop her. She pouted, then smiled when he went to her and reached for the fourth button. He said, "I better make sure you're in no danger of heat stroke. Your folks would be mad if I just stood here and watched you collapse."

Soon they were wrapped in a topless embrace, their skin slick with perspiration. They discovered they could slip and slide against each other. The sensation was incredibly pleasurable. And funny. When they parted, suction created a loud "smack." They giggled and then went back to slippin' and slidin' and kissin'.

Miz Braun's voice called, "Dolores?" It sounded like she was just outside the barn.

Panic contorted Lola's face. She whispered, "We're dead if she finds you here!" She stuffed her bra under a saddle, grabbed her shirt, pulled it on and buttoned like crazy.

He put his arms through his shirt sleeves and searched for a way out. Nothing but walls and one door. Trapped.

Miz Braun called again, nearer. "Dolores, I know you're down here."

Jesse looked up at the gap above, between the loft floor and the plank wall. He pointed, Lola nodded. They went to a side wall, she cupped her hands and boosted him up enough for him to catch the top of the wall.

"Dolores, you answer me this minute!"

Lola shoved Jesse up and shouted, "In the tack room!"

Jesse got a foot on top of the plank wall, grabbed the edge of the loft floor, pushed and rolled into the loft.

Lola rushed to the tack room door, grabbing up Fibber's bridle on the way, and yanked the door open. Her mother was reaching for the door. "Hi, Mom." She made a show of hanging up the bridle.

Her mother stalked through the doorway, her face furrowed in a harsh frown. She examined Lola. "Where is your brassier?"

Lola pulled it out from under the saddle. "I was so hot I couldn't stand it."

"Was that boy here with you?"

Lola gave her best wide-eyed look. "I haven't been near the boys in days."

"Don't give me that. Your father told me he sent some tea down with Jesse."

Lola struggled to keep her voice calm and casual. "Oh, yeah. He brought some, then I did some more runs. I don't know where he went. Did you look at the pond?"

Her mother seethed. "Don't you lie to me."

Jesse's toe stuck out over the edge of the loft floor—he shifted his foot—his shoe scraped with a sound that seemed like a sonic boom.

Miz Braun said, "He's in the loft, isn't he?"

"I don't know where he is."

"I'm going up there." Lola followed her mother out of the tack room.

Jesse looked for a place to hide. The orange and white cat crouched on a bale of hay, all tensed up like he was about to run. Maybe if it made a noise. He took a penny from his pocket and tossed it at the cat.

It thunked on the floor a foot short. The cat shied and leaped from the bale.

Miz Braun shouted, "I hear you, you little bastard!"

Jesse dug out a quarter, his last coin, and tossed. It struck the cat on the side; the cat scrambled down the stairs.

Lola laughed, "It was just Spot. I'm going to take a shower. Do you want me to tell the boys you're looking for them if I see them?"

Miz Braun snapped, "Don't you get smart with me!"

"No, ma'am."

"Dolores, you will stay away from him."

Lola's voice was surly. "Can I go take a shower now?"

The tack room door shut. Miz Braun's voice grew fainter. "I'm warning you, Dolores, I'd better not catch you with that boy. And it'll be him that pays the price."

Jesse relaxed. His heart slowed as his fear eased. But it didn't vanish. Neither did his determination to see more of Lola. He didn't care what Miz Braun did. She was his girl.

That night at supper, Miz Braun glared at him more than usual, but he pretended not to notice. Lola kept her hands—and feet—away from him, so they gave her nothing to get more pissed off about.

Just when they'd started in on a peach cobbler, Sheriff Webb came calling with a photograph to show. "This is the man the State Police picked up down by McAllen." He held out a grainy-looking fax.

Mister Braun shook his head. "Not Romero."

Miz Braun took a look and shook her head.

The sheriff sighed. "Then he's still out there."

Buddy said, "Bet he's five hundred miles away from here by now."

"Maybe so—but we don't know that. I advise you folks to take care. I'd lock my doors at night if I were you."

Mister Braun said, "You think we're in danger here, Carl?"

"With murder, there's no telling. Until we find that man, there's a killer on the prowl."

Buddy chimed in. "Or on the run."

"Yessir, we can hope so."

On the way to the cabin after supper, Jesse said, "Hey, Dudley."

"Hey, what?"

"Let's check out the hen house."

"What for?"

"Maybe we can find something that will help the Sheriff."

Dudley said, "Like a clue, Nancy Drew?"

Jesse blushed, but he said, "Yeah," and started for the hen house. He was relieved to hear Dudley follow him. They slipped inside, split up and paced the room, searching.

Dudley lifted the tattered rug by a corner. "Nothing under here." He dropped it, then leaned down and studied it. "Jess?" He pointed.

Jesse joined him. A trail of dark, red-brown dots cut across a corner of the rug. Trust Dudley's artist's eye to spot it. Jesse said, "Kinda looks like blood."

Dudley shrugged. "Or chili sauce. Reminds me of my room back home."

Jesse punched him. "This is serious. Where was Alejandro when Romero cut him?"

Dudley pointed to the bunk next to the far wall. "Over that way."

Jesse said, "So this isn't from that. Let's keep looking." He opened the drawers of a small dresser, finding nothing. When he pulled it out from the wall to look behind it, a piece of paper fell to the floor. He fished it out. He stared at a photo of Romero. Romero smiling. Smiling with his arm around a pretty Mexican woman. Two small children leaned against their legs.

"Dudley?"

Dudley came and looked.

Jesse said, "He wouldn't leave this."

Dudley nodded. "I wouldn't."

Jesse slipped the picture into his shirt pocket. They searched until the sunlight began to go, but found nothing more. Not wanting to turn on a lamp and risk revealing that they'd been sneaking around, they went to the cabin.

Jesse dug the red feather from under his shirts and laid it on the dresser next to the photo of Romero and his family. "Why are we finding pieces of Romero?"

"He was a sloppy packer?"

"Hey!"

"Because he was running for it?"

"Maybe. But *how* did he run for it? Nobody saw him go."

"The only person who went anywhere that day was Buddy, and he was searching for Romero."

The Chrysler racing past the barn that day came to Jesse.

"There was something blue. In the back seat." He picked up the feather. "Where I found this."

"Blue like what?"

Jesse pictured it. Beige car, Buddy's red shirt, and in the back . . . "Like Romero's blue-jean shirt."

Dudley shook his head. "Didn't see it. Why would Buddy help Romero get away?"

"Sounds nuts, doesn't it."

"Should we tell Mister Braun or the sheriff?"

Jesse pointed at the items on the dresser. "Tell 'em what? We found some trash, a rug is dirty, and maybe I saw something blue in a car?"

"Now that you put it that way . . ."

"Yeah." Jesse put the photo and the red feather under his shirts. As he closed the drawer, he remembered Buddy seeing him find the feather in the car. He hadn't seemed to care.

But after that he had taken Jesse on an unannounced visit to a snake nest.

It was Jesse's favorite part of the week—sleeping in on Sunday morning. Then Dudley's voice wormed its way into a dream of sweaty, slippery, salty girl. "Jesse? You gotta wake up!"

Go away.

Dudley yelled, "Jesse!"

Jesse snapped awake. Weak light came in the window, so it was morning, but it hadn't been for long. He leaned over the edge of his bunk and peered down.

Dudley's face twisted as he lay in his bunk, his hands gripping his bare belly. Sweat beaded his forehead, and his breathing was loud. As Jesse watched, a lump bulged under the skin on one side of Dudley's stomach and moved across it like a wave. Dudley moaned.

Jesse hopped down. "What's wrong?"

"I don't know. It's hard to breathe, and my belly's killin' me right here." He pointed to a red spot the size of a nickel.

"My back, too." He rolled onto his side and revealed a similar red spot halfway down his back.

There was a black something on the sheet—a dead spider.

"Don't move." Jesse got a piece of toilet paper and carefully picked up the spider. Its belly sported a red hourglass.

"You got bit by a black widow."

"Oh, shit." Dudley rolled onto his back and another spasm

or cramp or whatever it was traveled across his stomach. He gritted his teeth but couldn't stop a moan.

Jesse placed the spider on the table. "I'll be right back."

He pulled his jeans on and raced to the house. Consuelo was frying bacon in the kitchen "Is Mister Braun up?"

"I have not seen him. *Que pasa*?"

"A black widow bit Dudley."

Her eyes widened. "*Madre de Dios*!"

He ran to the hallway that led to the bedrooms and called out, "Mister Braun?"

"Yeah?" He sounded alert, awake.

"Dudley got bit by a black widow."

Mister Braun hurried out, barefooted, pulling on a shirt. "Connie, get me a washcloth."

As Consuelo rushed to the utility room, Mister Braun took an ice cube tray from the refrigerator freezer. When she returned with the cloth, he wrapped ice cubes in it, dampened the cloth, and ran out the back door. Jesse dashed after him.

In the cabin, Mister Braun knelt beside Dudley, studied the bite on his belly, and then put the cloth-wrapped ice on it. "How you feelin', son?"

"Awful."

"Just hold on, you'll be okay." He turned to Jesse. "Where's the spider?"

Jesse pointed, Mister Braun examined it and nodded. "You run up to the house and tell Miz Braun to call the hospital and let 'em know we're bringing in a boy with a black-widow bite."

Jesse's voice shook. "There's another bite on his back. Are two bites—is that—I mean, how bad . . ." Dudley couldn't die!

Mister Braun put a hand on his shoulder. "He'll be all right. Now go, then come back and help me with Dudley."

At the hospital, Jesse paced the waiting area while a doctor examined Dudley in the emergency room. On the drive in,

Alejandro's death had crashed back into Jesse's mind, and then his father's murder. Death was too real, too easy. He couldn't lose Dudley! He'd be alone in the world—his mother might as well be dead, there was nothing there of his real Mama, only the numb woman who pretended she was all right.

Why was it taking so long? A crazy panic was rising when Mister Braun put his hands on Jesse's shoulders. "He'll be all right, son. He's a big, strong boy."

Mister Braun seemed so certain that the knots in Jesse's mind relaxed a little. "Thank you, sir."

The doctor, a round man who waddled rather than walked, came out. "He'll be fine in a few days. But I want to keep him for observation, just to be sure there are no complications."

Jesse said, "Complications?"

The doctor smiled. "Don't worry, young man. It's not like a rattlesnake bite, but it can make you pretty sick, and that's why we want to keep him here."

Jesse edged toward the door the doctor had come out. "Can I see him?"

"Go right ahead."

Dudley looked pale, but he worked up a weak grin for Jesse. "Hey, Jess."

"Hey, Spider."

Dudley broke open the biggest smile Jesse'd ever seen on him. The nickname had happened.

Jesse grinned. "Still hurtin' . . . Spider?"

Dudley laughed and then winced. "Yeah. But the doc says it'll stop by tomorrow. Gotta rest for a few days, though."

"Man, you'll do anything to get out of work, won't you?"

"Ah, Jess, you know me too well. Took me days to find that spider."

Mister Braun came in and, after the usual how-are-you-I'm-okay stuff, said, "We need to go, Jesse."

"Okay." Jesse patted Dudley on the shoulder. "See you tomorrow, Spider."

Mister Braun raised his eyebrows. "Spider?"

Dudley nodded.

Mister Braun chuckled. "Take care, Spider."

For a boy in pain, Dudley looked mighty pleased with himself.

Lola, still in her pajamas and robe, nibbled at a piece of toast with honey on it and glanced at the front door every few minutes. Why didn't her father call?

Her mother, preceded by a wave of too much perfume, came into the kitchen wearing a church outfit. "You need to get dressed."

The front door opened and her father entered, trailed by Jesse. Lola dropped her toast and ran to her father.

"Is he all right?"

"He's fine. He'll be back in a day or so."

She shuddered with relief, a little surprised to realize how frightened for Dudley she had been. She glanced at Jesse, happy that he was okay. She wished she could be alone with him. She turned to Connie, "Let's bake up some cookies and take them in this afternoon."

Her father said, "I don't think he'll feel much like eating."

"Tomorrow then."

Her mother said, "There's time to make late Mass."

Mister Braun nodded. "Good. I could use a little peace and quiet." He eyed Lola. "You don't look quite ready."

"I'm so beat after workin' Fibber all week, I just want to go back to bed."

Her mother frowned.

Her father said to her, "She has worked awful hard."

"I'll go to the Wednesday-night Mass." She went to him and collapsed against his chest. "I'm sooo tired. Pleeeeeese?"

He smoothed her hair. "You'll go to bed?"

She yawned. "Absolutely."

Her mother glanced squinty-eyed at Jesse. "I don't like this, Axel. She shouldn't be skipping church."

"She won't be, I'll take her in Wednesday." Her father tousled Lola's hair. "Okay, honey."

Her mother turned to Jesse. "I want you out of the house."

Jesse responded with a wide-eyed look. "I'm going to search our cabin for spiders."

Her mother aimed a hard look at Connie. "You keep an eye on things."

"*Si, Señora.*"

Her father headed for their bedroom and her mother followed, saying, "When's Dudley coming back to work? Do we have to pay for the hospital?"

Lola brushed past Jesse and whispered, "I'll come help you." She caught Connie watching them and beamed her best innocent smile at her.

As Jesse walked to the back door, Connie handed a broom to him. "Don't forget to check the ceilings and corners, especially in the bathroom."

Lola forced herself to walk slowly; thinking of stealing time with Jesse made her want to skip.

Sure enough, Jesse found a spider community in a corner behind the tub and another under the bunk bed. Good old Buddy hadn't done much of a job—if he'd done one at all. Jesse pounded them with the broom. After sweeping the bodies outside, he sat in the chair beside Dudley's bunk to wait for Lola.

By the time she pulled open the screened door, his thoughts had spiraled downward until he felt as if he were submerging beneath the weight of Buddy's harassment, Miz Braun's hostility, and Dudley's scary spider bites.

Lola was barefooted, barelegged, and bare-shouldered in shorts and a brief top, but the sight of her caused only a momentary blip in his depression. He tried for a grin and failed. She sat on Dudley's bunk. "What's wrong?"

"Everything. What happened to Spider . . ."

"Spider?"

"Found a nickname for Dudley."

"Neat."

"Yeah, but he's so sick."

"Are you afraid Dudley—Spider will die?"

"Not now, but just thinking about it—I mean, he's my best friend in the world. We're going to ranch together." He trailed off and stared out the screened door. She leaned close and placed her hand on his leg. Warmth spread from that spot as they sat.

Lola wanted to banish Jesse's sadness. As she wondered how to cheer him, the feel of his leg under her hand rekindled the heat her mother had interrupted in the tack room. She inched her hand higher on his thigh. "I promised Daddy that I'd go to bed."

After a long moment, he turned to her; his eyes were no longer sad. He lifted her hand to his lips. He kissed the back, and then the palm. Shivers tingled her spine. She took his hand and pulled him with her as she lay back on the bunk.

Her feelings for Jesse transformed every touch, every caress, and she discovered the difference between having sex and making love. As she neared her peak, she felt him begin to withdraw. But she wanted all of him all the way. She locked her legs and arms around him and held him until they were both done.

Afterwards, they cuddled. She could not imagine anything better than laying touch on touch with the boy she loved, their breathing and sweet mockingbird melodies the only sounds.

"Jesse?"

"mmm"

"I could be like this for the rest of my days."

"Me too."

"In a place of our own."

He didn't answer.

She propped herself on an elbow to see his face. "Don't you want to?"

He grinned. Oh, those warm brown eyes. "Yes. I was just trying to figure out what to do with Dudley."

She smiled. "How about a cabin just for him?"

He nodded.

She lay back and followed her thoughts into the future.

A soft, persistent knock roused her. It took a moment for her to realize that she lay next to Jesse in Dudley's bunk. He was asleep.

They were naked.

Someone was knocking on the screened door.

Panic struck. Stifling a cry, she peered out and saw Connie's familiar shape, her back to the door, one arm behind her, knocking on the door frame. Oh, God, she must have seen them. But she was knocking, not yelling.

Lola worked up the courage to whisper. "What?"

"Your parents will soon be home from church." With that, she left.

Lola climbed out over Jesse and hurried into her clothing.

He stirred. "What was that?"

"Connie warning me my parents will be home soon."

He bolted upright. "Consuelo?

"I don't think she'll tell."

"I'm dead if she does."

"We both are. But she loves me. She won't."

Alarm still rattled her, but she drew strength from her

dreams of a future with Jesse. They would be all right. She leaned down and kissed him. "Don't worry." She ran to get back into her pajamas.

Jesse did worry. He dressed and then sat on Dudley's bunk. If the Brauns found out, he'd be sent home. Or worse. Maybe sent to jail for rape or something. But it wasn't rape. They loved each other. Footsteps passed by the window and came to the door. Dread tightened his gut.

Consuelo said, "Jesse?"

He went to the door. She looked up at him, worry in her dark eyes. "Lola is in her bed, as she promised. They will not know."

His relief made him weak at the knees. "Oh, thank you, Consuelo."

She shook her head. "You must keep away from her."

"But we love each other."

"I know you feel that way, but I think there will be trouble. Bad trouble."

Fright ran a cold finger down his spine. "What?"

She glanced toward the ranch house and then shook her head. "I don' know. I can't say." Her eyes pleaded with him. "Please, for Lola, stop."

"I don't know if we can."

She looked at him for a long moment. "Then God help you both."

With Dudley in the hospital, Jesse worked harder than ever, and he was glad of it. Even when he could hardly put one foot in front of the other, his only response to yet another order was "Yessir."

On Monday, Jesse rode with Mister Braun to check on grazing conditions for the livestock. Bone dry, the parched grass was sparse everywhere. Mister Braun decided the angora goats needed to be moved and dropped Jesse off to handle it while he scouted further. The yellowish-white goats had long, silky hair that would end up as sweaters and become soft, fuzzy coverings for the curves of pretty girls.

He found out the hard way that herding goats was like herding a flock of birds. He'd get them moving and then, for no reason he could see, they'd all suddenly turn at a right angle, like birds in the air did. He wondered, as he cursed and ran to head them off, if that was why it was called a flock.

Determined not to fail in Mister Braun's eyes, he kept after the contrary things. He finally got the hang of it, anticipating their moves and keeping them headed in more or less the right direction, though they went sideways as much as they went forward. It would have taken a half hour to walk from one pasture to the other. It took Jesse two hours to get the goats there.

When Mister Braun returned, he said, "Good job."

Jesse felt as if he'd just gotten an A on a test.

Mister Braun said, "Got one more animal I need to have moved today."

Oh, great, another animal adventure.

"It's almost time to take the bull down to Hondo to cover my sister Mary's prize heifer, and I want to move him up to the barn to watch his feed."

Oh, boy. A miniature roundup. Real cowboy work.

Instead of going back to the barn to get Jesse a horse, Mister Braun drove directly to the bull's pasture. The animal they'd dubbed "Mister Completely" stood near a water trough, chewing his cud.

"Just drive him to the barn. He's as gentle as can be; you won't have any trouble."

So Jesse's miniature roundup turned into a long, hot walk behind a plodding bull that refused to hurry no matter how many stones Jesse peppered its tail end with. It was not Jesse's idea of being a cowboy.

On Wednesday, they toasted cactus. As Mister Braun lifted the flamethrower from the truck, he said, "Jesse, want to try it?"

Wow! "Yessir!"

Buddy scowled. "I'd like to do some."

Mister Braun ignored him. He coached Jesse, and soon Jesse was singeing needles from prickly pear. He was working on the other side of a clump of cactus from Buddy when darned if his trigger finger didn't slip and loose a ten-foot blast of flame in Buddy's direction. Luckily for Buddy, it was a twelve-foot clump of cactus.

Buddy yelped like a kicked dog and staggered backward. "You idiot!"

Jesse shrugged. "Darn clumsy of me. Sorry 'bout that."

An amused look crinkled Mister Braun's eyes while he gave Jesse a mild chewing about safety. Buddy's yelp and the expression on his face when he dodged ten feet of flame had been well worth it.

The next day, Mister Braun took the truck to town and returned to the barn loaded with a couple of tons of oats and corn in hundred-pound burlap sacks.

He told Jesse and Buddy, "I've got to go see Mike Fletcher about the wiring for the addition, and then get Dudley out of the hospital. If you're smart, you'll get this unloaded and put away today. We've got a long drive to Pecos Saturday for the rodeo, and we're taking Independence Day off tomorrow. I won't mind if you work on a holiday, but you might."

Buddy grabbed a sack off the truck and hoisted it to a shoulder. "We'll get it done."

Jesse grabbed a sack and surprised himself when he didn't collapse under it. He had grown much stronger. They were headed into the feed room in the barn when Mister Braun drove away in the Jeep.

When they returned to the truck for more, Buddy leaned against the side of the truck and watched Jesse lug another sack in. When Jesse returned to the truck, he found Buddy sitting in the shade against the barn, his legs stretched out. Jesse didn't say anything, but he sure as hell thought it. He toted feed for another fifteen minutes, growing angrier with each sack. The heat was enormous, and every bag seemed heavier than the one before.

Jesse pulled yet another sack off the truck and then stopped. It wasn't right. Buddy would get credit for his work while not moving a single, lazy muscle.

Not this time. Jesse dumped the sack back on the truck bed and then went to the horse trough. He plunged his face in and out, and the shock of cool water helped. He collapsed against the barn wall, about ten feet from Buddy. Lord, it felt good to sit.

Buddy said, "What do you think you're doing?"

Thinking it should have been obvious, Jesse told him anyway. "Nothing."

"Get back to work."

Jesse gazed out at heat waves shimmering on the road. "Don't think so."

"We got to get this unloaded by the time Axel gets back."

"Well, we are tired of doing it by ourselves."

Buddy got up, stood over Jesse, and jabbed him in the leg with his toe. "You little turd, get to work."

Jesse looked him right in the eye and did not move.

Buddy leaned down, grabbed Jesse's shirt with both hands, and pulled. Jesse let his body go limp. Buddy dropped him and Jesse fell back against the barn. His head banged against the wall and it hurt, but he stopped himself from rubbing it. He wasn't about to let his tormentor know.

Buddy could have been spitting stones instead of words when he leaned close and said, "You little son of a bitch."

Jesse's heart was pounding by then and he feared Buddy would punch him in the face. But he'd had enough. He stared at the dead center of Buddy's eyes. One part of Jesse thought he was being stupid, another was beyond caring.

Buddy backed off and tried another tactic. "They'll send you back to Dallas."

Jesse gave him a lazy smile. "Then you'll have to do all the work all by yourself until Dudley gets well, and I don't think he'll stay here without me."

Buddy snorted, and then he walked to the truck and paced, looking up the road toward the front gate. Putting on a smile, he said, "Come on, Jesse. I'll do my share."

Jesse closed his eyes.

"Bastard."

Jesse listened for footsteps coming at him. He tensed, expecting a kick. He wasn't going to give on this one. Let Buddy try explaining bruises and injuries to Mister Braun. Jesse heard the slide of burlap on the truck bed, a sound he was intimately familiar with, and cracked his eyes open.

Wonder of wonders, Buddy had hauled a sack onto his shoulder. He glanced Jesse's way and saw him watching. He studied Jesse, and then carried the sack to the feed room.

Jesse relaxed and let Buddy labor alone until he figured they were about even, and then he got up and went back to work. They hauled sacks equally until the entire load was neatly stacked in the feed room.

They relaxed against the barn, shirts off to take advantage of a breeze. Buddy stared out at sun-baked fields. He didn't have his usual angry edge when he said, "Feel better now?"

Jesse glanced at Buddy. "Yeah."

Buddy nodded. "You showed me somethin' today." He shook his head and grinned. "With that flamethrower yesterday, too."

Jesse puzzled over Buddy's tone. It wasn't nasty or condescending. It was—man to man? "Yeah?"

"You got sand. Man's got to respect that."

Jesse looked at Buddy, wondering if he'd heard right.

Buddy leaned his head back and pulled his hat down over his eyes.

What the hell was happening?

The beep of the Jeep's horn sounded and up the driveway came Mister Braun, Dudley beside him.

Jesse shouted, "Hey, Spider!" and ran to Dudley. "How're you feeling?"

Dudley looked pale, but okay. "A little weak, but the doctor says I'll be over it in a day or two."

Mister Braun eyed the empty truck and said to Buddy, "Good job." Buddy nodded.

Buddy said, "Yeah, good job, Jess."

His remark provoked a second look from Mister Braun, eyebrows raised, and made Jesse wonder if the heat wasn't making him hallucinate. He clapped Dudley on the shoulder. "You too weak for a dip in the pond?" He looked at Mister Braun. "If, that is, we're done."

Mister Braun smiled. "You're done, I'm done, we're all done, and a swim is the best idea I've heard in a coon's age."

He slipped the Jeep into gear and Jesse hopped into the back. Mister Braun looked to Buddy, who waved them on.

Mister Braun limited his swim to a quick dip, but Jesse and Dudley lingered. Jesse caught Dudley up on the week, telling him how weird goats were and describing how he'd toasted Buddy with the flamethrower.

Dudley laughed at that. "I'm surprised Buddy didn't make you do all the work."

"He tried." Jesse told him what had happened when unloading the grain.

Dudley said, "Maybe the guy's got some sense of what's right after all."

"It'd be nice. It'd be fun to see pigs fly, too."

After Friday breakfast, Mister Braun went to a hall closet and returned with an American flag folded into a triangular shape. He led Jesse, Dudley and the family out front, where he and Lola unfolded the flag with care. He raised it on a pole attached to the house, then placed his hand over his heart and began reciting the Pledge of Allegiance. Lola, Miz Braun and Buddy did the same.

Dudley joined in and Jesse added his voice. He was proud to be an American, although he often thought it would have been neater if Texas had stayed an independent nation and never joined the Union.

Consuelo watched from the doorway, silent. In her eyes was a shadow of the hurt he'd seen when he'd almost called her a wetback.

Miz Braun had a sick look on her face and retired to her bedroom right after the flag ceremony.

Lola whispered, "The monthlies." That aspect of womanhood was a total mystery to Jesse, and one he had no desire to know more about.

Lola spent the day with her horse, training for the race and then washing and grooming him. At supper that night, Jesse could see she was running on fumes, with purplish circles under her eyes. He managed to get her out on the back patio for a quick kiss, but then her father came out to smoke his annual Fourth of July cigar. Buddy joined them for a cigarette.

Lola said, "Good night, y'all," gave her father a kiss on the cheek, and went inside.

Mister Braun puffed his cigar into life and silence settled. The sweet scent of Buddy's cigarette wrestled with the rank odor of Mister Braun's cigar, and lost.

Mister Braun broke the quiet. "We'll need to pull out by nine. It's over three hundred miles to Pecos, and we've got to get there early enough to settle Fibber in. It'll be a good seven or eight hours."

The light in Lola's bedroom window went on. Jesse smiled. "Yessir. We'll be ready."

Buddy said, "I'm takin' my car. A couple of friends are riding along, so I'll be sleepin' in."

The drive to Pecos was blistering hot, but a good time was had by some. The Braun's Chrysler had no air conditioning, so they cruised with all the windows down. With the horse trailer in tow, Mister Braun didn't drive over fifty, and cars kept passing them. Buddy passed them before eleven o'clock, two friends in the car with him, the pipes on his Chevy blaring.

Dudley said, "Bet I could take him." Jesse thought he probably could. The Caddy didn't look like it would be fast, but it had an engine the size of Rhode Island under the hood, and Dudley'd beaten a lot of cars street dragging.

Lola spent so much time on her knees in the middle of the front seat facing back to shout to them over the wind noise that her father finally whacked her on the bottom and laughed, "I'm tired of this thing stickin' up here. Get into the back seat if you're going to yak all the way there."

Lola giggled. "Yessir!"

Miz Braun frowned and opened her mouth, but she stopped and turned her head away. Jesse figured it was just too hot to raise a fuss, even about Lola sitting in the back with evil Jesse.

Mister Braun slowed and started to pull over, but Lola slid head first over the seat, twisting and curling like an otter. Jesse helped, oh so glad to get his hands on her when he, ahem, accidentally cupped her breast. She ended up between Dudley and him. That was when a good time was had by some.

Jesse'd had the sense to sit behind Miz Braun so she'd have to have been an owl to swivel her head around and send him sour looks. Still, she might be able to see enough to catch them holding hands, so he avoided that, as tempting as it was. Lola slid one bare foot over to play footsie. Jesse had his boots on, so it was more like "leggie," a fine variation.

Dudley grinned at them and shook his head; Lola stuck her tongue out at him, and Jesse didn't care what he saw. By the time they reached the rodeo grounds in Pecos, he was truly hot and bothered.

The mound in Jesse's jeans relaxed as they unloaded Fibber to take him to a stall. Mister Braun went to the office to make sure Lola was entered for barrel racing. Miz Braun stayed in the car to nap. The smell of mustard and hot dogs led Dudley away in search of food, claiming the doctor had told him to eat whenever possible. As if anyone ever had to tell Dudley to do that.

It was even hotter than Kerrville, and a pall of dust rose above the rodeo arena. The warm smell of it all enveloped Jesse; it was one of the things he liked best about rodeos. The mixture of dust, sweat, animals, and manure somehow added up to rich and pleasant. Horse droppings had hardly any scent when the sun had baked the moisture from them. The rounded pieces were also a handy size for throwing—Dudley and he sometimes had horseshit fights in the pasture where they kept their horses. Jesse always won. He just kept coming, and Dudley couldn't stand up to him.

It was the day after the Fourth but the holiday was still kicking up its heels. Red, white, and blue bunting decorated the stands, and the place was crowded with people moving livestock, chatting, and laughing. Firecracker explosions punctuated the happy noise now and again.

Jesse was glad he'd shined his boots and worn his Western shirt, although he was no match for bowlegged men who had to be veteran riders. The shine on his boots didn't last long—Pecos was pretty much desert, and the ground was dirt and dust dotted by occasional piles of horse droppings.

He walked beside Lola as she led her horse to the stables. On the way, they passed Buddy and his friends up on a fence, checking out the hump-backed Brahman bulls Buddy was entered to ride. Jesse thought Buddy was nuts to voluntarily sit on top of a ton of angry meat with horns.

Suddenly a string of firecrackers went off six feet away, popping like a playful machine gun. Fibber reared, yanking Lola off her feet and slamming her into a fence. She fell and the lead rope whipped out of her hand. Jesse dove and caught the rope as the panicked horse wheeled to run. Fibber gathered himself to drag Jesse all over hell and half of Texas—then Buddy appeared, holding his arms wide to head the horse off. Talking in a smooth, calm voice, Buddy eased close and got a hold on the halter.

Jesse dropped the rope and stood. Lola sat on the ground, rubbing her side. He pulled her to her feet. "You okay?"

"Yeah. Got the wind knocked out of me, and my ribs hurt a little."

Two boys, maybe twelve years old, one of them a carrot-top redhead, ran away laughing. People smiled at their mischief. A cowboy with a rope threw a loop at them, but missed.

Buddy led Fibber to them. The horse had calmed, though his eyes showed more white than usual. As Lola reached for the lead rope, Buddy asked, "Sure you can handle him?"

She grasped the rope snug under the halter to keep the horse on a tight lead to make it a lot harder to lift his head and rear.

"I'm ready for anything, now."

Jesse took a grip on the rope just under her hand. "We've got him."

She smiled at his touch and said to Buddy, "Thanks."

Jesse had to admit that he had been headed for a rough time until Buddy stepped in. As much as he hated to, he said, "Yeah, thanks."

Buddy nodded and went back to his friends and the bulls.

Lola made sure Fibber was comfortable in his stall, with plenty of water and a ration of oats, plus an armful of hay to munch on when he got bored. Her ribs hurt when she picked up the bucket of water. Jesse saw her wince and immediately took it from her. She surely did like having him around, and not just for toting buckets. He was increasingly good to look at. The little bit of extra tummy he'd had when he arrived on the ranch had gone the way of hard work, and he was now as lean as Buddy.

Satisfied that Fibber was settled in, she planted a kiss on his velvety nose and they went back to the car. Dudley was there, finishing a hot dog, a dribble of mustard on his shirt. Her father had the number she would wear in the race, a lucky seven. She started to ask if they could look around, but her mother looked like death warmed over, so miserable that Lola felt a brief moment of pity. Then her mother glared at Jesse and the pity evaporated.

Her father drove them to the Pecos Inn—a better name would have been The Pecos Crematorium. Neither of the wheezing window air conditioners dented the heat stored up in the two rooms, one for the three Brauns and one for Dudley and Jesse.

There was no swimming pool, so the only option was to sit and sweat and hope darkness would bring relief. Which, her daddy kept assuring them, it would.

Her mother, who was so cheap she'd pinch a nickel until the buffalo hollered, surprised Lola by suggesting they all go to a movie to cool off. Lola guessed her cramps must have been somethin' awful. Cramps had never troubled Lola, though her period was well-established and regular. Come to think of it, she was due. She prayed it would hold off until after the race.

They piled into the Chrysler and found the theater, not difficult since it was the only one in town and right on the main drag. It featured *Damn Yankees.*

Lola turned to her father. "What's it about?"

"Baseball."

She said, "Phooey."

Her dad chuckled. "It's also a musical, based on a big Broadway hit."

Lola brightened, and her interest grew with the sight of a poster featuring a dancer with incredibly long legs in a remarkably short costume. Her name was Gwen Verdon.

The theater was good and chilly, especially after the hundred and ten degrees outside. Her father bought treats—Dudley got a giant popcorn, Jesse went for Junior Mints, and she chose Milk Duds.

Her mother made sure she and Daddy sat between Jesse and her. Luckily, the movie was fun, with a nutty devil, great sports action, and that dancer. When Gwen Verdon danced and sang *Whatever Lola Wants,* Lola grinned so hard she thought her face would break. She applauded at the end of the song, and her dad chuckled. She leaned forward and caught Jesse looking at her. Then her mother shifted to block her view.

When they left, she learned that her father had been right about the temperature—the sun had gone down and taken the worst of the heat with it. The air was easy and cool.

Her father proposed that they walk to a nearby restaurant for dinner and got no arguments. She felt full of life, and Lola's song still played in her mind. She danced ahead of the others, imitating Gwen Verdon's moves, and sang,

"Whatever Lola wants, Lola gets, and little man, little Lola wants you . . ."

She gave Jesse a bump with her hip and then, seeing the quick frown on her mother's face, did the same to her father and Dudley. They laughed. Her mother didn't.

"I always get what I aim for, and your heart and soul is what I came for. Whatever Lola wants, Lola gets . . ."

Her mother grabbed her by one arm and shook her. "You will *not* act like white trash!"

Lola clenched her teeth. She wrenched her arm free. Tears formed, but she fought them back and glared up at her mother.

People on the sidewalk stopped to watch. Her father stepped close to her mother and gripped her arm. "Now, Margaret, it's just a song."

Her mother raised her hand as if to slap Lola. Lola flinched back, then straightened and lifted her chin, daring her mother. She'd be damned if she'd run and cry.

Instead, her mother rubbed the scar that cut through her eyebrow. Then she pointed at Lola, her face knotted up like Buddy's did when he was pissed off. "I don't want to hear any more 'Lola,' either. *Dolores*."

Lola opened her mouth to protest but stopped when, out of her mother's sight, her father shook his head. She sniffled and turned away. Shame kept her gaze from Jesse and Dudley.

Her father moved her mother on by her arm, then put his arm around Lola and hugged her to him as they walked. Dudley and Jesse fell in behind. Although her father's embrace felt good, like it always did, she found herself wanting Jesse's arms around her. But she didn't want to think about what her mother would do to him if she saw him so much as touch her.

She was quiet at dinner, but no on else had much to say, either. Finally, when dessert was about done, Jesse asked her, "How are your ribs?"

Her father said, "What's this?"

She said, "Oh, I guess I bruised a rib when I fell."

Her mother glanced at her, but said nothing.

Her father wasn't going to let this go. "Fell when?"

She started to roll her eyes in her usual "Give me a break" expression, but thought better of it. "A firecracker scared Fibber and he reared, and I fell and hit a fence. It's okay."

"Show me where."

She pointed to a place low on her side. He probed gently; it hurt and she winced.

"Maybe you should withdraw."

"Daddy, don't you always say quitters never win?"

"Yes, but . . ."

"I'm not quittin'."

He grinned. "That's my girl."

When they got back to the motel, Lola wasn't surprised to hear her mother say, "Dolores, you need your rest. Get to bed now." It was only nine o'clock, but there was no arguing. At least it was dark and she could pretend it was really bedtime.

She lingered in the doorway, her hand on the frame. Jesse came close and, out of her parents' sight, touched her fingers.

Her mother called, "Dolores?"

Jesse whispered, "Hey."

What he said was I love you. She beamed at him and whispered, "Hey."

A hand grabbed her arm and yanked her inside. Her mother shut the door hard enough to make the window rattle.

Her mother pointed her damned finger. "I told you . . ."

Lola turned her anger loose. "Don't you ever do that to me again!"

Her mother loomed over her, cheeks flushed, scar red. "I'll do what I have to, you little alley cat."

Her father stepped between them, facing her mother. "What's wrong with you? She hasn't done a thing."

Lola ran into the bathroom and slammed the door with all of her strength. She sat on the stool and muffled her sobs with a towel. She ached for Jesse, only one wall away, but it might as well have been a jillion miles with that monster between them.

At Sunday breakfast at the Denny's, Jesse watched Lola fidget with nervous energy, and it sparked his own excitement about the rodeo. Lola chattered to everyone but her mother, who didn't seem to exist in Lola's eyes. There was something brittle and edgy about Miz Braun, but Mister Braun was his usual unruffled self. Dudley was his usual hungry self.

When they got to the rodeo grounds, Jesse and Dudley went with Lola to check on Fibber, who was munching hay. Lola took it away from him and said, "You got to be light on your feet today. I want you hungry."

They joined Mister and Miz Braun in the stands to wait for Buddy's event. Dudley entertained them with wise cracks about people in the crowd. Mister Braun sometimes chuckled along with them, but Miz Braun's mouth never lost its bitter downturn.

Buddy climbed up to them a few minutes before the bull-riding event. His eyes were bloodshot; Jesse figured a few bottles of Pearl had gone down his gullet the night before. But Buddy looked good in his red-checked western shirt and leather chaps over his jeans. His riding gloves stuck out of a hip pocket. He wore a new black hat with a peacock feather in a snakeskin hatband. Looking at that shirt, Jesse couldn't help a nasty thought about bulls going after red.

Mister Braun said, "Good luck."

Miz Braun gave him a big hug. "You be careful. Don't take any chances out there."

"I won't."

She clung to his arm. "I don't like you doing this."

He frowned and pulled his arm away. "Yeah, yeah."

Lola added, "Ride him hard."

Buddy nodded his thanks and then greeted Jesse. "Hey." His expression was, well, friendly.

Jesse said, "Yeah, good luck."

Dudley added, "Break a leg."

Buddy laughed. "Good to know you're with me, Spider."

The announcer boomed, "Will all bull riders please report in?" Buddy left, and they settled back to watch.

Dudley said, "Jimmy Smith told me bronc riding is more dangerous than the bulls."

Jesse shook his head. "Naw. A horse doesn't have horns to gore you with."

Lola added, "You can break a hand easy on a bull, too. You got your hand stuck under that rope wrapped around the bull's belly, and you don't let go quick enough when you get tossed, well, I've heard bones snap from up here."

Miz Braun frowned at them. "That's enough of that kind of talk. Buddy'll be fine."

The clown, Jesse's favorite part of bull riding, rolled a big padded barrel into the center of the arena, then stirred up chuckles by miming a boxer with his dukes up, ready to fight. He wore a flaming red shirt and baggy jeans several sizes too big, held up with bright yellow suspenders. Red sneakers were on his feet; boots wouldn't do for the running and dodging he'd have to do. The clown signaled "come on" at the first bull in a chute, and then he shadow boxed until he pantomimed knocking the bull out and raised his hands in victory. The crowd cheered.

The announcer called, "And now, ladies and gentlemen, bullll ridinnng! Our first contestant is Bill Atkins on Terrible Trouble." The bulls always had better names than the riders.

Bill was a long, lean cowboy. Hands on the top rails of the chute, he carefully lowered himself toward the back of a big brown Brahman bull. Halfway down, the bull thrashed from side to side, and the cowboy jerked his legs up. The bull calmed, and the rider lowered himself. He gave a nod, and a cowboy yanked the wide gate open. The bull was penned sideways to the arena, so it turned and lunged out, then kicked its rear hooves high and twisted its back.

The rider flopped back and forth like Raggedy Andy while trying to hold his free arm high. He had to stay on for a total of eight seconds, holding on with only one hand. The judges would award points based on style—how he kept his seat, how he kept his arm up—and how the bull bucked. Riders didn't want a calm, easy-going bull; cowboys liked bulls that bucked hard but in a consistent way so they could get a rhythm going when they raked the bull's sides with their spurs from high on the withers to the flanks.

Bill managed to hang on for the full count, but he was riding sideways and holding on with both hands when the buzzer went off. He let go and sprawled in the sandy dirt, then scrambled to his feet and ran for the fence. A few folks offered up mild applause. It hadn't been much of a ride.

The clown dashed in front of the bull and caught its attention. The bull lowered its head and started after the clown as two cowboys rode into the arena to herd the bull out. The clown made the safety of his barrel and stood behind it, taunting the bull. The barrel didn't stop the bull; it lowered its head and charged, and both barrel and clown went down.

Before the bull could take advantage, though, a rider on a cutting horse headed it off. He and his partner drove the bull out of the arena. The clown chased after the bull, and then he strutted back into the arena with his thumbs hooked under his suspenders as if he'd bested the beast.

The announcer blared, "Tough ride, Bill, but you earned yourself sixty-seven points. Comin' up, Buddy Pritchert on Do-o-o-omsday."

Buddy lowered himself onto a nasty-looking cream-colored animal and then gave a nod. The bull was turned loose and old Doomsday did well by Buddy; he bucked straight ahead, kicking hard with enough twisting to be truly troublesome. Buddy was able to stay upright and wave his free arm round and round over his head as if he was having fun. He had a darn good ride going.

The eight-second buzzer sounded, Buddy slipped his hand out of the rope and hopped off to land on his feet, making it look easy, and the crowd applauded. His back to the bull, he tipped his hat. Then the crowd drew in its breath; the bull had spun and now bore down on Buddy.

Miz Braun's long, quavering scream soared over the crowd's murmur. "Buddyyyyyyyyy!"

He turned and saw the bull charging. Blocked by the bull from the fence, he ran for the barrel. With the clown flapping his arms to distract the bull, Buddy dove head first into the barrel. The bull didn't go for the clown; it rammed the barrel with its horns and toppled it. The bull battered the barrel again and again, rolling it across the dirt until it slammed against the wall, Buddy's legs sticking out the open end.

The clown whacked the bull on the rump with his hat. The bull turned, the clown ran, and the bull pursued.

Buddy wriggled out of the barrel to cheers from the audience and climbed to safety on the fence.

The clown wasn't so lucky. A horn caught his suspenders and the bull threw the clown a dozen feet to land on his back.

The cowboys who herded the bulls out spurred their horses into a run. Buddy, who was closest, hopped off the wall and dashed past the bull, hitting it on the nose with his hat. The bull wheeled, Buddy hotfooted it for the fence, and the cowboys came at a dead run.

The bull closed fast, put its head down, and scooped Buddy off his feet. Tossing its head up as though Buddy were a twig, it threw him back. Buddy landed on the bull's rump, bounced off, and hit the ground tumbling. He rolled to his feet and took off running while the bull turned.

A cowboy rode hard straight at Buddy, one arm held out. As the rider passed, Buddy grabbed the arm and swung up behind him. The other cowboy cut his horse in front of the bull before it could charge again.

The crowd cheered, and Buddy rode out smiling and waving his hat. The clown got to his feet, another cheer went up, and he resumed his act, once again "chasing" the bull out and acting as though he were the victor. The clown was the toughest guy out there. With the possible exception of Buddy.

Jesse glanced at Miz Braun. Her eyes were closed and her lips moved as if in silent prayer.

Lola jumped up. "Come on!"

Dudley said, "Where?"

"To see Buddy."

Dudley waved her on. "I've seen him before."

She scampered toward the exit. Jesse followed.

They ran all the way to the bull pens and arrived to find Buddy receiving pats on the back from other riders.

Lola said, "Buddy, that was great!"

Jesse thought so, too. Buddy didn't have to do what he had done to help the clown, and it took guts. Like Buddy had said to him, a man's got to respect that. He said to this new Buddy, "Yeah." He stuck his hand out for a shake.

Buddy gave him three manly pumps. "I appreciate that."

The announcer called out, "The score for Buddy Pritchert, ninety-eight! Helluva ride, Buddy."

The crowd whistled and applauded. The best a rider could do was a hundred points. Well, he deserved it. Buddy's friends ran up whooping and shouting that he'd earned a "tall cold one." Jesse didn't think they were talking about a Coke.

Miz Braun bowled her way through and wrapped Buddy in her big arms. "Baby!"

Buddy pried himself loose. "I'm fine."

She laid hands on him. "Where does it hurt?"

He batted them away. "Nowhere." His voice grew impatient. "I'm fine."

Miz Braun stopped her fussing and glanced at his friends. "I don't think you ought to ride bulls any more, honey."

Buddy bristled just as Jesse did when his mother pulled something like that. "I'll ride what I want to ride."

All eyes were on Buddy. Jesse took Lola's hand and pulled her away. They stole into the crowd, leaving behind the commotion around Buddy. Miz Braun's strident protestations faded as they escaped.

It felt good to be alone with Lola. True, there was a crowd all around, but there was no Miz Braun to cast a shadow over their sunshine. Jesse held her hand, and the feel of her warm skin sent his emotions surging. They walked lazily back toward the stands until something smashed into their hands and broke them apart.

Her mother bellowed, "Dolores!"

They whirled to find Miz Braun glowering at them. Jesse got one of those sinking feelings in his stomach.

Miz Braun said, "What did I tell you?"

"Yes, Mommy."

"I don't have to let you race!"

Lola looked as though she could bite through a nail. "Yes, Mommy."

"Get up there, now!" She gave Jesse a major scowl and followed Lola into the stands.

Jesse wondered why she was so down on him. He'd understand if she knew what they'd been doing, but they'd been careful—she didn't know, or he'd be dead meat. Did she suspect? Had Consuelo told her? No, there'd be nothing left of him by now if she had.

It didn't seem like a good idea to be in Miz Braun's neighborhood right then, so he yelled up to Dudley, "Come on, Spider, let's look around."

Dudley put a hand to his forehead as if he were going to faint. "I don't know, Jess—I'm so weak."

Jesse had to laugh. "So let's look around for some food."

Dudley grinned. "Why didn't you say that the first time?"

After Dudley joined him, Jesse glanced back up at the stands. Miz Braun stood at the rail, glowering down at him. There was no sign of Lola. Surely her mother would still let her ride.

22

Jesse and Dudley found a corn dog vendor and then killed time by the corral where the broncos were kept, each selecting a string of horses they'd like to have for their someday ranch. At last the announcer bellowed, "It's tiiiiime, ladies and gentlemen, for those courageous gals of barrrrrrrellll racinnnnnng!" Jesse led a run for the big entry gate into the arena where the racers would start.

Lola arrived, leading Fibber through a clutter of observers, contestants, and horses. Jesse had never seen her costume—her pink western shirt sparkled with rhinestones and white fringe swayed from the sleeves. Her pink pants showed the smooth curve of her hips, and white fringe down the outside seams flashed as she walked. Her turquoise boots, belt, and hat contrasted perfectly. For Jesse's money, she was the prettiest girl there.

Best of all, her parents weren't in sight. Jesse ran to her, gathered her in his arms, and put a lot of stored-up loving into his kiss. She broke the kiss with a laugh and pushed him away.

"Are you crazy? Somebody will tell my mother."

"It was just a good luck kiss."

Dudley joined them. "Hey, don't I get one too?"

She punched him on the arm and he said, "That's not exactly what I had in mind."

She laughed and then sobered as a big blond girl on a big blond horse readied herself at the starting line. Lola patted Fibber. "I'm a little nervous."

Jesse gave her a quick hug. "You'll do great."

The announcer boomed, "And now our first rider, Miss Virginia Marston, riding Sure Fire."

Jesse liked how the animals got credit in a rodeo. Heck, they did most of the work. Virginia kicked Sure Fire into a run and dashed into the arena. They couldn't see the whole course from where they were, so they couldn't tell how her run looked, but she made it without a fall. Shortly after she burst back out, the announcer called, "Virginia Marston on Sure Fire, fifteen and five-tenths seconds."

Lola rubbed Fibber's nose and said to him, "We can beat that." Extra white in Fibber's eyes showed his excitement. He was ready to race.

Three more riders came and went. The second rider, a long, lean redhead all in black, took with lead with a time of fifteen and three-tenths seconds. Finally the call came. "Dolores Braun, riding Fibber."

Jesse boosted Lola into the saddle, and then he and Dudley ran to climb the fence so they could see inside the arena. Lola nodded at the timer, kicked Fibber in the ribs and thundered in, her face fierce with determination.

She rounded the first two barrels, her horse leaning at a scary angle, her leg brushing one barrel and leaving it rocking but upright. Knocking a barrel over cost a rider a five-second penalty, but good riders cut it close enough to make the crowd say o-o-o.

As she headed for the far barrel at full speed, movement to Jesse's right caught his eye. On the fence sat the two firecracker boys from the day before—the redheaded one was launching something into the arena in a high arc. Jesse prayed it wasn't a firecracker, but knew it was.

Judging by the blast that went off just as Fibber rounded the third barrel, it was a cherry bomb. The horse shied, his front hooves skidded, and he went down hard on his side, landing on Lola's leg.

Jesse was off the fence and running to her before Fibber had begun to struggle to his feet. As Jesse ran, he looked where her parents had been sitting and caught sight of Mister Braun racing down the grandstand steps.

Fibber had gotten to his feet and was trotting away when Jesse reached Lola. She raised herself onto one elbow. He landed on his knees next to her and gently put his arm under her back. "Are you okay?"

Dust coated one side of her face, and a streak of a tear ran through it. Her smile trembled, but it came. His heart swelled up a size or two at her guts.

She said, "I think so. Help me up."

Mister Braun arrived just as Jesse stood. Mister Braun took one side, Jesse took the other, and they lifted her to her feet. The crowd applauded. Lola smiled and waved, but Jesse knew she had to be miserable. A fall meant no time, so she was out of the competition.

Her father peered into her eyes. "Do you hurt anywhere?"

"Some. Let's go see if Fibber's okay."

She stepped forward, cried out and took her weight off a foot. "Fibber landed on my ankle."

Mister Braun said, "I'll carry you."

Lola's first impulse was to say yes, sweep me off my feet and carry me to someplace soft. Her ribs hurt worse than ever. Her ankle was on fire. But she was damned if she would give in to injury. "No, let me try."

Leaning on Jesse and her father, she took a couple of steps. Sharp pains streaked upward from her ankle, but she could bear it. She hoped. She gritted her teeth. "I can do it."

The crowd applauded again as Jesse and her father helped her limp out of the arena. When they reached the exit gate the announcer said, "There will be no time recorded for Miss Braun, but the judges have ruled interference and the little lady can have another run if she and her horse are able." The crowd cheered encouragement.

She looked around for Fibber. Dudley had rounded him up and stood waiting for them. They stopped beside the horse and she said, "Is he okay, Daddy?"

She held onto Jesse while her father went over Fibber with his hands, lifting each leg, squeezing and probing, looking for signs of pain.

Jesse seemed to be searching the crowd for someone. He asked Dudley, "You see where that kid went?"

Dudley pointed toward the parking lot. "Long gone. He tore out that way with a big red-haired guy chasing him."

Her father finished checking Fibber and smiled at her. "Seems sound. But you can't ride with that ankle."

She thought he might be right. When she didn't put weight on it, her ankle merely throbbed, but lean on it and pain lanced up. There was no way she could make tight swings around barrels without putting her weight on the stirrups. Dammit, she wasn't ready to quit. "I want to try taping it."

Her father gazed down at her for long seconds. She could see "No" taking shape in his expression. She added, "Quitters never win."

He smiled. "Guess you're right about that." He hustled away, headed for trailer with a red cross on the door.

Jesse said, "You are some kind of girl."

She bumped him with her hip. "You're not so bad for a boy, either."

Her father ran back with a roll of white adhesive tape. He lifted her and set her sideways on her saddle to work her boot off. Lordy, it hurt, but she clenched her teeth and kept a yelp inside; her father might not let her go if he got an idea how much it hurt.

He examined her ankle. “Starting to swell.”

“You better get to taping, then.”

He smiled up at her, respect in his eyes, and then he wrapped the two-inch tape tight around her ankle and under her arch.

The last racer went. She got a time of fifteen seconds flat, the best so far by three-tenths of a second. The crowd cheered. Lola wondered if this was worth it. But she wasn’t quitting.

Her father slid her boot over her foot, and then it jammed on her swollen ankle. She said, “Brace the boot.”

He gripped the tops of the boot and she shoved. Her foot slid in. The boot was tight, giving additional support. She swung her leg over the saddle horn and slipped her feet into the stirrups. She cautiously stood in her stirrups. And was surprised—the injured ankle was tender, but it supported her without making her want to give way. She smiled. “It’s as good as new.”

Her dad said, “You sure?”

She nodded; he looked her over, and then he grinned. “I’ll tell ’em.” He ran to the tower that housed the announcer and the judges.

Jesse reached up, took her hand, and squeezed it. She squeezed back, and they held hands until her father returned. He said, “All set.”

The announcer called out, “Hats off now to a little lady with real courage, folks. Miss Lo-o-o-o-la-a-a . . .”

Lola laughed and mouthed “Thank you” at her father. He smiled, his eyes twinkling.

“. . . Braun rides agiiiiin!”

He said, “Good luck, Princess.”

Jesse put his hand on her knee. The emotion in his eyes gladdened her heart. She turned Fibber toward the gate.

"Hold up!" Buddy trotted up to her, his two friends right behind him. "We caught the kid that did it and gave him to his old man." He grinned. "I wouldn't want to be that boy's butt." He looked away and then back, as though embarrassed that he'd come. "Well, uh, ride him good."

Her feelings were so tangled she didn't know what to say, but she was glad of his words. So she just said, "Thanks."

She rode to the start line, focusing on Fibber, straining to sense any trouble. He seemed okay. She leaned forward, patted his neck, and aimed a whisper at his ear. "We can do it, boy."

She settled into position. Her ankle hurt, but there was no turning back now. She nodded to the starter, got the signal, and lashed Fibber's flank with the reins. Fibber charged the first barrel and they cut around it, Lola able to put her weight on the good ankle.

Second barrel. Pain shot up her injured ankle and tears formed. She finished the turn and kicked at Fibber's sides, ignoring the hurt. He ran like a champion for the third barrel. Praying he wouldn't remember the fall, she cut close and hauled on his reins. Fibber hugged the barrel, her bad leg brushed it, the barrel wobbled, but she felt no pain now.

They straightened out for the run home. Leaning low over the saddle along Fibber's neck, she whipped his flanks with the reins. "Go! Go!"

No firecrackers came, and the crowd roared as she flashed across the finish line.

Reining in next to her father, she patted Fibber's sweaty neck, then reached up and scratched the bump between his ears. "That's my horse." He was the best. She threw a leg over the saddle and slid off, her father catching her on the way down. She tried her bad ankle. Now it hurt to put weight on it, so she stood on her good leg and leaned on her father.

Jesse stepped next to her. "That was a great ride!"

But was it good enough? "We'll see."

The speaker boomed, "Fifteen point one five seconds for one plucky little lady!"

Pure joy! Over the crowd's cheer, she squealed, "I got second! I got second place!"

Dudley let out a Rebel yell, her daddy gave her a big hug, and Jesse beamed. When her father released her, Jesse slipped in and gave her a small hug, which she thought her father would see as appropriate under the circumstances.

Just as he whispered "I love you" in her ear, two hands grabbed his shoulders and yanked him stumbling backward to land on his back.

Her mother stood over Jesse, her expression like a runaway truck bearing down on him. She sounded like a snake when she said, "You keep your filthy hands off her." She lifted one foot, it looked like to kick him.

Lola shouted, "No!"

Jesse rolled away and jumped to his feet.

Her father grabbed her mother by the arms and twisted her to face him. "What the hell are you doing!?"

She stared up at him, but didn't answer. Wrenching herself from his grip, she turned to Lola. "What'd I tell you?"

Lola wasn't going to take any shit, not this time. "He was just sayin' congratulations. Somethin' *you* haven't brought up."

Her mother tightened her eyes. Lola stood her ground, matching glare for glare.

Her mother said, "We're leaving." She grabbed Lola's arm, but she pulled free.

Her father stepped between them. "That's enough, Margaret." Though his voice was calm, a flush rising on his neck was all Lola needed to see to know her father was terribly angry. "This is not right."

Lola backed away and stood close to Jesse. He edged in front of her as if to shield her, his face grim. Her mother gave her one last, evil look, and then she marched away.

Her father turned to her, his expression a mix of anger and puzzlement. "I don't know what's gotten into your mother." He shook his head.

Jesse took her hand. "You okay?"

His concern brushed her anger aside. She smiled.

The announcer called out, "Will Barb Petura, Lola Braun, and Virginia Marston please report to the area?"

Lola said to Jesse, "Give me a hand up?"

Jesse lifted her at the waist until she got her boot in the stirrup. All in all, she felt good. She'd had a great ride, and her mother would never buffalo her again. Never. She smiled at Jesse, trying to put her love into it. "Thank you." If his grin meant anything, he got her message.

After the judge handed her the incredibly beautiful Second Place ribbon, she rode Fibber out of the arena, loving the applause. Somebody in the stands even yelled, "Go Lola!"

Her father and Dudley joined her. Her father said, "Why don't you ride Fibber over to the trailer and we'll get him loaded up? I want to get you home and treat that ankle."

She thought that was a great idea, and they started off. When Jesse hung back, her father stopped and asked, "Aren't you coming?"

Jesse gazed after her mother, and then said, "I guess." She could tell he hated the idea of being in the car with her mom. Heck, so did she.

Buddy said, "He's welcome to ride back with me."

Her father nodded. "I think that would be best. See you back home."

Lola stayed on her feet, though mostly on one leg, until Fibber was secure in his trailer. Then her father had her stretch out on the back seat of the car and worked the boot off her injured ankle. As gentle as he was, it hurt like hell. She moaned, but turned it into a grunt.

Her mother, already sitting in the front seat, never glanced back. Which was fine with Lola. Her emotions about her mother were so confused she didn't know what she would do, cry or scream.

Her father examined her. "We'll leave the tape on, it'll help the swelling." He backed out of the car and said, "Dudley, would you fetch the blanket in the trunk?"

"Yessir."

When Dudley arrived with the travel blanket, her father took it and told her, "Take a seat."

Lola pulled her feet out of the way, Dudley got in. Her father folded the blanket, placed it across Dudley's knees, and gently placed her ankle on it.

"Dudley, you okay with this? I want to keep her ankle up."

"Sure." He smiled. "I'm pretty good at sittin'."

Lola jerked her ankle when she laughed, but the pain was worth it.

On the way out of the rodeo grounds, trailer in tow, they passed the redheaded boy, sprawled face down on the fender of a pickup, a red-headed man whipping his butt with a belt. Lola said, "Slow down, Daddy."

She smiled at the slap of leather on denim. The kid yelped. She yelled out the window, "Harder!"

Her father said, "Damn right."

On the long ride home she enjoyed the hours of peace, stretched out on the back seat with her bad leg propped up on Dudley. She grinned at the memory of putting her feet in Jesse's lap at the drive-in.

Her parents weren't talking to each other, and wind noise prevented them from talking to her. Her ankle throbbed, but she forgot about it as she admired her Second Place ribbon. She relived her ride and thanked her lucky stars for having a horse with heart.

She wished her mother had a heart. Then she'd understand. Whether she ever did or not, Lola vowed to be with Jesse, no matter what it took.

Jesse slumped in the back seat of Buddy's Chevy, lulled by the heat and the car's motion. They'd only been on the road an hour, and it already seemed like forever.

Buddy's friend Steve, riding shotgun, pulled a Lone Star from a cooler at his feet and offered it to Jesse. "Cold one'll do you good."

While it felt good—and grown up—to be asked, Jesse hated the taste of beer. "No thanks."

Steve shrugged. "More for us."

Jesse drowsed. His gaze drifted to Buddy's hat, the peacock feather fluttering in the wind. He wondered if it would blow out of the hatband. He surely did like those snakeskin hatbands. Jesse slid into a daydream of walking with Lola at the rodeo, sneaking little kisses. Then, bam, Miz Braun glared down from on high in the rodeo stands.

She pointed at Jesse and boomed in a voice as big as God's, "GET OUT!" Then she lifted a Brahman bull over her head and threw it at him. It fell head first, horns aimed at his heart. The bull wore a black hat with a snakeskin hatband, a red feather tucked in it. The tip of a horn touched his chest—he startled awake.

It took a moment to remember where he was. He sat up and saw that they were in the hill country, nearing the ranch, Buddy and his friends were singing along with the radio—*It was a one-eyed, one-horned, flyin' purple people eater . . .*

He stared at Buddy's black hat. Romero'd had a snakeskin hatband like that.

That night, Alejandro invaded Jesse's dreams. Lying dead on the barn floor, the Mexican's staring eyes shifted to Jesse. His mouth shaped a word, but no sound came. As Jesse strained to hear, he realized that the pitchfork was missing from Alejandro's chest. He heard footsteps behind him, turned—and broke out of the dream.

He lay wide-eyed; a shiver of fear faded away as the night's gentle sounds returned him to the real world. He hadn't had a nightmare since he was a little kid sick with double mumps—fever had cooked up a dream in which Captain Marvel turned into a bad guy and threw him and his father into a dungeon. He had awakened screaming, his father taking him into his arms to calm him.

Being awake wasn't much of an improvement—all he could think about was being kicked off the ranch and leaving Lola. The way Miz Braun was acting, he figured he was a goner. Unwilling to imagine life without Lola, he wrestled with how to live in Kerrville. He'd get a job, and see her at school, and sneak visits with her through her friend, Cindy. He couldn't go back to Dallas; his life was with Lola now. His mother would never notice, anyway. She had her drinks to keep her company.

The alarm clock sounded. Miz Braun would be waiting for

him at breakfast. He expected she'd give him marching orders right after she removed her foot from halfway up his butt.

She wasn't waiting for him.

Mister Braun was.

He signaled Jesse to go to the utility room. Dudley joined Buddy at the breakfast table—Lola wasn't there. Jesse hoped he'd get a last minute with her before he had to go.

Mister Braun closed the door and Jesse steeled himself.

"Jesse, Miz Braun is sorry for the way she acted yesterday."

Jesse thought he'd heard wrong.

"With the bull attacking Buddy and the horse falling on Dolores, well, she was just real upset. I'm sorry it happened."

Jesse recalled Miz Braun's face when she had raised a foot to kick him, and he couldn't imagine her saying she was sorry. Seemed to him the apology was actually coming from Mister Braun. He didn't care; he was just glad he hadn't been told to pack up and haul ass.

"That's all right, sir. We were all pretty shook up, I guess."

Mister Braun gripped Jesse's shoulder. "You're a good boy, son. Let's get some breakfast, got plenty of work to do."

It was well after ten o'clock before Lola opened her eyes enough to check the clock. It had been a bad night. Her ribs hurt, her ankle hurt, and her heart hurt. After her anger had worn itself out the night before, she had wondered over and over why her mother hadn't been glad about how great she'd done in her race. Why was she so mean to Jesse?

Why doesn't she love me any more?

There was one person who would know. Connie had worked for her mother's parents and had helped raise her. Nobody knew her better.

Lola ran her hands over her ribs and winced when she found bruises. She continued down across her flat belly. She'd been expecting the distended, uncomfortable feeling that came this time of the month. She checked her Western Horsemen calendar on the wall. She was three days late.

She was never late.

It was the excitement of the rodeo. And her mother's craziness. She had to talk to Connie.

Lola dressed and limped into the empty kitchen. As she made a piece of toast and slathered it with grape jelly, she peered out the window. Her mother hoed furiously in the garden. Connie was not in sight.

She called out to the house, "Connie?" No answer. Munching her toast, she checked the utility room. Not there. Must be in her cottage.

Lola left through the front door and circled around the house to avoid the garden. When she came to Connie's place, she could hear her humming inside. She tapped lightly on the screened door, hoping her mother wouldn't hear.

Connie opened it almost immediately and smiled when she saw Lola. "*Niña!* I am so proud of you." She pulled Lola into a hug. It felt so good.

Lola whispered into her ear, "Connie, can I ask you about something?"

Connie released her and smiled, "*Si*, of course." Then she looked closely at Lola. "So serious. Come in."

Lola got the feeling she always did in Connie's little house—safe. It had been a haven for Lola as long as she could remember. It was perpetually dim inside, the Venetian blinds set to keep the heat of the sun out, and crowded with hand-me-down but scrupulously clean furniture.

Connie led her to a loveseat and sat beside her.

Lola told Connie what her mother had done after the movie in Pecos, and what she hadn't done after the race, and how she had knocked Jesse down. Connie's expression grew darker with each part of the story.

Lola ran out of words. A tear leaked from one eye. She wiped it away and asked, "Why?"

Connie thought for a long moment. "I think—she tries to save you."

"From what?"

"She have a—a terrible trouble when she was a girl like you. She would not want it to happen to you."

"Not want what to happen?"

"It was a boy . . ." She fingered a dainty gold crucifix on a fine gold chain around her neck and shook her head. "I can't tell. I make a promise." She put her arm around Lola. "But I know your mother loves you. And I think she try to protect."

Lola shook her head. "It sure doesn't feel that way."

"Let time come and go. It will be better."

Lola hoped so. But down deep, she felt something was wrong, and she was afraid it would never be right again.

Jesse's love life that week was like Mother Hubbard's cupboard, with not even a romantic bone to gnaw on. Miz Braun was chilly to him, and she never let Lola out of her sight. Lola had told him her mother had somehow known about Alejandro, and now she didn't dare sneak out at night to meet him. But Lola's smiles still warmed Jesse from afar.

Wednesday morning, Mister Braun drove to New Braunfels for a meeting at a bank and left Buddy in charge. After loading axes and the chain saw into the Jeep, Buddy carted Jesse and Dudley to the goat pasture and parked near a collection of live oaks.

Buddy grabbed the chain saw and said, "I'm going to cut some trees down, y'all trim off branches that stick up so the goats can get to the leaves."

Jesse asked, "The goats?"

"We need extra food for them just like we did for the cows. The goats like leaves, and the government pays us by the acre for clearing the land." He cranked up the saw, toppled a tree, and then he lopped off especially thick branches. When he moved on to another three, Dudley and Jesse each attacked with their axes.

Jesse swung hard, the blade sliced through a branch he'd thought would need a couple of chops and buried itself in the dirt inches from his foot. He tested the edge with his thumb and whistled.

When they finished a tree and moved on, goats gathered and munched leaves, some walking up a downed trunk to get at them.

On Jesse's fifth tree, his axe glanced off the trunk and the blade cut through the steel toe of his shoe. He could feel the warm metal between his big toe and its neighbor, but nothing hurt. He released the handle, and the axe stood upright. He called out to Buddy, "Hey, check this out."

Buddy came over and laughed. "You must be all right, or you'd be yellin' by now."

Dudley ambled up. "This is no time to be trimming your toenails."

Jesse pulled the axe out and Buddy squatted for a closer look. "Didn't cut you?"

"I don't feel anything."

Buddy looked around. Goats munched on the leaves of ten toppled trees. "That's enough for now, anyway. I'll run you into town for shoes."

Dudley said, "What about me?"

"You take some hay out to the yearlings."

Dudley groaned and Jesse laughed.

Buddy parked the Jeep on Water Street, in front of Bledsoe's Tavern and a couple of blocks from the Sears. "I'm gonna get a cold one. Meet you back here in twenty minutes." He hopped out and headed into the tavern.

On the way to Sears, Jesse heard giggles across the way. Cindy and two friends walked toward a dress shop. Leroy, the creep from the drive-in, accompanied by two equally cruddy-looking boys, followed the girls. Jesse couldn't make out what they were saying, but he had an idea. Well, it was none of his business.

Leroy noticed him; he turned toward Jesse, his friends following. Jesse hightailed it into the Sears.

The clerk tsked when he saw what Jesse'd done to his shoe and tried to sell him a pair with even thicker steel in the toes. Jesse figured he'd learned his lesson and stuck with the kind he'd gotten before.

When he headed back to the Jeep, working his toes in his new shoes, the old pair in the box, he found Leroy sitting on the hood and one of his cronies leaning against a fender.

Leroy said, "Hey, it's the white wetback."

Jesse stopped.

Leroy stood. "What's the matter, greaser? This is your ride, ain't it?"

Jesse took a step back. Leroy slid off the hood and strolled toward him. He held up a fist. "I got somethin' to settle with you." His friend followed.

Jesse didn't want to tackle two-to-one odds. Behind him, an alley beside the tavern led to who knew where. He decided to retreat to Sears and wait until Buddy came looking for him. But when he turned he found Leroy's other friend waiting for him. He was a big guy, Dudley's size. He started toward Jesse.

Jesse searched for help, but the only people in sight were a couple of old ladies inching across the street. He threw his shoe box at the big guy and cut into the alley.

Footsteps raced after him, but he thought he was holding his own. One of his old shoes flashed past him. The other one tumbled just in front of him, his foot came down on it, he tripped and slammed into a pair of garbage cans. Soggy paper napkins and empty beer bottles from the tavern spilled over him. He struggled to his feet and stumbled forward, and then a fist hit him in the back and sent him falling.

Scrambling up, he faced the three of them. They spread out and herded him toward a brick wall. He backed, searching for a weapon, a stick or a rock or anything, but found nothing.

Leroy said, "You think you're pretty tough, don't you?"

Jesse shook his head. "Actually, no, I don't."

"Seemed like it at the drive-in when you came to your girlfriend's rescue. Lord knows why, though—there's not enough meat on her for a decent screw."

The insult to Lola stirred Jesse and brought a hot feeling of strength. He lifted his fists. Leroy closed with Jesse, his friends holding back. Leroy feinted with his left, Jesse raised his arms to block and Leroy drove his right into Jesse's ribs.

A shock wave of pain exploded through Jesse. He hunched over and Leroy swung at his face. Jesse managed to jerk out of the way and staggered back to the wall.

Leroy danced like a boxer. "Come on, chicken, fight."

Jesse faked a moan and stumbled to Leroy's left. Leroy moved to cut him off, Jesse pivoted and swung his right, catching Leroy flush on the nose with a satisfying crunch.

Leroy staggered back, howling, hands to his nose. His big friend steadied him. Leroy's hands were bloody when he took them away from his nose.

Jesse's anger was at full boil; he felt powerful and unstoppable. He charged, catching Leroy off guard, and buried his fist deep in his skinny belly. The big guy holding Leroy wobbled, but kept his balance. Jesse stepped back, waiting.

Leroy sucked wind. When he could breathe again, he gasped, "You're dead."

Though Jesse felt strong, he knew he was in trouble. He backed toward the wall so they couldn't get behind him. They moved toward him.

Buddy's voice came. "Hold on there, boys." He strode down the alley.

Relief rushed through Jesse. Leroy didn't seem threatened, although he did turn to face Buddy.

Buddy strolled, no hurry, until he was at Jesse's side. "Why don't y'all just move on?"

Leroy wiped at the blood from his nose with the back of his arm and then grinned. "'Cause there's only two of you, and I feel like beatin' the living shit out of somebody today." He raised his fists and his two friends shadowed his movements.

Buddy said, "Can't let you do that. Axel left me in charge, and he'd be upset if his hand got too beat up to work."

Leroy said, "Too bad he's not here to help you, then."

Buddy grabbed something from his jeans pocket. "I got all the help I need." Sunlight flashed from steel. He lunged forward and slashed, Leroy leaped back, a hole gaping in the belly of his shirt.

Leroy eyed the straight razor in Buddy's hand. Buddy crouched, ready.

Leroy raised his hands and backed up a step. "I don't want no quarrel with you. I'll get him another time." He spat on the ground in front of Buddy, but not so close that he hit Buddy's shoes. Leroy led his cronies away.

Jesse turned to Buddy. "Thanks."

"You'd have done it for me." He grinned.

"I guess." Jesse's gaze dropped to the razor. It looked like the one Romero had carried. Maybe everybody around there carried a razor.

Buddy saw him look. As he folded the razor and put it into his pocket, he said, "It used to be one of the wetback's. I found it in the hen house after they were gone."

It had to be Romero's. If Alejandro'd had one, he'd have used it when Romero pulled his. A picture of the last time Jesse'd seen Romero popped into his mind. They were being introduced in the front yard. He could see the shape of the razor in Romero's pocket, an outline worn there because he always carried it. Jesse couldn't imagine that razor ever leaving that pocket, especially when he ran for it.

Jesse groped for words. "Yeah, uh, lucky for me you did."

When they piled into the Jeep, Buddy said, "You showed some guts back there. You ever think about bull riding?"

"Not really." Jesse was forced to chat about bull riding on the drive back. But all he could think of was the flash of Romero's razor.

At breakfast on Thursday, Jesse wondered why Lola's eyes were swollen and red. Mister Braun asked her about it, and she said, "Nothing." Then she spilled her orange juice and ran crying to her room. Mister Braun raised his eyebrows at Miz Braun.

Her mother said, "It's probably that time."

He nodded.

What time? Jesse worried about Lola, and ached for her in his heart and below his belt. Nights in the cabin with Dudley had become boring. Even Jesse's books held little interest for him now. He needed to put his arms around Lola. But how?

Lola had supper in her room that evening, and didn't appear at breakfast Friday morning. He was dying to ask why, but knew better than to show interest in front of Miz Braun. Hope for an answer came that evening with an after-supper cookie. Consuelo stopped Dudley and Jesse on the way out the door. "I have a treat for you."

She handed each of them a stack of peanut butter cookies. Her eyes were on Jesse's as he took his, and he understood why when he felt a folded piece of paper under the bottom cookie. "*Muchos gracias*, Consuelo."

She smiled. "*De nada*."

In the cabin, he unfolded the note. It read, "Meet me in the hen house at midnight. Lola." Jesse didn't know if hearts could really sing like they said, but he was pretty sure his hummed for the next few hours.

The air was cool when he left the cabin, and the night spoke with the voices of bugs and an occasional toad. His wait in the hen house wasn't more than five minutes old before Lola slipped in. He opened his arms, expecting the ready, willing, and able girl he loved.

She put her hands up and held him back. "No." Her voice seemed stiff and cold.

Funny how you could go from a peak to a pit in absolutely no time at all.

She stepped past him and went to the table. A match scratched, and she lit a candle. The pale glow painted her face and downcast eyes with soft, loving strokes. He soared back to his peak. She had only wanted a romantic setting. She tilted the candle so a drop of wax fell onto the table, then set the candle's base into the wax so it would stand upright.

Jesse slid his arms around her from behind, his hands coming together on her belly. She leaned back against him, and he began to harden. Then she pulled his hands apart, stepped away, and turned to face him. The look on her face wasn't love.

It was fear.

Back into the pit.

She said, "I'm late."

"You were right on time."

Tears filled her eyes, and one ran down a cheek. "No, my period's late."

Somewhere in his head he knew what that meant.

"I think I'm pregnant. I'm so scared, Jesse."

This time she didn't resist when he put his arms around her. He held her close, and she sobbed into his shoulder. He was afraid, too, but he kept his voice calm. "You're not sure?"

"I'm never, never late, not even a day, and it's almost a week."

"Isn't there . . . a test?"

She stepped back and her voice turned bitter. "Yeah, just ask my parents to take me to the doctor for a pregnancy test."

"Maybe if you went for something else—"

"The doctor would tell 'em!" She wrapped her arms around herself and huddled as though under assault.

All right. They'd find a way. He'd take care of her. "Maybe we can find a way to—"

"No!" Her voice took on a shrill edge. "I'm Catholic! I can't get rid of it!"

He reached for her. "I meant we could have it."

Lola pushed away. "She'll kill it!"

"Who . . ."

Her voice grew louder. "She'll drown it like—" She clamped her teeth together and moaned, then tossed her head side to side. Her voice escalated toward a scream. "She'll drown my baby in the sink! She'll drown my baby! She'll—"

"Quiet!" Jesse took her shoulders. "They'll hear you!"

She screamed. "She'll kill it!"

He shook her.

She wailed.

Instinct took over. He slapped her.

Silence was instant and complete. Sanity came back into her eyes. She sniffled and shuddered. He reached out to smooth her hair. "Honey, we'll . . ."

She slapped him. "You bastard!"

"But I had to stop you!"

She spun and went to the door.

He followed. "You were, I don't know, you wouldn't stop, I'm sorry, I had to . . ."

She turned, her face twisted with fury. "You son of a bitch. Never. Touch. Me. Again." She burst out the door.

Jesse stood frozen, as empty of thought as if he'd been hit in the head with a brick. Going after her would do no good. If they fought outside, her parents would hear for sure, and that would make it worse. The glow of the candle intruded on the darkness of his thoughts. He put it out and took it with him.

He wanted to hit something.

He wanted to cry.

He couldn't do either.

It was just too much. He wandered back to the cabin, confused, hurt, and afraid.

Lola fumed in her room. She kicked her wastebasket. Her crazy mother was right. She couldn't trust any boy. Jesse had betrayed her, he had hit her, for Christ's sake!

She hated more than anything to be pushed around. She'd always been small, and people had always taken advantage of her size. But no more. Not her mother, not Buddy, not Jesse, not anybody. They'd keep their hands off of her. And she'd get even with Jesse, too.

She picked up her favorite stuffed animal, a pink elephant her father had won for her at the county fair, and flung it against a wall.

Then she rushed to it and cradled it in her arms. It didn't take long for tears to come.

That night, a re-enactment of Lola's slap replaced Jesse's dream of Miz Braun ordering him to go away. Close on its heels came the Alejandro dream—it looked like the corpse mouthed one word over and over. His dream self struggled to make out what Alejandro was saying.

It was after ten when he awoke Sunday morning. Dudley was gone. Jesse dressed and went up for breakfast. No Dudley there. He asked Consuelo, "*Dónde está* Dudley?"

She smiled at his use of Spanish. "*No sé.* I don't know, I feed him, he leave."

Back in the cabin, he lay on his bunk and tried to think of what to do about Lola, but nothing in his experience or imagination told him how to deal with an angry girl.

Dudley returned at one in the afternoon, slapping dust off his jeans. Jesse was in his bunk, reading, wearing only underwear in a vain attempt to escape the heat.

Dudley grinned when he entered the cabin. "Did you know that Dusty bucks when you run him?"

"Lola told me. Where you been?"

"Rode down to the river."

"I'd've gone with you."

"You were dead to the world, and I kinda wanted to just

take it in for myself, you know."

Lola's voice came. "Hey, Spider." Her face and bare brown shoulders appeared outside the cabin window. She wore her bathing suit.

"Hey."

Jesse leaned out from his bunk and smiled at her. "Hi."

Her eyes didn't even flicker in his direction. She grinned at Dudley. "I'm going down to the pond for a swim. Wanna come?"

Dudley said, "That's a cool idea."

"So come on."

He glanced up at Jesse. She still refused to acknowledge his presence.

Dudley said, "Ah, what about Jesse?"

"Jesse who?"

That hurt.

Dudley shrugged. "Okay. Just let me change."

She stayed at the window, and an impish look appeared.

"Excuse me? I'm about to get naked here?"

She giggled. "See you there." She turned and left.

"Weird girl." Dudley went into the bathroom to get his swimming trunks from the floor where they'd been since the last time they'd swum. He shook them out and inspected them for bugs.

As he changed, he said, "What's going on with y'all?"

"Nothing." That was the literal truth.

"You have a fight?"

"I guess you could say that."

"Well, I'm hot." He grabbed a bath towel and went to the door. "See you later, alligator."

The traitor left.

A half hour passed. Jesse couldn't read a word. All he could see was Lola's face in the window. Her smile. Her naked shoulders. Her snub. It was too damn quiet. He turned on the radio. Elvis Presley sang about the heartbreak hotel at the end of Lonely Street.

Thanks for nothing, Elvis. He snapped the radio off. He would bust if he didn't do something. What the hell, he was hot, and he had as much right to swim as they did. So he changed into his swimming trunks, slipped on his loafers, grabbed a towel, and left for the swimming hole.

Slipping through the trees, he heard laughter and splashing. He peeked around the tree at the top end of the pond.

Lola knew she looked good as she sat at the pond's edge, kicking her legs in the water, slim and brown and wet, her hair plastered to her head. She watched Dudley climb out. He was fat, but he was fun. She'd invited him to swim to punish Jesse, but he was helping keep her mind off of . . . things. She put a hand to her belly, and then she shook off the thought of what might be going on in there.

Movement by the big oak caught her eye; she glimpsed Jesse peeping around the trunk. Not letting him see that she'd spotted him, she stood and stepped close to Dudley. He towered over her. "So, do you have a girlfriend in Dallas?"

"Naw. Nobody steady, anyway."

"Who wants to go steady? That always goes bad, sooner or later."

"Yeah. I just want to have fun."

She grinned up at him. "Me, too."

"How about this, then?" He scooped her up in his arms and tossed her in the pond.

She shrieked, went under with a splash, and then she shot up and whacked water at him. She laughed, "You bastard!"

He laughed and dove in. She cut her gaze to the tree for a quick measure of the effect she'd had. Jesse looked like he hurt. Good. He turned and ran back through the woods.

As she sent another splash at Dudley, though, the wounded expression in Jesse's eyes troubled her. She wasn't liking what she was doing as much as she had thought she would.

Jesse had been back in his bunk an hour before Dudley returned. His former best friend grinned when he stepped through the doorway. "Hey, you shoulda come down."

Jesse's anger had been building the whole time; he jumped down from his bunk and shoved Dudley. "You son of a bitch."

Dudley's grin dropped off his face. "Now, Jess, you got no call to be mad at me."

Jesse shoved again, both hands, and slammed Dudley against the wall.

Dudley's cheeks got red and his eyes narrowed. "Don't you touch me again."

Jesse lunged with a roundhouse swing. Dudley slid the punch off a forearm and spun Jesse around, then shoved him right at the screened door. It burst open, he staggered outside and turned to go back. He didn't need to; Dudley came out.

Jesse charged and locked his arms around Dudley's middle. He drove Dudley back until he fell. Jesse straddled him with his knees and pinned Dudley's wrists to the ground with his hands. Dudley bucked up with his belly and heaved with his arms. He threw Jesse off. Jesse rolled to his feet and Dudley got up. Dudley was powerful, but slow.

They circled, fists up. Dudley said, "What put a burr under your saddle?"

"You."

"Me?"

"Stay away from her."

"We were just swimming."

"I saw what you were doing." By which he meant what *she* was doing.

"I wasn't doing nothin'."

Jesse tried to surprise him with a jab; Dudley knocked his strike aside like Jesse was a little boy. That made Jesse madder, so he yelled "Bastard!" and charged, head down.

Wrong thing to do. Dudley pivoted and caught Jesse in a headlock. Jesse struggled; Dudley tightened his arm around Jesse's skull, crushing his ears. The pressure hurt his temples. Jesse swung wildly and connected beside Dudley's crotch.

Dudley shouted, "You little shit!" He wheeled, spun Jesse off his feet, and let go. Jesse flipped through the air to land on his back. The wind exploded out of him, and he was gulping for air when Dudley knelt, straddling him, pinning Jesse's arms to his sides between his knees.

Wondering what Jesse would do, Lola had followed Dudley from the pond and was watching from the gazebo when the cabin door crashed open and Jesse burst out.

Now she watched Dudley pin Jesse to the ground and slug him in the ribs. Slowly, left then right then left, he pounded Jesse's ribs. Then he slapped Jesse's face. Every blow struck her. She hadn't meant to cause this. Her feelings of being a curse gathered. Instead of the triumph she'd thought she would feel when Jesse got what was coming to him for hitting her, she felt shame. She pressed her hands against the screening and mouthed a silent "Don't, Dudley, please don't."

Dudley finally quit when Jesse finally cried out, "Stop! Stop!" She heard gasps as Jesse struggled to breathe. Dudley looked like he wanted to hit Jesse again. In a low, mean voice, he said, "You done?"

"I'm done."

"You don't call me that."

Jesse nodded.

Dudley got off and went inside. Jesse lay in the dirt, beaten. It shamed her to see him like that. She slipped from the gazebo and ran for her room.

When Jesse came in to breakfast Monday, Lola was sitting between Dudley and Buddy. That left the chair beside Miz Braun for Jesse. It was like sitting next to a block of ice and across from a rain cloud. Lola mostly kept her eyes downcast, although he caught her sneaking a quick look at him, her eyes red and narrowed. He understood then that a girl can make it possible to go to hell before you die.

On top of all that, his ribs hurt from the pounding Dudley had given him.

When Mister Braun finished his coffee, he said, "Aunt Mary called last night. Her prize heifer is ready, so it's time to take the bull down to Hondo."

Lola brightened. "Aunt Mary? Can I go? I haven't seen cousin Katie in months."

Mister Braun looked to his wife. She said, "Sure." She glanced at Jesse. "It would be good for Dolores to get away. And you could bring back a couple sacks of pecans, too."

Mister Braun nodded. "That's it, then. Buddy, hitch the trailer to the Chrysler and put Mister in it."

Buddy said, "Mister?"

Mister Braun grinned. "Oh, just a nickname for the bull the boys came up with. Now, we'll be back in two or three days. And I'm only an hour away if you need me.

"Buddy, while I'm gone, I want you and the boys to cut more live oak for the goats. And there's a stray heifer in the gully pasture I want brought in."

The gully pasture was a half hour's ride to the south. There hadn't been any work for Jesse or Dudley to do there yet.

Buddy nodded. "I'll get it before we do the trees."

Mister Braun eyed Jesse. "I was thinking Jesse here's good at rounding up and herding."

Great, another exciting animal adventure.

Mister Braun asked, "You a good rider?"

Rider? Hope stirred. "Yessir."

Buddy frowned. "Better let me. Lotta snakes in that gully, awful dangerous for somebody from the city. And that cow's gonna be pretty wild."

Miz Braun chimed in. "I think Buddy's right, Axel."

Jesse said, "I can ride just fine."

Mister Braun aimed an irritated squint at Miz Braun and Buddy. "I trust Jesse to do a good job. Buddy, I want you get started on the oaks with Dudley. Jesse, there's a holding pen in the corner of the pasture by the gate. Take Dusty and move the heifer into it. Buddy'll pick you up back here after you've had lunch."

Jesse kept his face serious as he said, "Yessir," but inside he grinned at a chance to be a real cowboy.

Buddy looked like he'd just bitten into a turd.

While Buddy got the bull into the trailer, Jesse saddled Dusty. He was mounted by the time Mister Braun and Lola were ready to go. He rode out and they left at the same time. Jesse got a wave from Mister Braun and nothing from Lola.

As he walked his horse down the drive through drifting dust raised by the car and trailer, Buddy yelled from the barn, "Jesse! I'll get the heifer later, come on back."

Jesse just grinned and kicked Dusty into a lope.

For a time, Jesse's ride through the warming morning was a happy one. There was no hurry, and he was living his dreams. He held Dusty to a walk so he wouldn't have any urges to buck, and his awareness dwindled to the rhythm of his horse's walk and the scuff of hooves in the hill-country quiet.

Too soon, his mind started gnawing on his troubles with Lola and their "problem." He had no clue how to get through her anger and give her the love he felt. But no matter what she said, he would figure out a way to stick by her. Her and the baby. His baby.

It was a relief to arrive at the gully pasture; there was a job to do, and his mulling had to wait. Careful to close the gate behind him, he stood in his stirrups and scanned the area. He saw five acres of meadows and live oak trees with a deep gully across the center, but no heifer. The only movement in the still heat was two vultures circling overhead.

Maybe he'd be able to see the heifer from the rise at the west end of the pasture. He kicked Dusty in the ribs, gave him a slap on the rump with his reins, and the horse took off running. Jesse enjoyed few things more than riding a horse at a full gallop. The ride was smooth and level, like sitting astride a living chair, but fast and exciting.

As Lola had warned, Dusty kicked his heels up in midstride, but Jesse was ready. He flexed his knees and rode with it, and Dusty settled back into his run. Jesse pulled up at the top of the rise and searched for the red-brown of the cow's hide amid the greens and tans of the pasture. He found it about two hundred yards away, between him and the gully.

A wild urge took hold of him; he slapped Dusty's flanks with the reins and yelled, "Yeeeeha!" Dusty knew what to do and took off running in a beeline for the heifer. She turned tail and trotted away. Dusty raced closer. The heifer lumbered into a run.

Man, this was fun! The heifer cut through a copse of live

oak and ran under a low-hanging tree limb. Dusty stayed with her. Jesse bent as low as he could, the saddle horn digging into his belly; the limb caught his shirt just below the collar and ripped the back off, raking his spine down to his belt. It stung, but not much. The heifer plunged into the gully. Jesse leaned forward and urged Dusty to run even faster.

Ten feet from gully's edge, without a hint of warning, Dusty turned at a right angle and shot away from the trench. Jesse left the saddle and flew straight ahead, riding air. He twisted to hit the ground on the side of one leg and rolled, picking up a mouthful of dust along the way.

He spat, struggled to his feet, and stared at Dusty's departing rump. He grinned. "You got me, you son of a bitch."

The horse was headed for the gate. Jesse started after it, but then a nasty smell stopped him. The air was ripe with a sick-sweet odor he recognized. Back home he'd come upon the bodies of three big dogs someone had dumped in the woods. The same putrid smell had come from their bloated corpses. It had made his horse nervous then, and now it had spooked Dusty into throwing him.

The stench of death came from the gully. He glanced up; the vultures circled directly overhead. Checking the ground and rocks, alert for snakes, he edged toward the slope and peered down. Erosion had created an overhang beneath a rock outcropping near the bottom. Under it, a patch of blue caught his eye. It wasn't a flower. Prickles went up his spine. He didn't want to go there.

He had to.

He edged down the slope, planting his feet sideways, loose shale spilling down before him; the smell got stronger.

The blue became the sleeve of a faded denim shirt. A body lay face down.

Shaggy black hair.

Dusty black hat on the ground beside the body.

He couldn't see the face, didn't want to see the face, but it had to be Romero. Jesse turned away and vomited his breakfast. When there was nothing left to come up, he stumbled out of the gully and ran toward the gate to find his horse. The strength and joy he'd been feeling had turned to shaky weakness all through his body.

Jesse ran Dusty all the way back to the ranch house, wishing he could get away from what he'd found, but there was no leaving it behind. Maybe Dusty was scared, too, because he didn't buck once. Jesse hoped, by some miracle, to find Mister Braun at the house, but he wasn't due for heavenly intervention that day. He rode onto the lawn, flung himself off his horse, and ran inside.

Miz Braun was alone in the living room, sewing trim onto a pink Western shirt. She looked up in surprise.

"I found—" He caught his breath. "I found Romero."

Her eyes widened. She frowned and shook her head. "He's gone. You saw somebody who looked like him."

He shook his head. "No. I found his body."

Her eyes got even wider. She started to speak, then glanced around, put her sewing down, stood and signaled for him to follow her. "I don't want Connie hearing this. It'll upset her."

She led him into the utility room and closed the door behind them. Rubbing the scar on her eyebrow, she said, "What did you find, and where?"

Jesse told her.

She asked, "Are you sure it wasn't just some old clothes?"

"I saw his hair."

"Did you see his face?"

He shuddered at the thought of what it might have looked like. "I didn't get that close."

"Then you don't know for sure it was Romero."

"But the clothes . . ."

"You didn't see the face."

He had to say, "I guess I don't know for sure, ma'am." But it was him. His shirt. His hat.

She checked her watch. "I'll call Mister Braun, they ought to be in Hondo by now. It would be better for him to talk to the sheriff." She stepped closer. She seemed angry. Her scar had become red. She put both hands on Jesse's shoulders, close to his neck. "But he's the only one's going to hear about this. I don't want you saying a word to anybody."

He nodded.

"Nobody. Not Dudley. Not Dolores. Not Buddy. Not even Mister Braun when he gets back, somebody might overhear you. Nobody." She tightened her grip; her hands were powerful, and it hurt where her fingers sank in. She glared into his eyes. "You understand?"

He didn't, really, but she was so intense that whatever she said seemed right. "Yes."

"You promise?"

"Yes."

At that she let him go. "All right. Axel seems to think you're honest."

"What about the heifer?"

"It'll be fine where it is. We shouldn't go back and take a chance of messing up the area around whoever that is you found. If it is Romero, I bet he ran into a rattlesnake trying to go cross-country. Maybe you've found the killer."

"What do I do now?" His voice sounded weak to him. Maybe it even shook a little. He became aware of stinging down his back and reached behind him. His hand encountered the dangling back of his shirt. He pulled it around and stared at it. What had happened?

Miz Braun asked, "What happened to your shirt?"

Oh, yeah. He remembered it tearing. "I was chasing the heifer and went under a low limb . . ."

"Turn around." She looked and then said, "I'll tell Buddy you hurt your back and had you take the rest of the day off."

That was a break. He didn't think he could act normally right then.

"Get Connie to take care of that scratch, then you can stay in your cabin."

"Yes, ma'am."

She put on a smile. "I'm sure you're upset. You can just rest." Her smile went away and her eyes narrowed. "You will not whisper a word about this."

Jesse nodded. He wanted no trouble with Miz Braun.

After Consuelo had washed his scratch and put Merthiolate on it, he trudged to the cabin. Gazing at the hen house, he gave thanks that it was over. Now all he had to deal with was an angry girl, a baby on the way, and the dust-up sure to come when they told her parents about it.

He slid a loose T-shirt on, then lay on his belly in his bunk and tried to read, but something nagged at him, distracting him enough to make him close the book and let it come. There'd been something wrong about Romero's hat. He pictured it. Black. Dusty. Except for a band of dark, clean black at the crown's base.

Where a snakeskin hatband had been.

Lola wandered through the pecan grove behind her Aunt Mary's house, her steps leading no place, her thoughts getting nowhere. The tall pecan trees ordinarily brought to mind playful memories of autumn harvests, scouring through fallen leaves for fallen nuts with cousin Katie and cousin Nelson from San Antonio, with giggles and shouts peppering the afternoon. The one who found the most got extra whipped cream on their pecan pie at supper.

Today they were just trees. Gloomy trees.

The visit had started out fine; on the drive down she had felt as though she were on her way to a safe haven, her troubles behind her. It had been great to see Aunt Mary and Katie. For a while she'd felt like her old, happy self. Then she and Katie got to talking and Katie ran on about her boyfriend, which made Lola think of the pain on Jesse's face when he'd watched her flirt with Dudley. And the beating he'd suffered because of her catty little game.

She'd excused herself, saying she needed to stretch her legs. But walking hadn't helped. She came to the tree house where she and her cousins had played dress-up for what seemed like a whole lifetime at the time, when the moment was all that there was. She climbed up, and was amazed at how small the tree house—once a castle filled with maidens and heroes—felt.

Sitting on the floor, the weight of the last few weeks pressed upon her.

The summer had started so well. She had worked up the courage to have no more to do with Buddy, even though she'd been afraid he would hit her. He'd done that to girls, but the threat of her father finding out what he'd done with her stopped him. And kept him away.

Then Alejandro had come, and it was fun to flirt with him. Until he got grabby. She told him no more, and he was killed.

Now she had done terrible things to Jesse. In her panic and anger at being pregnant, she'd put all the blame on him. But that wasn't right, was it? And then she'd caused a fight between Jesse and his best friend. A sense of dread darkened her thoughts. Was she a really curse? She wanted to call Jesse. Sure, nothin' to it, just call and ask her mother to bring him to the phone. Tension tightened her stomach; something was going to happen. She wished they were home. She climbed down to find her father. Maybe he would drive her back. It wasn't far.

When she stepped to the ground, she became aware of the pressure low in her belly that signaled the start of her period. She focused on her insides. Yes. She wasn't pregnant! Relief filled her like helium in a balloon. She couldn't wait to tell Jesse the good news. Then she cursed her stupidity—she had killed his feelings for her. She walked back to Aunt Mary's house, shoulders slumped in defeat. She had screwed up the one good thing in her life, and there was no hope of getting it back.

Now she wished she never had to go home.

28

Jesse's fears dwindled, and frustration built through the long afternoon after finding Romero's body. How could he not tell Dudley? As suppertime crawled within reach, he decided the hell with the sheriff and Miz Braun, he had to talk to Dudley about what he'd found. Buddy was part of it, and Dudley could help figure out how he was. And what to do.

But Dudley hadn't shown up by the time Consuelo's call of "Supper!" drifted down from the house, and Jesse was worried. Dudley was out alone with Buddy.

His tension turned into a grin when he found Dudley lounging on the patio, finishing a cigarette. "Hey, Spider."

Dudley gave him a wintry look and flicked his cigarette butt at him. Jesse batted it aside and said, "Listen, I have to tell you . . ."

The screened door opened. Miz Braun sent a hard glance Jesse's way. "Supper's getting cold."

Dudley went in and Jesse followed, but she stopped him at the door. Speaking low, she said, "Mister Braun called, and he says not to worry. Sheriff Webb got the body."

"Was it . . .?"

"It was Romero. He fell into a nest of rattlers." She sighed. "I'm glad it's over, aren't you?"

"Yes, ma'am. Can I tell Dudley about it now?"

She frowned. "The sheriff said we can't say a word until it's official. And I really don't want it to get back to Connie or Dolores and upset them before I have a chance to talk to them." Her gaze hammered at him. "Nobody'd better hear it from you."

When he sat next to Dudley at the supper table, Dudley moved to the farthest chair away. Jesse was the Invisible Boy to Dudley while they ate, but Buddy acted friendly. Miz Braun did a great job of not giving the tiniest clue that something was going on.

Jesse felt like Lola's horse must have after the firecrackers went off: wound tight and ready to bolt.

When supper was done, Buddy said to Miz Braun, "I'm going into town for a couple beers, you need anything?"

She pressed her fingers to her temples. "Pick me up some aspirin? My head's been killin' me today and I'm out."

He went to her and massaged her shoulders, up high by her neck. "Sure. Why don't you lie down for a while?"

"I think I will."

Dudley said "G'night" and left. Jesse followed, nobody to talk to.

They'd just stepped off the patio when Buddy came to the back door. "Wait up, Spider."

Dudley stopped. "Yeah?"

Jesse stepped past him, and then he stopped and waited on the path.

"With Lola gone, Margaret wants you to come up early tomorrow morning and feed Poko and her puppies."

Dudley said, "Sure."

"She said be sure you do it at five sharp. Poko's nursing a lot of puppies and gets pretty hungry."

Dudley's shoulders sank. Getting up was hard for him at the regular time; this was going to be a killer. "Five. Right."

Buddy went back into the house and Dudley started for the cabin. Jesse desperately wanted to get back together with him. "Spider . . ."

Dudley walked by, staring straight ahead. He said, "Don't call me that."

"I have to talk to you."

"I don't have to talk to you."

"It's really important."

Dudley kept walking.

"C'mon, Dudley, you've got to listen!"

"Screw you."

"I'm sorry, Dudley!"

Dudley stooped, grabbed a rock and hurled it at Jesse. Jesse dodged. "This is serious!"

"So is this." Dudley scooped up more rocks and started throwing. One grazed Jesse's ear. He was forced to run for it. He stopped at the big maple on the front lawn and plopped down on the grass. The longest Dudley had stayed pissed off at him before was two weeks. He would come around, but would it be in time?

Maybe Jesse could call the sheriff. The trouble was, he'd have to ask to use the phone in the house, and there'd be questions about what for, and even if he told a good lie, Miz Braun would probably stand there and listen.

And he didn't really know anything. All he had was a feather that could have come from anywhere, and a left-behind picture. He'd seen a snakeskin hatband on Buddy's hat that might not be Romero's, and a razor that Buddy could have found. And Miz Braun could be right about the snakes.

In the distance, Buddy's Chevy fired up. He racked his pipes and then drove away.

Dammit, Jesse *knew* he'd seen the bulge of Romero's razor deep in his front pocket that morning, its shape outlined in a place it never left. He wouldn't drop it, much less leave it behind. It had come from his pocket. And that hatband hadn't just up and walked off of his hat. Both had ended up with Buddy. But, still and all, it didn't seem like enough to convince the sheriff.

What if Buddy had taken more?

Jesse lifted his head like a bird dog catching a scent. Buddy's trailer. As soon as it was dark, he'd find out. He trotted to the cabin for his flashlight. Maybe he could get through to Dudley before he started throwing things. As he passed the patio, he heard Dudley's voice and then Consuelo's laugh. Through the kitchen window he could see Dudley having a helping of cobbler. Maybe it was best to wait. Dudley would listen to hard evidence.

He got his flashlight and went to the barn to wait for the sun to go down. He climbed to the loft, where he could see most of the driveway. While he waited, he patiently wooed the barn cat, Spot, and managed to get him close enough for a scratch behind the ears. A loud purr rewarded him; it felt good to have something be friendly.

At last darkness swallowed the long shadow cast by the barn, and he walked to Buddy's trailer. It felt creepy and wrong to go inside; his father had taught respect for the property and privacy of others. He wished his father were there to help him know what to do. The door wasn't locked; he winced at a loud creak when he eased it open.

Inside, the first thing that struck him was the acrid stink of body odor. His flashlight revealed dirty socks and shirts littering the floor of the small living room. Empty beer bottles and cans surrounded Buddy's bull-riding trophy on a coffee table. There were no books in sight, but on the couch a Playboy magazine lay open to the centerfold. A small television sat on an overturned cardboard box, tinfoil wrapped around its rabbit-ears antenna.

A quick rummage through the mess turned up nothing that looked like it would be Romero's. It occurred to Jesse that he didn't know what he was looking for. Passing by the kitchen off the living space, he wrinkled his nose at piles of dirty dishes in the sink.

He pawed through the single bedroom. There was nothing suspicious in sight. He dug into a narrow closet across from the tiny bathroom. Metal clinked when he shifted a muddy boot. He upended it and poured something onto his palm.

The flashlight showed a half-dozen silver dollars—and a heavy silver ring with a turquoise eagle. Sunlight had flashed from that ring when Romero removed his hat the morning they met.

Tires crunched on the drive. Jesse poured the money and ring back into the boot and flicked off the flashlight. The rumble of Buddy's car stopped outside the trailer; a car door opened and shut. Jesse stepped inside the closet and pulled the door closed, leaving it ajar just enough to peek out.

The front door creaked open, and lights turned on. Buddy's footsteps shook the trailer. Jesse braced his feet and raised his flashlight to use as a club. He'd fight his way out if he had to. The footsteps stopped, and then a long sigh accompanied the sound of pee hitting water in the toilet.

Jesse opened the closet door a few inches, Buddy's stream masking the sound. He could see the back of Buddy's shoulder; the bathroom door blocked the rest of him. Jesse slipped out of the closet and tiptoed past the bathroom. As he stepped toward the front door, the splash in the toilet stopped. Jesse rushed to the front door. It creaked when he opened it and Buddy called out, "Who's that?"

Jesse slipped out. A porch light lit the area, and there were no bushes or trees near enough to get to in time. Buddy had backed the Chevy up to a few feet from the steps.

Buddy called again, "Hey?"

Jesse dove to the ground and rolled into the darkness under the rear of the Chevy. The front door opened and Buddy thumped down the steps. He stopped at the rear of the car; Jesse shrank against the axle.

Buddy belched and then grunted, "Hmph." He turned and started back in, then stopped. "Oh, shit, the aspirin." He got into the car and started it. Jesse winced as Buddy racked his pipes. The car rolled forward, exposing Jesse. He lay flat, hoping Buddy wouldn't look in his rear view mirror. When the Chevy's taillights turned toward the ranch house, Jesse ran for the barn.

Jesse climbed into the loft, lay on the floor in front of the open upper doors, and watched for pursuit. None came. His breathing slowed and his heart stopped trying to jackhammer its way out of his chest. He rested his head on his arm and closed his eyes for just a second . . .

Jesse jerked awake from a dream of Alejandro and Romero; he thought the dead men had been mouthing "*señor.*" *Señor* who?

His body was stiff, and the hay tickled—hay? He realized he lay on the loft floor, the cat curled against his side. A predawn glow grayed the darkness outside. He sat up. Buddy's car was back in front of his trailer. No lights on. Saying goodbye to the cat, Jesse climbed down.

Excitement thrummed in him as he ran for the cabin. He'd discovered something important, and he was eager to tell Dudley. Even if Romero had been snaked to death, how did Buddy come up with Romero's stuff? Something was wrong.

Consuelo's house was dark as he ran past, but the kitchen light in the main house was on.

Puffing from his run, he opened the cabin door and found Dudley snoring in his bunk. The alarm clock read four forty-five, almost time for Dudley to get up to do his chore for Miz Braun. Thinking maybe it would help get him and Dudley back together if he did it instead, Jesse let Dudley sleep and went to the house. After he fed Poko, he would get Dudley up, and they'd head for town and the sheriff. He wished Mister Braun was home.

Consuelo was in the kitchen, mixing up pancake batter. Feeling good, he said, "*Buenas dias*, Consuelo."

As he got dog food from the utility room, she said, "You are up early. It's five o'clock."

He checked the kitchen clock. Dudley's alarm clock was running slow again. "I'm going to feed the dog. Dudley was sleeping hard, so I thought I'd help him out."

She smiled. "You are a good boy."

Sure he was. He'd knocked up the boss's daughter, hit her, and then attacked his best friend.

When he got to the dog run, Poko wagged her tail so hard a hind foot left the ground at times. Jesse filled her bowl and then patted her while she dug in.

The glow of dawn was slipping into the cabin by the time he returned to the cabin. Dudley's snores were as strong as ever. Jesse stepped toward the table to shut off the alarm before it woke Dudley up.

A sound that didn't belong surfaced between snores. It was a dry, scratchy, buzzing noise. The hair on the back of Jesse's neck rose; he froze.

Coiled a few feet from the bed, a rattlesnake as thick as Jesse's forearm pointed its triangular head at him, rattle vibrating. Its tongue flicked at him, tasting his scent. His old fear of snakes shivered him. He tried to think of how far a rattler could strike. Half its length sounded right—but how could he tell how long a coiled snake was? It was maybe five feet away.

He wanted to escape. But he couldn't leave Dudley.

Dudley shifted in his sleep, his hand slipped off his belly and fell over the side of the bunk to dangle a couple of feet from the rattler. The snake startled and jerked its nasty eyes to focus on the new threat.

Oh, God, don't move, Dudley. Panicked, Jesse searched the room for a weapon. The broom he'd used on the spiders stood in a corner next to the bathroom. He stepped back.

The snake swiveled its head to look at him, the sound of its rattle like dried seeds swirling in a hollow gourd.

He inched his way to the broom, and then he raised it to a striking position in slow motion. Moving with care, he got within range. He would knock the rattler into the bathroom, then get Dudley up and run for it. As he worked up the gumption to swing, Dudley snorted, rolled over, and pulled his hand back up onto the bed.

The snake turned its head toward the motion and then settled back to a ready position.

Okay, now that Dudley was out of immediate danger, what? The trouble with using the broom was that the rattler might come at him if he didn't hit it just right. As scared as he was, hitting it just wrong seemed more likely.

Maybe if he threw something on top of the snake, he could get Dudley out of the cabin and then they could deal with it. Moving in slow motion, a step and a pause, a step and a pause, he backed into the bathroom. The snake's rattle slowed, and then silenced.

He got the bath towels to throw over the snake. Thinking heavy would be better, he wadded them under the tub faucet and soaked them with water.

Holding the two dripping towels hanging together to form a single mass, he crept back into the bedroom. The rattler stayed quiet; maybe it had gotten used to his slow movement. Dudley's snore had stopped when he rolled over.

Jesse crept to within six feet of the snake. He couldn't make himself get any nearer. He readied to throw the towels. The silence was so complete Jesse could hear his pulse pounding in his ear.

Dudley's alarm smashed into the quiet.

Jesse flinched, the snake tightened its coil and its rattle started up.

Dudley mumbled, "Oh, shit, the damn dog," and swung his feet onto the floor.

Jesse shouted, "Dudley, no!"

The snake struck the meaty part of Dudley's bare thigh. He cried out and hit at it. The rattler struck again, this time catching him high on the left arm. Dudley screamed and lifted his arm in the air, the snake hanging from him.

Jesse dropped the towels, leaped forward, and grabbed the snake's tail. He yanked with all the strength and fear in his body. Its fangs ripped out of Dudley's arm and Jesse crashed its head against the log wall behind him. He slammed it again and again until it hung limp. Its muscles contracted where he held its tail, but its head was a bloody mess. He flung the snake out the screened door. He turned to Dudley.

His friend's eyes were wide and scared. "Jesse?"

The clock alarm screamed. Jesse silenced it with his fist. What should he do? Stop the poison—a tourniquet!

Dudley's jeans and socks were on the floor beside the bed. Jesse grabbed a sock. "Hold still, man." He tied it above the bite on Dudley's arm and then tried to get another sock around his leg. It wasn't long enough. He snatched Dudley's jeans and used a pant leg.

Dudley's voice rose toward a scream. "It hurts!"

"Don't move. I'll get help. You'll be all right."

Dudley laid back, his expression dazed.

Jesse slammed out the door. The snake lay where he'd thrown it, still writhing. He jumped over it and ran to the house, screaming. "Consuelo!"

Buddy and Miz Braun were having coffee at the dining table when Jesse ran in. They looked surprised, then shocked when he yelled, "A rattlesnake bit Dudley."

Consuelo gasped, "Oh, no!"

Buddy said, "Oh, shit."

Miz Braun said, "Where is he?"

"In the cabin! You've got to do something!"

Miz Braun hurried out the door and ran to the cabin with Jesse and Buddy at her heels.

Dudley lay limp, his eyes closed. Miz Braun took a quick look at the tourniquets. "Two bites?"

"Yes'm."

"That one's awful high on his left arm."

Buddy's eyes were wide, and his gaze darted all around, like the day Alejandro was killed. He muttered, "Oh, shit."

Jesse sat on the edge of the bunk. "Dudley? Dudley?" Oh, please be okay.

Dudley moaned. The pain must be bad.

Jesse turned to Miz Braun, "What can we do?!"

She snapped, "Buddy, get the Jeep. We gotta get him to the hospital for antivenom."

At the hospital emergency room, Dudley moaned on a gurney. The doctor who had dealt with Dudley's spider bites looked up from his examination. He seemed worried. He turned to a nurse. "Antivenom."

Her eyes widened. "We don't have much. It's on order since we used it to save that guy that got bit at church."

"Damn. Get me all we have, call around."

He closed a curtain around Dudley and, for the second time, Jesse spent an eternity in a waiting room.

The eternity and life as he'd known it ended in less than an hour. The doctor walked in, his stricken eyes and down-curved mouth telegraphing bad news. Jesse's stomach knotted. Dudley must be really sick.

The doctor went to Miz Braun. "I'm sorry, ma'am, we did everything we could. But he was weakened from the spider bites, and too much venom reached his heart . . ."

Dudley was dead?

Miz Braun stared at Jesse, her expression as blank as if she were looking at a shoe.

Black, bitter anguish filled Jesse's mind. "No!"

The doctor said, “I’m sorry, son, we did all—”

Jesse ran into the treatment room. Dudley looked like he was sleeping. Jesse grabbed his arms and shook, “Spider! Wake up!” Dumb, sure, but Jesse had failed him, and he had to try something, anything.

Dudley wobbled, and then he lay strangely still.

Jesse realized that the stillness was because he wasn’t breathing. Breath is life. Jesse’s friend had no life.

Jesse stared straight ahead, his life with Dudley flashing past and ending with bitter words and a stupid fight. Red rage erupted. “It’s not fair! You’re not supposed to be dead!” He punched the mattress.

Dudley’s head wobbled as if he shook his head no in disagreement.

On the trip back to the ranch, Jesse slumped in the back of the Jeep, forearms across his knees, face buried in his arms. Tears squeezed from his closed eyes. Over and over he saw the fear on Dudley's face, his eyes wide, saying, "Jesse?"

Do something, Jesse.

Help me, Jesse.

Jesse hadn't helped. He'd let his friend die. His thoughts circled viciously—*I-let-him-die-I-let-him-die-I-let-him-die* . . .

Miz Braun's voice intruded. "Those tourniquets were a good idea, it's just bad luck they were so short on antivenom."

It wasn't bad luck; if he'd been there instead of sleeping in the barn, maybe he'd have seen the snake in time. *I-let-him-die-I-let-him-die-I-let-him-die* . . .

At the ranch house, Jesse slumped in a living room chair, his stare seeing nothing, his emotions a wasteland. His life had come to an end with Dudley's. Consuelo laid a gentle hand on his arm, but he had no response to give.

Buddy sat at the dining room table, eating. The smell of food nauseated Jesse.

He heard Miz Braun calling Mister Braun in Hondo. She hung up and said, "Axel is coming right away. He says not to do anything until he gets here."

It was too late to do anything. Jesse thought he ought to call Dudley's mother, but he couldn't imagine being able to get the words out of his mouth. He ought to call his mother, but he was empty of will.

After an hour of despair had trickled by, the front door opened and Mister Braun walked in, followed by Lola. She darted glances at him, her movements stiff. The sight of her stirred only an eddy in his emptiness.

She fled down the hall to her room.

Mister Braun put his hand on Jesse's shoulder for a moment, and that felt good. Mister Braun said, "I'm sorry, son."

The doorbell rang. Consuelo admitted Sheriff Webb.

He was somber, but intense. "Sorry to trouble you folks, but I'm required to turn in a report. I need to see where it happened."

Jesse didn't move.

Mister Braun said, "Jesse?"

"Yessir." He stood. "In the cabin."

There was sympathy in Sheriff Webb's eyes when he said, "I'm sorry, son, but I need you to take me through it."

Jesse led the sheriff and Mister Braun to the cabin. Buddy started to follow, but the sheriff told him the fewer the better.

Outside the cabin, they examined the dead snake while Jesse said, "I'm sure the snake wasn't in the cabin when I went to feed Poko, but it was there when I came back." He didn't feel right about telling the sheriff he'd spent the night in the barn, or why, until he'd talked to Mister Braun about it.

Sheriff Webb asked him, "Was the screen door open?"

"No, sir."

The sheriff studied the door. A spring held it shut tight to keep bugs out. He opened the door and let the spring snap it closed. Then he knelt and peered at the bottom.

The screen was pulled away from the frame at a bottom

corner. He poked his fingers through a hole large enough for a snake to get through.

The sheriff looked up at Jesse. "What about this?"

"I never noticed it." It could have happened when Dudley shoved him out the door.

The sheriff led them inside, and Jesse took them through what he'd done with the broom and the towels. And then about the alarm going off, and Dudley sitting up, and the snake striking . . . he choked up and could say no more.

Mister Braun put a hand on Jesse's shoulder and looked to the sheriff, who nodded and said, "Go on outside and wait for us, son."

Jesse stepped out and leaned against the cabin wall, careful to keep his gaze away from the rattler. He could hear Mister Braun and the sheriff.

The sheriff said, "Well, Axel, I don't think we'll need a formal inquest. It looks like an unfortunate accident."

"Yeah. With the drought, we've seen more snakes around the house than normal, and I guess this one was just looking for a cool place to spend the day."

"That boy can't stay in this cabin."

"No. I'll put him in the guest room in the house until I figure out what to do next. I'll have to send Jesse home. God, I hate the thought of making the call to Dudley's mother."

"I'll do it."

"No, it's mine to do."

"You've had a black summer, Axel."

"Yeah. First the wetback, and now this."

The screened door opened and they came out. The sheriff said, "Thank you, Jesse. I won't trouble you any more."

They trailed the sheriff back to his car, Jesse in a daze, there and not there. Sheriff Webb started to back away, then stopped and leaned out the car window. "I almost forgot to tell you, Axel, we finally located Romero's sister in Reynosa."

"She any help?"

"No. The man has just disappeared. I thought sure we'd have found him by now."

"Well, you will."

The sheriff nodded and drove away. Mister Braun gave Jesse's shoulder a pat. "I need to see to things. Why don't you go on in the house?"

Jesse nodded, his gaze locked on the sheriff's car. Mister Braun left him standing there with no idea what to do next.

Jesse stared at the sheriff's car until it left his sight. He should have told him about Romero's ring in Buddy's trailer. And the feather in the Chrysler. And the razor Buddy had. But he owed it to Mister Braun to talk to him first. He'd know what to do.

Then what he'd just heard sank in. The sheriff didn't know Romero's body had been found.

Jesse's eyes tightened. Mister Braun hadn't told the sheriff about Romero's body. Fear pulled him out of his muddle.

What if Buddy had told Mister Braun about Jesse knowing that he had Romero's straight razor? It hit him. He knew how dangerous Buddy was, and Buddy went to a church where they passed rattlesnakes around. Dudley's death had been an accident, all right, but not the way the sheriff thought. The rattler had been meant for Jesse. While Dudley was out feeding the dog, he would have climbed down from his bunk . . .

Would they come after him again? Maybe not for a while, not so soon after what they'd done to Dudley. Could be he had a chance to get away before they figured out how to make another "accident" happen. He settled his thoughts. He could do it as long as he didn't panic. And stayed alert.

He forced himself to be calm when he went to the ranch house. But he couldn't meet Mister Braun's eyes. He'd had his gaze on the ground all morning, though, so he didn't think it would make him suspicious. "I need to call my mother."

"Sure."

"I'd like her to come get me today."

"I understand. Whatever you want."

Jesse dialed his mother, but there was no answer even though he let it ring twenty times.

He spent the rest of the day trying to call his mother, but she wasn't home. He thought to sneak in a call to the sheriff, but the only phone he had access to was in the kitchen, and somebody was always around. Maybe he could do it after they went to bed.

Belatedly, while Consuelo was preparing supper, it occurred to him to call his mother's best friend. "Vicky, I tried to call Mama all day, but she's not home."

Vicky said, "Oh, darn, I told her she ought to tell you, but she wanted it to be a surprise. She's in a hospital, but everything's fine and she'll be out tomorrow."

"She have another 'accident'?" Meaning too many drinks on the highway.

Vicky must have heard the scorn in his voice. "Not this time, Jesse. She went in to get help for her problem."

He'd believe it when he saw it. "I gotta come home."

"Isn't the ranch fun?"

He didn't want to get into what had happened. Actually, that wasn't true. He wanted to spill everything to a grownup who would take care of him; he was about to break wide open. But he couldn't. "Uh, they just don't need me any more."

"Well, I'll make sure she calls first thing tomorrow. Okay?"

"Can't you just give me the hospital number?"

"She can't make calls or receive them, doctor's orders. First thing tomorrow, I promise."

Trapped by his little white lie, he couldn't say it had to be now. So he said, "Okay. Tell her as soon as she can."

"Is Dudley coming home too?"

"Yes." Forever. "Listen, I gotta go." After goodbyes, he hung up. He turned and found Mister and Miz Braun standing behind him; she had that blank look on her face.

Mister Braun said, "Well?"

He couldn't tell them he hadn't reached her. "My mother, uh, she'll be down to get me in the morning. Real early." Maybe that would stop them from doing anything.

"Good." Mister Braun stepped close and put a hand on Jesse's shoulder, who forced himself not to cringe away from the treacherous touch. "Why don't you get some rest? The guest room's the first one on the right down the hall."

"Yeah."

Jesse went to the room, which was next to Lola's bedroom. The bedsprings squeaked when he flopped down. She must have heard, because a minute later she came into the room. His feelings about her were so tangled with Dudley dying it hurt to look at her—he turned his back and stared out the window. He could see Consuelo's cottage.

Her weight on the double bed tilted him toward her; he rolled away. Her hand rested lightly on his shoulder. "Jesse. I'm so sorry."

Hurt and anger kept his mouth shut.

Lola's hopes of helping Jesse shriveled when he turned his back to her. What could she say? I liked Dudley a lot? That was dumb; it sounded like she was still playing her game. Shit.

His best friend in the world had died. She hoped they'd been okay with each other before . . . before . . . This time she couldn't stop the tears.

She did love Jesse. She wanted to tell him. But she didn't think she could bear the cold silence she'd get. He had good reason to hate her. He'd go home tomorrow, and that would be the best thing for him. Her curse couldn't reach all the way to Dallas. He'd be safe there.

And she'd be so alone here.

She sat next to him for long, quiet minutes. She ached to lie beside him and hold him to her; no matter what he said or did, at least he'd know she cared.

Her mother's voice came from behind her. "Dolores?"

Don't yell at me, just don't yell at me, I couldn't stand it. She stood, cast one last longing glance at Jesse, and left. She avoided her mother's gaze and went into her room, closing the door behind her. Hurt overwhelmed her. Every part of her life was pain.

The thought crossed her mind that it was too bad killing yourself was a mortal sin. God, what a selfish bitch. Jesse was the one who hurt. She had to tell him what she felt. She searched for something to write on.

Jesse missed the warmth of Lola's hand. He regretted not saying anything to her.

He dozed. Images chased each other in his mind, blurred with speed like the tigers circling the tree in the story of Little Black Sambo. The bed was soft. Jesse's eyes drooped. He fought to keep them open. He wasn't safe. He ought to get up and lock the door. He would, in just a minute.

Jesse stands in the barn, beside the truck. The heat is roasting, and sweat seeps down his face. Wood in the barn crackles with expansion. Before him on the barn floor lies a man. A big man.

Dudley. Ghost-pale, his once ruddy, fat cheeks sallow and sunken. Dudley lumbers to his feet and faces Jesse.

The hand of fear pierces Jesse's chest and grips his heart. Dudley's arm lifts and aims at Jesse. His index finger points.

Jesse shakes his head. I couldn't stop it. I couldn't.

Dudley's mouth forms the word "you."

The hand in Jesse's chest squeezes, his heart will burst—

Jesse broke from the dream with a shout. "No!" He jerked upright on the bed. It was dark. A cricket chirp came through the window. A coyote howl found its way into the room.

There was a huge, sore sorrow in him. The shame of failing Dudley would never go away. He tensed. Whoever had set the rattlesnake trap might try again. He wanted home. He wanted to feel safe again.

His stomach rumbled. He hadn't been able to eat all day and he needed food. He thought of the phone in the kitchen, and his pulse quickened; he might be able to sneak a call to the sheriff. Was it late enough for everybody to be in bed? He went to the bedroom door and listened. The night was still.

As he steeled himself for action, into the quiet came the scrape of clothes against leaves outside the window. His scalp prickled. A ghostly face appeared outside. Fright shot down his spine and he tensed to fight—or run.

Consuelo whispered, "Jesse?"

He released a long breath, then went to the window and knelt. "You scared me to death."

"You have money?"

Puzzled, he said, "Some. Maybe twenty bucks."

"Bring it and come to my house." The rustle of leaves marked her disappearance.

He was still fully dressed, and his money was in his pocket. He unlatched the screen and slipped out.

Consuelo's lights were out. She waited in her doorway, holding open the screened door. He stepped through; she followed and closed the door after her. He could barely make out shapes of furniture in the living room. She took his hand and led him to a door with a sliver of light showing beneath it. "Quick."

Inside, she shut the door behind them. Her bedroom was clean and crisp in pastel colors. A small table was set up in one corner as an altar, with a crucifix on the wall above it. Three votive candles beneath the cross provided the only light.

She looked up at him, concern in her eyes. "You must leave here."

He nodded. "My mother will come get me tomorrow."

"Go tonight."

"Why?"

"I don' want no more 'accident' to happen."

"What do you know?"

She took his hand and placed the keys to Dudley's car on his palm. "That you must go."

He gripped the keys. A memory flashed—Dudley at the wheel of the Caddy, laughing. Jesse forced himself to think about what Consuelo had said. She was right. He needed to be out of there. “All right.”

She took a paper sack from her bed and held it out to him. “This is food for you.”

The sack was unexpectedly heavy with something hard inside, and it almost slipped from his hands.

She said, “Careful, it will break.”

“*Gracias*, Consuelo.”

Her smile didn’t quite remove the sadness from her eyes. “*De nada, niño.*” He turned to the door, but she stopped him with a hand on his arm. “This way.” She led him to an open window. She whispered, “*Vaya con Dios.*”

Thanking her one more time, he climbed out. Fighting an urge to bolt, he circled behind the garden, careful to make no noise that would alarm the dog. The cabin Dudley and he had shared huddled in the night—small, empty, and sad. He thought of his stuff, but there was no way he could go in there.

As he neared the back of the house, he stopped to listen and look. He needed to go around the utility room end of the house to get to the Cadillac. He saw no lights or movement. His gaze lingered on Lola’s window. Remembering her slim legs coming through it when she’d slipped out in her pajamas, he longed for her.

Poko barked and he startled. He ran for the car, skidded to a stop by the car door and listened for pursuit. Even the insects had gone silent.

He opened the door and the dome light blazed. He felt like an escaping convict, a spotlight hitting him just as he went over the wall. He jumped in and slammed the door shut. He cringed—hell, why not just fire a cannon?

He jammed the key in and cranked the engine. The pipes roared and rumbled. There was no sneaking away now. Turning on the lights and dropping into reverse, he floored the gas pedal and whipped the car back and around. He crashed into the wall of sandstone rocks he and Dudley had stacked, ready for building a fireplace. His foot slipped off the accelerator, the motor died.

He stabbed the gas pedal and turned the key. The engine ground on and on. Maybe he'd flooded it!

A backfire boomed and the car started. He slammed into drive and peeled out.

A shape rushed at him from the darkness, arms extended—he was past it! He was gone!

Buddy's trailer was dark and his Chevy was there, parked pointing outward. Jesse raced for the gate to the highway and turned toward Kerrville.

Free!

As Jesse sped through the dark, his elation faded. Hunger gnawed at him, and it was hard to keep his thoughts focused on driving. He eyed the sack Consuelo had given him. A side road appeared; he turned in and drove up it for a quarter mile, then parked behind a cluster of cedars.

He cranked down his window and listened for pursuit. There was only the whisper of wind through cedar boughs. He could eat and then, well, he had gas money and was only five hours from home. He'd call the sheriff when he got there and tell him everything he knew.

He was so hungry he could have eaten the sack. He reached in and felt a sandwich wrapped in wax paper. He unwrapped it and took a giant bite. Tuna fish. He exhaled long and loud. Fear eased from him like sweat evaporating in a breeze.

As he ate, the burn of anger kindled in his gut like a rising sun. It dawned into the full glare of rage. But at what? He couldn't sit. He flung open the car door.

The goddam dome light went on. He slammed his fist into it, splintering the plastic cover and smashing the bulb. His knuckles hurt. He felt better for it.

In the grim grip of anger, he got out. He kicked a tire. Lola had thrown their love away.

But that wasn't it.

Jesse wanted to smash his fists into . . . into . . . himself. Because he was running away. Somebody had killed his best friend in the world, and he was running home to Mama. He closed his eyes, and his father's face rose in his mind.

His dad had noticed the bruises on Jesse's arm when he picked Jesse up from Jefferson Elementary School. "How did you get those?"

Jesse had cast his gaze down. "I dunno."

"Jesse?"

He had to tell. "It's Ryan. He's big, and the teachers never catch him."

His father had thought, and then he'd shook his head. "I'll talk to the principal about it."

"Please don't, Daddy. I'll stay away from him."

"It's not right, son, it's not *right*."

The next morning, his dad had gone to school and told the principal all about it.

The following day, Ryan's father had stomped up the steps to their front porch and hammered on their door. He yelled, "Your kid's a goddam liar!"

Jesse's dad had said, quietly, "Bruises don't lie." Later, Jesse had thought maybe it was his father's calm that made Ryan's father grab Jesse's dad by his tie and yank him off the porch.

Jesse's father hit the sidewalk wrong and broke his neck. He had died right in front of Jesse, surprise in his dead eyes. He died because he hadn't been able to rest knowing a wrong needed righting.

There'd been a time Jesse raged at his father for leaving him. But after a while he had realized his father was still with him, looking over his shoulder, nodding with a faint smile when his son did something right, frowning when Jesse was about to do something that didn't fit the code of honor his father had lived.

His father wouldn't be smiling now. Jesse couldn't let his dad down. Before the night was over, he would tell Sheriff Webb what was wrong at the ranch and then do whatever the sheriff said.

His anger simmered down into simple hate for Buddy and Mister Braun. He got back into the car. His mouth was as dry as a bucket of dust. Hoping Consuelo had packed something to drink, he dug into the sack and found a Mason jar of iced tea—and a folded piece of paper.

After a long drink of tea, he held the paper out the car window. There was enough moonlight to see writing, but not to read it. Smooth move, busting the dome light.

He found Dudley's emergency matches in the glove compartment. Dudley'd said a cigarette without a light was as useless as a kiss without a pucker. Striking a match and holding it close to the note, he recognized Lola's writing.

"Dearest Jesse,

"I saw Connie packing this food and figured it was for you. You looked so peaceful while you slept. I wanted to curl up next to you like we did in the cabin.

"I'm so sorry for being mean to you. I realize now you had to do what you did when I was crazy that night. And now you're going away. Even though I love you, that's the best thing, for you to get away from me. I told you I was a curse.

"I will love you always, and miss you forever.

"Lola."

He shook the match out and dropped it in the ashtray. The memory of her soft, warm kisses made his heart ache. He wouldn't leave Kerrville until he'd seen Lola again. But he had to get to the sheriff before anything more happened. He drove to the highway and turned toward town.

As his gaze followed the headlights down the road, he

pictured Lola. She faced away from him, in front of a small house. Their house. She turned to him with a broad smile, her dimple showing. In her arms she cradled a baby. His baby. He punched the accelerator, looking forward to holding her safe in his arms.

A dark shadow fell over Lola and the baby. Her smile dropped away, fear took its place. Jesse slowed. There was no guarantee she was safe at the ranch. How many times had he seen Buddy glare at her, fists clenched? He stood on the brakes, slammed through a u-turn, floored the Caddy, and raced toward the ranch.

Jesse rolled through the front gate, using only enough gas to creep forward. Keeping the Caddy's sound to a low rumble, he eased up the driveway and parked beside the barn. He carefully closed the car door with no more noise than a horse's hoof pawing a stall floor.

Staying on grass to avoid the driveway's noisy crushed rock, he trotted toward the house. He slowed as he passed Buddy's trailer. The Chevy sat in front; he saw no lights and heard no sounds. Jesse was sure he'd awakened them all when he left but, as far as they knew, he was long gone. Surprise was on his side.

Lights were out at the house. Jesse crouched low and hurried to Lola's window. He scratched on her screen. He was about to chance a whisper when her sheets rustled. Her face appeared behind the screen. Her whisper was hardly louder than a breath. "Oh, Jesse. I prayed you'd come back."

Her words told him everything he needed to know.

She said, "I couldn't sleep, and then I heard you go away, and I thought I'd never . . ." Her voice choked off.

"Come on."

"Where?"

"With me. To figure out what to do."

"Let me put some clothes on."

He turned his attention to listening for noises that weren't Mother Nature's, but he wasn't completely successful; the smooth sounds of pajamas sliding off her skin and clothes being pulled on aroused memories of their lovemaking.

The window screen lifted and a foot wearing a moccasin appeared, followed by a blue-jeaned leg. He helped her out and wrapped her in his embrace. She circled his waist with her arms, and they held each other, she soft and warm against him. When he released her, she looked up at him. Moonlight gleamed on tears in her eyes. He took her hand and led her away. As they crept past the end of the house, a light went on in her parents' window. They froze.

Mister Braun's voice came. "What is it?

Miz Braun said, "I can't sleep."

Sheets rustled and floorboards creaked, the sound of footsteps faded and silenced. Jesse tugged on Lola's hand; they ran. As they passed Buddy's trailer, Lola tripped and fell. Jesse tumbled over her, and a loud grunt burst from him when he hit the ground. They held still.

A light came on in Buddy's trailer; his door creaked open. Jesse watched Buddy peer into the dark. They were fifty feet away; with the porch light blinding Buddy's night vision, Jesse didn't think he could see them. Buddy closed the door and his lights went off. Jesse waited for a long moment, and then he led the way toward the barn.

He headed for the car, but Lola said, "The tack room. Nobody can see us there."

When he shut the tack room door behind them, a match flared and Lola took a candle from her pocket and lit it. God, it was so good to see her face. She dripped a spot of wax on an empty saddle rack, stuck the candle on it, and turned to him.

She didn't have far to turn. His arms were instantly around her, and hers around his neck. He poured all of his longing and love into his kiss, and that's what he got back.

At last they parted. She put her head on his shoulder and he held her for a long moment. He whispered, "I love you."

Her voice soft and low, she said, "I love you."

He pried her away. Her eyes were red and puffy. He smiled. "That allergy's going around."

She laughed. "Yeah." She sobered. "I thought you were gone home."

"I'm going to go see the sheriff. I have to tell him about finding Romero's body."

Her eyes widened. "He's dead? You found him?"

Jesse nodded. "Four days ago, in the Gully Pasture, the day you went to Hondo. I told your mother. She said your father told the sheriff, but I found out today that he didn't."

"No, that can't be."

He shook his head. "This morning the sheriff said he hadn't found Romero. Your father acted like he didn't know anything about it."

She pushed back from him, her hands raised in denial. "My father? No!"

"Buddy's a part of it, too."

"This sounds crazy."

"You've got to believe me. Buddy has Romero's straight razor. And that eagle ring Romero wore, I found it in Buddy's trailer."

"Maybe there's a reason. I want to ask my father."

"But what if I'm right?"

She whipped her head side-to-side and moaned.

He took her hands. "The sheriff will figure it out. Come with me."

"I don't know what to do."

The sound of a car intruded. Jesse snuffed the candle. The sound escalated into a roar. Intense light speared through gaps in the plank wall. Tires skidded in the dirt outside the barn.

The car's engine shut off, but the lights remained on, streaming through gaps in the wall. A car door opened and slammed shut. He pulled at Lola and pointed up; maybe he could boost her up to the loft through the gap between the tack room wall and the loft floor. She resisted and whispered, "No. We're together."

He searched for a weapon. The best he could find was a bridle with a heavy steel bit.

Lola grabbed a quirt and held it ready. Side by side, they faced the door. Lola's hand stole into his.

The door jerked open and Buddy stood there, shirtless, silhouetted by headlights. The glare made Jesse's eyes water. Buddy said, "You were dumb to come back."

Buddy reeked of beer. Jesse stepped in front of Lola. "We're leaving."

"You're half right. You're leaving, permanently." Buddy's hand lifted; Romero's straight razor gleamed.

Lola stepped beside Jesse, her face set to fight. "You leave us alone."

Buddy shook his head. "Can't do that now."

Jesse swung the bridle at Buddy's hand and knocked the razor to the floor; Buddy grabbed the bridle with his other hand and hauled Jesse out the doorway. Jesse fell onto the barn floor, still gripping the bridle. He scrambled to his feet. Buddy slammed the door closed and clicked the padlock shut.

Lola shouted, "Let me out."

Buddy grabbed a machete from the tool wall and rushed Jesse.

Jesse backpedaled toward the big doorway to the outside, swinging the bridle to keep Buddy at a distance.

Buddy angled and cut him off, slowing his advance. "You're dead meat."

Lola cried, "Jesse?"

Jesse threw the bridle, Buddy dodged; Jesse dashed to the tool wall and grabbed an axe. He took a swing at the padlock, but only dented the hasp. He spun to face Buddy—barely in time to block a blow from the machete with the axe handle.

Buddy chopped, Jesse had no time to swing the axe. He could only hold it in out with both hands to block the machete. Buddy hacked, driving him away from the tack room.

Lola jammed the quirt handle in a hip pocket and climbed onto a saddle rack. She jumped for the top of the wall. It was too high, and she fell. Her injured ankle twisted and pain knifed up her leg. Fighting panic, she struggled to her feet and searched for something to help her climb.

Her gaze swept across an old curb bit shaped like a steel "H"—if she could hook it on the top of the wall maybe she could climb out. She grabbed it and tied a leather rein to it. Climbing onto the saddle rack, she tossed the bit over the wall. Praying for it to catch, she gently pulled it back. It hooked on the top of the wall! She put her weight on the rein. It held.

Slipping out of her moccasins, she set her bare feet on the wall and pulled herself upward, hand over hand. A foot slipped and a toenail ripped. She gritted her teeth and climbed.

Outside, the chop of metal on wood picked up pace. She reached the top of the wall and clawed her way onto the loft.

The cat stood at the edge, looking down into the barn. It eyed her and then returned to watching. Below, Jesse held an axe up to block a machete that Buddy swung down with a huge, overhead blow. The axe handle broke in two. The force knocked Jesse backward onto the barn floor. Buddy lifted the machete high over his head.

Lola screamed "No!" and threw the quirt at him. It flashed past his head; he whirled.

Jesse rolled and sprang to his feet.

Buddy's eyes glittered madly up at her, and then he turned to Jesse and raised the machete.

She grabbed the cat and threw it at Buddy's naked back.

The cat hit Buddy and dug its claws deep into his shoulder. Buddy screamed and twisted. Jesse grabbed a pitchfork from the tool wall and spun. The machete crashed down, but Jesse caught it with the fork, and steel rang on steel.

They circled, Jesse jabbing with the pitchfork, Buddy slashing with the machete. Jesse said, "You don't like somebody using a pitchfork on you for a change, do you?" He charged.

Buddy parried with the machete and danced to one side. "You're full of shit."

"The pitchfork was still in Alejandro when you drove Romero out in the car. What did you do, knock him out and feed him to the snakes?"

Buddy lunged and chopped. "I didn't lay a hand on either one of them."

Jesse swung the pitchfork and landed a blow to Buddy's shoulder. Buddy staggered and recovered. They circled.

He risked a glance up at Lola. She signaled him to drive Buddy in her direction. He stabbed his pitchfork at Buddy and forced him back a step.

Buddy said, "Too bad you saw that razor. Hell, I even started to like you a little once you showed some backbone."

"But you didn't mind sending a rattlesnake to kill me."

"I minded. But I did what I had to do."

Jesse lunged and shouted, "You killed Dudley!" Buddy staggered backward, toward the tack room wall.

Lola launched herself from the loft and crashed onto Buddy. Buddy fell, the machete flew from his hand and hit the dirt at Jesse's feet. Jesse grabbed it and threw it behind him.

Lola curled up on the ground, grabbing her ankle. When Buddy leaped up and reached for her, Jesse jabbed at him and yelled, "Back!" A tine pierced Buddy's biceps and he backed away. Blood welled from the wound.

Jesse went to Lola. "Can you make it to the car?"

"Yeah."

Buddy sidled toward the tool wall, but Jesse aimed the pitchfork at him and said, "Don't move." Buddy stopped. Jesse dug the keys out of his pocket and handed them to Lola. "Get it started and leave the door open. Honk when you're ready." He helped her to her feet. She hopped on her good leg toward the barn door.

Buddy clenched and unclenched his hands, leaning forward as if he were going to charge. Jesse tightened his grip on the pitchfork. "Why'd you kill them?"

Buddy's face closed, his mouth a slit, his eyes narrowed.

Jesse looked to see where Lola was. She fell and cried out when she hit the barn floor. He said, "You okay?"

Lola nodded and got to her feet. Jesse turned back to see Buddy running to the tool wall—he grabbed the flamethrower. Cussing himself for an idiot, Jesse rushed him with the pitchfork. "Drop it."

Buddy lit the pilot flame. "I'm gonna do some toastin'."

Jesse wheeled, ran to Lola, and helped her hop out the door. A hiss, and then flame shot between them and the Caddy. Jesse swerved toward Buddy's car. He dropped the pitchfork to help her in. "Stay inside!"

He slammed the door and ran behind the car. In back of him was the boat shed, almost lost in darkness. Buddy closed in on him, dragging the flamethrower tanks by the harness.

Lola honked the horn. Buddy aimed the flamethrower nozzle at her and yelled, "Stop that!" She shrieked and threw herself down on the seat.

Jesse shouted, "Leave her alone!"

Buddy leveled a blast of flame across the Chevy's trunk. Jesse dropped; it passed over him and hit the boat shed. Flame flowed over the dry planks and caught.

Jesse crawled to the passenger side of the car and stood.

Buddy stared at the boat shed, firelight flickering in his eyes. He turned to Jesse. "Look what you made me do, you little pissant. Won't be any more trips to the lake this summer."

He started around the car. Jesse circled away from him.

A gas can in the burning boat shed exploded, blasting away part of the roof. A pillar of fire shot into the sky.

Buddy laughed. "Yahooo!"

Jesse stepped on the pitchfork. He picked it up to throw at Buddy, maybe distract him long enough to run for it. But he couldn't leave Lola behind.

Lola pointed at the Chevy's ignition. "The keys!"

Jesse yanked the door open. As she scooted over, Buddy thrust the flamethrower through the passenger window, inches from Lola. The burnt stench filled the car. She screamed.

Jesse pulled Lola out, put one arm around her waist, and they hobbled toward Dudley's car.

Buddy grabbed the tanks and ran around the Chevy to block them. Caught in the open, they had nowhere to run.

Lola pleaded, "Uncle Buddy, stop this."

"I'm just getting started." He shot a flame at the barn. The wood caught and fire raced up the wall.

A wailing scream turned their heads. "Buddyyyyy!"

It was Miz Braun; the Brauns ran down the driveway toward them, Lola's mother in the lead.

Buddy stared at them, and Jesse saw a chance. He let go of Lola, reared back, and hurled the pitchfork at Buddy. It flew true. The tines sunk into Buddy's midsection. He staggered back and the flamethrower slipped from his hand. Triumph soared in Jesse.

Buddy pulled the fork free and dropped it. Blood spilled down his belly. He collapsed to his knees and them fell back.

Miz Braun ran to Buddy and dropped to the ground beside him. She cried, "My baby! My . . ."

The words popped into Jesse's mind as she said them: "little boy." Lola gasped.

Miz Braun slid her arm under Buddy's shoulders and hugged him to her.

Buddy whispered. "I tried, Mama, I tried."

Miz Braun looked at Lola and Jesse, her eyes wild in the firelight, the scar on her forehead blood red. She snarled, "You." She shifted her gaze to the bloodied pitchfork. She eased Buddy to the ground and then rose and grabbed it.

Leveling it at them, she advanced, step by deliberate step, her voice low and flat. "I heard you out there with that greaser, you little tramp."

Lola moaned. "Oh, no."

Jesse flashed back to the night he'd heard Lola and Alejandro. Miz Braun had been awake.

Miz Braun's voice rose. "I tried to talk to him, but he laughed! I knew what that meant." With grim satisfaction, she said, "So I stopped him! And the other one." She came on. "You were safe!" Her next words were a scream of rage. "Then this punk came after you!"

The pitchfork's tines swung toward Jesse. He lifted Lola into his arms and backed away.

Miz Braun's stare found his. "Take your filthy hands off my daughter."

Lola said, “Mommy. No. Please, no.”

Jesse turned to run. Mister Braun was right on top of them, his arms spread wide.

Lola cringed against Jesse. “Daddy?”

Jesse set her down and raised his fists.

Mister Braun walked past them, his eyes on his wife. “Stop.”

She advanced step by step until the pitchfork pressed against her husband’s shirt.

His voice gentle, he said, “Margaret, stop this.”

Buddy coughed.

Fire crackled.

Mister Braun pried the pitchfork from Miz Braun’s hands and dropped it, then wrapped his arms around her.

Consuelo’s shout came from behind. “*Niña*!” Breathless, she ran to Lola.

Lola said, “I’m okay.”

Consuelo saw Buddy. “*Madre mio*!” She hurried to him.

A horse screamed inside the barn. Lola cried “Fibber!”

Jesse ran into the barn. Smoke billowed, but flames hadn’t reached the interior; he raced to Fibber’s stall and threw the door open. The horse crashed into him as it charged out, sending him tumbling. Fibber bolted out the front door, Jesse struggled to his feet and released the other horses, careful to stand wide of the stall doors.

He ran back to Lola and clutched her tightly to him.

Mister Braun held his wife in his arms. She wept with deep, shuddering sobs. He looked like he was a hundred years old.

Buddy lay deathly still; Consuelo tore a strip of cloth from her nightgown and pressed it against his wounds.

Lola stared, first at Buddy, then at her mother.

Mister Braun told Jesse, “Take Dolores up to the house. Call the sheriff, tell him to get an ambulance and a fire truck out here.”

As Jesse drove Lola to the house, he heard a crash. He looked in the rear view mirror to see the boat shed collapse. And Mister Braun, his arms around Miz Braun, their lives in flames.

Jesse rides perched high atop the back seat of a Cadillac convertible, smiling and waving to a throng crowding both sides of the Braun's driveway. The sun is bright and hot.

At the edge of the crowd, his father clasps both hands over his head in a victory gesture. Behind him, Alejandro and Romero toast him with longneck bottles of beer.

The car comes to Dudley, who beams and waves. He holds a rooster under his arm. The rooster crows . . .

Jesse woke, disoriented for a few seconds until he recognized the Braun's guest room. Morning sun brightened the window, and the rooster stopped crowing. Still feeling the elation of victory, his lips curved up. He replayed the night before with a sense of disbelief, and gratitude. He had to smile at the fierce expression on Lola's face when she leaped at Buddy from the loft. She was one to ride the river with.

His thoughts turned to Dudley. There was a knot of sorrow that he didn't think would ever go away. But the smile Dudley had sent him in the parade turned him loose to face forward. He eased out of bed, clear-headed, ready for the day.

His belongings were still in the cabin, so he dressed in his dirty clothes and then found Consuelo in the kitchen, drinking coffee. It was surprisingly late, eight o'clock. She smiled when she saw him. "Are you hungry?"

He realized he was starving. "*Mucho!*" She fetched him orange juice, and, while she fixed a mess of scrambled eggs and bacon, Mister Braun came in. His steps were slow, his expression distant. He declined food and sat at the round table. He stirred sugar into a cup of coffee and sipped. Jesse didn't know what to say, so he kept quiet.

Jesse had just finished eating when Sheriff Webb came calling. Mister Braun answered the door. "Come on in, Carl."

"I'm sure sorry to be botherin' you, Axel."

"No helping it. How's—" His voice choked off.

"She rested well. And Buddy pulled through. He's got a deputy at his door, though he ain't needed much."

A fear inside Jesse eased.

Lola walked in, dressed in jeans and a shirt. She wrapped her arms around her father and put her head to his chest. He cupped her face with his hand, and his expression warmed.

As they gathered at the dining table, Consuelo brought the sheriff a cup of coffee and then hovered nearby. Lola sat next to Jesse. He took her hand; she gripped his and leaned close.

The sheriff opened his mouth, and then shut it. Mister Braun said, "Tell me, Carl."

The sheriff grimaced. "I hate this, Axel."

"I need to know."

Sheriff Webb sighed. "Well, you know Margaret was, uh, worried about Lola and that Mexican boy. Seems she got after him about it when he was alone in the barn." He gazed intently at Mister Braun. "She says she went kinda crazy when the kid laughed at her."

Consuelo darted a look at Mister Braun, and Jesse followed it to see new pain on his face. What was it?

The sheriff pulled out a Pall Mall and lit up. "She believed Romero was . . . how'd she put it?" He pulled a note pad from his shirt pocket and consulted it. "She said, 'a danger too.' She killed him back in that hen house."

Mister Braun said, "So Buddy wasn't part of it."

"No, he found her there, cleaned up as best he could, and took the body away to that pasture."

It struck Jesse that Buddy had been protecting his mother.

Just the way he would have done.

The sheriff looked to Jesse. "She never told Axel about you finding Romero. She told Buddy, and together they came up with the idea of using a rattlesnake to . . . well, you know."

Mister Braun said, "Buddy put it in the cabin?"

"Yep. This mornin' he seemed relieved to tell me what he'd done. Said last night he was drunk and crazy scared." He took a long time sipping his coffee. "You'll hear this sooner or later. If the snake hadn't killed Jesse outright, they planned to take a little too long to get him to the hospital." He shook his head. "It was a nasty business."

Lola clenched Jesse's hand. He looked at Mister Braun. The pain the man controlled was carved into his expression. All he did was nod.

The sheriff asked, "Axel, is that snake still out back?"

"Haven't gotten around to disposing of it."

"I'll take it. It's a murder weapon, now." He drowned his cigarette in the dregs of his coffee. "Jesse, it's clear you acted in self-defense. There won't be any trouble for you."

He stood and held his hand out to Jesse. As they shook, he said, "Son, I don't know if I could have done as well. I'm pleased to know you."

Jesse felt a little guilty for the pride that sprang up, but he was glad of it. "Thank you, sir."

The sheriff left through the back door to collect the snake. After a long pause, Mister Braun asked Jesse, "Did you call your mother?"

He hadn't. She'd want him to come home right away, but he didn't see how he could leave Lola, her being pregnant and all. He needed time to think. "I'll do it in a little while."

"It's too late for her to drive down from Dallas and back in a day, so it'll have to be tomorrow, anyway. Do you want to stay in town tonight?"

Jesse glanced at Lola. "Ah, could I stay here? In the house, I mean?"

Mister Braun said, "Sure. Maybe you can help me with Dudley's things." He gazed in the direction of the cabin. "I just couldn't make myself get to it yesterday."

Jesse's throat tightened. "I'd like to do it."

Mister Braun nodded. He stood and gazed down at Lola's hand in Jesse's. His voice was strained when he said, "I figure you saved my daughter's life last night. There aren't any words to say what I feel about that." Tears pooled in his eyes, and he turned away.

In the cabin, Jesse changed clothes and packed Dudley's things and his own in their suitcases. He was efficient, and didn't get too emotional. He checked under the bottom bunk and spotted Dudley's sketch pad.

He sat at the table and flipped through it. On the next to last page he found a half dozen drawings of spiders. With each drawing was a carefully lettered "Spider." Jesse groaned, "Oh, Spider." He turned to the last page. Dudley's neat printing said, "Our Brand."

The page was filled with sketches of brands. There were variations on "Bar DJ" and "Bar JD." Also included was a circle with eight short spokes sticking out from it.

A spider brand.

Blinking tears back, Jesse said, "I promise you I'll get our ranch someday, pardner. And I'll call it the Lazy Spider." He took a shuddering sigh to catch his breath. "I'll never forget you, my friend. Never." He tore the last two pages from the notebook to keep, grabbed the suitcases, and went up to the ranch house.

He called his mother. Her voice sounded clear and bright. He explained what had happened, and then had to stop her from coming down immediately.

"No, Mama, things aren't finished here. Don't do anything until I call you." He held firm, and at last she agreed. Her voice was shaky; he hoped she wouldn't dive back into a bottle. He was afraid that without him there she would.

Consuelo came to him with a picnic basket. "Lola said to tell you she is down at the corral. Take this with you."

He thought of Consuelo giving him Dudley's car keys the night before. He said, "Without you, I don't think I'd be here."

"I am very glad that you are." She gazed out the kitchen window. "You know, even though she do very bad things, I feel sad for the *Señora*."

Señora. That was what Alejandro and Romeo had been saying in his dream. "Why?"

"I was with her family when she get pregnant. She was just a girl, fifteen like Lola. The boy would no marry her. He say the baby wasn't his. He call her a slut and, and he laugh at her."

She touched her right eyebrow in the place Miz Braun had her scar. "Her father beat her so bad. Her face . . ." She trailed off and shook her head as if she wanted to expel that memory.

"She go crazy. She take a shotgun to the boy's house and kill him. The sheriff back then was brother to her father, so she go to a hospital for a while, and that was all. She had the little boy, and he was raised as her brother."

Jesse said, "She thought it would happen to Lola."

Consuelo looked up at him. "You are not like the one who fathered Buddy."

He smiled and gave her a small bow. "*Gracias*, Consuelo."

She smiled. "*De nada*. Now you go."

He found Lola sitting on the corral fence, waiting for him. Fibber and Dusty were saddled and hitched to the fence—the fire truck had arrived in time to save most of the barn. She smiled. "How about a ride?"

That felt just right. He tied the picnic basket behind his saddle and they rode out. She led him to an area of the ranch he'd never seen, a golden meadow on the top of a high hill crowned by a lone live oak tree. A steady breeze countered the wrath of the sun. They staked their horses out to graze. Consuelo had included a blanket in the picnic basket, and they set up a picnic in the shade.

The hill country spread out before them, rolling toward the horizon, forested and pastured, green and gold. "I wish Dudley could see this."

"He's looking down on it right now."

He wished he could believe that. He looked up at the sky, a bright blue with fluffy clouds. It could be true. He whispered, "Hey, Spider."

A silence settled as they ate.

Jesse lay back and watched Lola pack up the basket. She caught him looking, knelt beside him, and kissed him. It was a sweet, loving kiss, not one of passion. He gazed up at her, and loved everything he saw. He placed his hand on her belly. "We have to figure out what to do."

She put her hands over his. "I never had a chance to tell you—I got my period while I was at Aunt Mary's. We're okay."

Relief spread through him like a slow wave of warmth. But disappointment followed. He'd been picturing a happy life with Lola and their baby on a ranch of their own. The Lazy Spider. He grasped her hand. "I don't want to leave you."

"Me neither."

He thought of his mother, living alone, drinking her life away. "But I gotta help my mother get through, well, what she's got to learn to live with."

Lola's face tensed. She bit her lip and looked away.

He realized he hadn't thought much about what had happened to Lola. She'd lost her mother and her . . . brother in one terrible night. "I'm sorry about what happened to your mother."

"I just wish I knew why."

He thought of the story Consuelo had told him. "She did it for you."

Lola frowned up at the sky. "Connie says my mother loves me. Maybe she does. But how could it go so wrong?"

He opened an arm to her. "Come here."

Lola lay next to him, her body rigid with tension. She cried, "She's my *mother*, Jesse!" She rolled away from him. He shifted to be close to her, and put his arm around her. She shook with sobs.

He stroked her hair. She quieted and relaxed against him. He rose onto an elbow, and she rolled to her back and looked up at him. He watched a tear run down her cheek. He kissed it. He was a man, and this was his woman.

A wisp of breeze jostled a bluebonnet not far from her head. He plucked it and handed it to her. She smiled and tucked it over her ear.

He said, "I have to go home, but I want to, I mean—"

"So I'll see you next summer, and then in college."

He grinned at the thought of Lola taking on college. Watch out, college. "I'm going to Sul Ross so I can have a ranch."

She smiled. "*We* are going to Sul Ross College so *we* can have a ranch."

He lay back and she snuggled into the hollow of his shoulder. Lola draped her arm over his chest, and he loved the warmth and weight of it. They lay together, sharing dreams until the sun started to fade and it was time to ride home.

Jesse called his mother that evening and asked her to pick him up the next day. Her voice was crisp and clear, colored with relief and happiness. He was surprised at how much it warmed him.

Late that night, when Mister Braun's snores echoed down the hallway, his thoughts ricocheting from longing for Lola to mourning Dudley, Jesse tossed and turned for an hour. He needed . . . he needed—he swung out of bed and slipped on his jeans. When he stepped into the hallway, he met Lola coming from her room, wearing jeans and a T-shirt. They reached for each other, and he took her hands and led her into his room. After wrapping their arms around each other for long minutes, they lay on his bed and settled in to rest, her head on his shoulder.

They woke that way the next morning. For once he was glad for the rooster, whose crow roused them in time for her to get back to her room before her father appeared.

His mother arrived just before noon. She was clear-eyed, and she wrapped her arms around him. Her embrace was fierce and protective. He hadn't expected to be happy to see her or want her hug—but it was exactly what he needed.

There was a liveliness in her eyes he hadn't seen for a long time. When he put his stuff in the car he looked for the ever-present drink holder. It was gone. Oh, God, please let it be really, really gone.

Mister Braun, Lola, and Consuelo came out to the driveway to see them off. Consuelo gave Jesse a brief hug, then handed him a paper sack. "Cookies for your trip."

He smiled. "*Gracias.*"

Mister Braun shook Jesse's hand. "If you ever need a friend, son, you know where I am."

Jesse's throat threatened to close up. He'd known only one other man with as much heart as Mister Braun. He managed to say, "Thank you, sir."

And then, right there in front of her father and his mother,

Jesse took Lola in his arms and kissed her, a long, strong, I-love-you kiss. He felt brave and bold and at same time feared that they'd grab them, yank them apart, and spank them.

They did nothing at all.

Later, in the car, his mother glanced at him and said, "You seem to like that girl."

He thought of that last kiss and smiled. "She's okay."

An invitation for book clubs and readers

Let's talk. I love to talk with readers about *The Summer Boy,* so, if your club would like to chat with me about it, email me at ray@rayrhamey.com and let's set up a phone call.

Give feedback: if you've anything you'd like to say to me about *The Summer Boy,* please do. Just use the email address above. And, if you liked it, online reviews are very helpful to auhors.

Many thanks for reading my story. Even though my other novels don't fit into standard genres any better than this one does, if you liked the storytelling here you might also like *We the Enemy, Finding Magic,* and *The Vampire Kitty-cat Chronicles.* There's information about them on following pages.

About Novels of Texas

The Summer Boy is one of a group of novels that reflect the grit and character you find in the people who live and love in that great state. They range from the days of the old West to more contemporary times.

Hope to see you again.

About the author

Ray Rhamey has been a writer for all of his professional career, beginning with writing programmed instruction training manuals for an insurance company (mind-numbing). He moved on to advertising and had a terrific time doing that. Storytelling crept into the ads he wrote, and he started working on screenplays.

Screenwriting lured him out of advertising and to Hollywood. Although he mastered the art of crafting a professional script and had an agent, he didn't concoct a story that anyone was interested in spending millions of dollars to produce. Ah, well. Although, on the kid side, you can still get his film adaptation of *The Little Engine that Could.*

So he moved on to become a novelist, a freelance fiction editor, and a book designer.

Ray grew up in Dallas, Texas, but has since lived in Chicago and much of the Midwest, and now calls the Pacific Northwest home with his amazing spouse, Sarah. His four terrific kids are equally scattered—but connected.

He has four websites that serve readers and writers:

- crrreative.com is his book editing and design site
- rayrhamey.com features his fiction and non-fiction
- ftqpress.com is the home of his publishing company
- floggingthequill.com is his blog on storytelling craft

Next, some of Ray's other novels.

Pogo was only a cartoon character, but he said it best: "We have met the enemy and he is us."

Revolving-door courts spit felons back onto streets uncaught, unreformed. Madmen, madchildren, and criminals kill us with terrifying firepower.

But in *We the Enemy* that's changing in the Pacific Northwest—until the forces of the status quo strike back.

Not too many years from now, the very nature of criminal justice and self defense is changing in the Pacific Northwest—criminals compelled to tell the truth in court, guns converted to nonlethal weapons.

But there's fierce opposition, and the president, in danger of losing reelection, aims to win votes by taking down the man behind it all, Noah Stone. His weapon is Jake Black, an ex Secret Service agent.

Now a cold-blooded gun for hire, Jake lives an emotionless existence after his wife and little girl were killed. A fog of numbness in his mind smothers everything—especially the grief he cannot bear. Scoring a million dollars for taking care of what he sees as a con man is no problem.

But the closer he gets to his target, the more he's drawn to Stone. When a treacherous attack threatens to destroy the good Stone seems to be doing, Jake is the one man who can keep Stone's mission alive, and he faces the question of his life—who is the real enemy, Noah Stone or Jake Black?

5-star Midwest Book Review *"We the Enemy* is a unique thriller with plenty of twists and turns, highly recommended."

Free sample at rayrhamey.com.

Annie is a gifted healer in the Hidden Clans, descendants of a Celtic ancestress with a genetic inheritance of mental abilities that enable them to do magical things. She can slow aging, cure disease, heal a heart from the inside . . . or crush an enemy's as it beats.

They hide to escape persecution that has haunted them through the ages, and they've moved safely among us since the Salem witch trials. But a Homeland Security agent penetrates Annie's disguise, and she's forced to flee. On the run as a suspected terrorist, Annie is desperate to protect her kin from discovery.

Then a greater threat arises when a clansman bent on avenging the murder of his son creates an unstoppable killer plague. Annie is the only hope for billions of people . . . if she can evade capture.

With high-stakes conflict and human drama, *Finding Magic* explores loss, prejudice, family, and the human magic within each of us.

Free sample at rayrhamey.com.

The Vampire Kitty-cat Chronicles turns vampire mythology on its head when Patch, a calico tomcat, is turned into breakfast—and a vampire kitty-cat—by a starving vampire.

Narrated by Patch in a deliciously snarky cat take on the world, Patch struggles to find a new life, as it were. In the process, he's tried for murder, just about shotgunned into undead pieces, comes inches from having his tail cut off and seconds from being fried by the sun, and kidnapped twice. Oh, yeah, and turned into a (shudder) politician.

On the other paw, he does hook up with a sweet Siamese, and it looks like he's on the way to winning that election . . .

5-star Midwest Book Review "Superbly crafted by an inventive and skilled storyteller, *The Vampire Kitty-cat Chronicles* is enthusiastically recommended for anyone who would enjoy a terrifically original and thoroughly entertaining action/adventure fantasy yarn!"

Tess Gerritsen, bestselling author of *ICE COLD* "What a pleasure! Quirky and laugh-out-loud fun. Ray Rhamey takes the vampire novel where it's never been before, into the realm of sheer hilarity."

Sample chapters, reviews, and more at vampirekittycat.com.

CPSIA information can be obtained
at www.ICGtesting.com
Printed in the USA
LVOW08s0008130617
537900LV00001B/53/P